HOLLY DATES

HOLLY DATES

Megan Becker

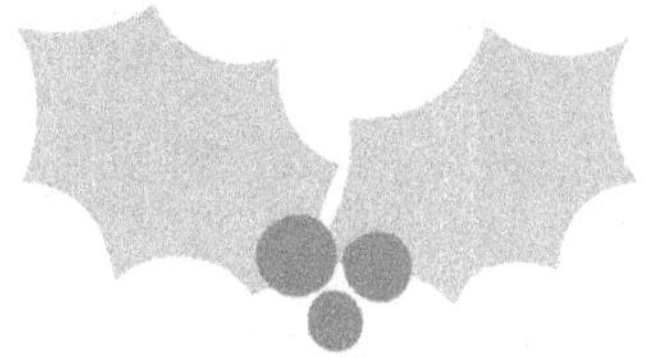

LATTES & LOVEBIRDS LITERATURE

Printed in the United States of America

Lattes & Lovebirds Literature

Print ISBN: 979-8-9898118-2-3

This one's for me.

And for everyone who's ever been told they're too much,
or felt like they're not living up to others' expectations for them,
or felt like they didn't belong.

You do.

I do.

And we're exactly the right amount.

A Note From Holly

Let's set a ground rule right now: None of what I'm about to tell you gets shared with the IRS. Got it?

Good.

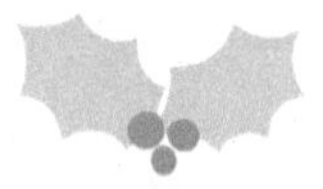

4 CARATS

Holly

I'M JUST A GIRL, standing in front of a boy, asking him to pay her.

For a date.

During which he already paid for my meal, two cocktails, and dessert.

Okay, sure, it sounds odd, but it all makes perfect sense when you get the backstory. I promise. Don't believe me? Allow me to share.

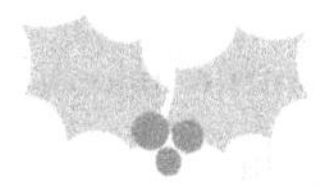

It was a dark and stormy night.

Just kidding. It was spring, and it was dusky, with the soft glow of the setting sun still creeping up from the horizon in a golden fuzz, and a warm breeze blew through the outdoor seating area of Pepper & Pour, one of our favorite spots to meet up for dinner.

It started over a nacho platter and sangria and a little gift bag, under a patio heater and strings of glowing bulbs, across from my best friend since we were assigned to the same shift at our campus library sophomore year.

"What's this?" I asked as she nudged the bag toward me, the massive diamond on her finger nearly blinding me.

"Open it."

So with a belly full of chorizo and tortillas, I pulled out a sheet of floral tissue paper and a mesh sachet containing a pair of dainty friendship bracelets.

"Ooh, they're pretty."

"Read them," Jasmine said with a nod toward the pouch.

I took out the bracelets and squinted in the dim light at the tiny cubic beads with delicate lettering. The first one seemed to read *BRIDE SQUAD* and I made out *MAID OF HONOR* on the second. Putting aside for a moment that the word "squad" ranks up there with words like *tribe* and *vibes* and *moist* on the list of words I detest, I was totally here for the maid-of-honor thing.

"Are you serious?" I asked, thrusting the bracelets toward her face like she hadn't seen them before.

She smiled and nodded. "Of course! I wouldn't think of asking anyone else."

I slipped the bracelets onto my wrist and admired them. Yes, even the *Bride Squad* bracelet.

"Is that a yes, then?" Jasmine asked, a little smile playing at her lips as she took a sip of sangria.

"Yes! Duh!" I raised my glass to hers and offered a toast. "To the best wedding ever!"

"So how'd you get into doing all this, anyway?" he asks, tucking a handful of twenties into my palm.

All this is dating for money, offering companionship to people who don't want to spend the holidays alone, who want to ward off the questions from nosey aunts about settling down, and who are willing to pay a few hundred bucks to make it happen.

All this is scrambling to put the money together to pay for my part in a wedding I agreed to be in—because of course I'm going to be my best friend's maid of honor—without doing my due diligence by asking questions like 'Is your wedding going to be at the Holiday Inn Express or the most expensive resort in the Caribbean?' or 'I'm sorry, did you say you wanted *designer* bridesmaids' dresses? Can I interest you in the clearance rack at David's Bridal?'

All this is pivoting to something unexpected when my very steady source of income—the one that allowed me to live in my own little townhouse and not my childhood bedroom—was ripped out from under me in the name of efficiency. Corporate golf outings get to stay in the budget, but administrative assistants don't. Got it.

I've told the story a few times before, mostly to quell fears that I'm actually a movie-villain seductress who plans to tie up my prey and abscond with their wallets and Timex watches, but Eddie seems almost bored by the whole transaction, more relieved than anything that his parents didn't question him or me too thoroughly at dinner.

"Just kind of happened," I say. I bounce between my feet and shiver in the late-November chill. "People don't want to face things alone, you know? So I'm a friend for hire."

He chuffs at this, his shoulders rising and falling with a jerk as he snorts a little white cloud into the air. "Just a friend, huh?" He doesn't bother to disguise his judgment.

But since I've done nothing wrong (except the whole not-telling-the-IRS thing that we've previously mentioned), and because the money is already in my hands, and because we're on a well-lit, heavily traveled street bustling with dinner-goers, I shrug it off and reply, "Yeah, when people don't have one of their own to call."

Don't come for me, Eddie, is implied. *I will roast you.* I count my money and shove it into my purse, then take out my phone, which

I've found to be a great deterrent for bad behavior. "I should get going. Pleasure doing business with you." Then I turn on my heels and march toward my car.

Mom's still in her jeans and sweater instead of pajamas when I walk in the door after nine, so it's pretty clear that she knew I was going on one of my 'Really wish you wouldn't do this, honey' dates again and has been waiting in her recliner, her slip-on sneakers at the ready by the door, just in case the police came knocking with news of my body being hacked into tiny bits.

"How was your night?" She sets her book down and watches as I hang my coat on the rack.

"It was great." It wasn't great, but it wasn't the absolute worst night I've had, either, and there's no reason to worry Mom.

"Was he nice?"

Sometimes I think what she's really asking is, 'Do you think he'd be nice enough to settle down with?' because heaven forbid I be unmarried in my thirties. Or maybe she's trying to find me an eligible man with his own house so that I am one less person taking up space in hers. Though, I think she likes having me around to help balance out the presence of my dad and twenty-something brother.

"He was nice enough for the job."

Mom winces, then sighs. "I wish you would find something else, Holly. There has to be another way."

Mom didn't like it when I started driving for Pickup CARtist, either, but she absolutely loathes my Holly Dates site. I know she's not thrilled that her college-educated child is surviving (sort of) on rideshare income, but she's made plenty of comments about my dating services in the past few months, all under the guise of worrying about my safety. Unfortunately, if there *is* a magical, mysterious 'other way,' I don't see it.

I yawn and stretch, more as an excuse to bail on the conversation than from sudden-onset sleepiness. "Well, I'm beat. I should probably get to bed."

She shakes her head and rises from her chair, then follows me upstairs. "In case I don't see you during the day, don't forget about tomorrow night," she says, and I try to summon a response that someone who totally remembers plans might say.

"Remind me what time?"

"Six. Sharp."

"Perfect. I'll make sure I'm home by six."

"Holly Grace." She says it in the same way she said it when I was growing up and talking too much or too loudly or just generally being annoying.

"What?" I reach the hallway at the top of the stairs, ready to turn right toward my room before she turns left toward hers, and she sighs.

"It's your grandmother's birthday. Sunset Diner. Six o'clock."

I feel blood rush to my cheeks, always a little embarrassed when I live down to my reputation as the flighty forgetful child. I'm smart—I swear I am. I have a psychology degree and *cum laude* after my name in my graduation program to prove it. But the little things have always slipped through the gray matter, if you will, especially with gig-economy work that leads me to make very few plans because I never know when work will pick up, and I want to be ready when it does.

"Just testing you, Mom." I try for the laugh, but it doesn't come.

Instead she rolls her eyes, not cruelly but a little exasperated, and turns down the hall toward her room. "Goodnight, Holly."

"Night, Mom."

In my room, I exhale before collapsing on my bed. I add Grandma's birthday dinner to my calendar so I won't forget about it, then go through all my apps to clear notifications. My brain may be cluttered, but my lock screen should not be. I'm fifteen minutes into doomscrolling strangers' lives on Instagram when my phone dings and a notification slides down from the top of my screen: I've got a new email through my Holly Dates site.

It's the Most Wonderful Time of the Year

Holly

THE GOOD THING ABOUT having a big family is that you can almost always slip out undetected from family functions, and nobody will notice. Especially if there's alcohol involved. That's what I'm banking on when I arrive at Sunset Diner at 5:58 with a card in my hand and a dinner date scheduled for 7:30 across town.

The bad thing about having a big family is that sometimes they choose to make you the center of attention. Especially if you're still single and still working a weird job that nobody understands and you're nowhere near as successful as your brothers who are all killing it in endeavors like law school, tech start-ups, and Being the Best Grandson in the World.

That last one is very specific to my kiss-ass older brother Micah, whose perfectly wrapped gift makes everyone swoon as he enters (three minutes late, mind you). I have an inkling that under the floral paper is a gift that Mom probably bought online and had shipped to his house for him.

Anyway.

I tear away from an aunt who is overly informative about her recent bunion surgery and drop my card with the stack of others on the gift table before finding a tray of hors d'oeuvres and devouring a bacon-wrapped scallop. I don't really like scallops, but that might tell you how much I love bacon.

Mom—already somehow champagne tipsy—finds me and puts an arm around my shoulders. She gestures with the other to the room, which is covered in evergreen *everything*, including a giant artificial tree in the corner and swags with velvety red bows draped over every window. "Isn't it beautiful?" she asks. "They did such a great job decorating." Then she kisses my cheek and takes off in the direction of one of her brothers.

I wonder if, in Grandma's eighty-five years, she's ever grown tired of her birthday decor being whatever people have set up for Christmas. I wonder if she's ever gotten bored by red and green, and I wonder if she ever had a unicorn party growing up, or a birthday without a Christmas tree, and I wonder if she feels like an afterthought, like people don't go out of their way to make her day just about her. I add a note to my calendar app and pocket my phone to mingle.

Mom's deep in conversation with Uncle Jack, whose third wife is leaning in a little too close to a waiter much too young for her, so I sneak away to find my youngest brother. Landon's my favorite for a myriad of reasons, but right now it's because he's found a table in a corner near an exit, and he's saved me a seat and a plate of bruschetta and scallops.

"You avoiding everyone, too?" I ask, unrolling a piece of bacon from its scallopy innards.

He shrugs. "Just watching, trying to figure out who's going to cause the drama this time."

Our family is famous for dramatic gatherings, like the time my cousin's baby had a blowout in her white dress at her baptism, and the time my aunt fainted at her son's wedding because she absolutely couldn't stand his new bride (R.I.P. that marriage, which lasted all of four months), and the time my uncle was asked to leave a toddler's birthday party because he didn't realize his ear buds weren't connected while he was watching some questionable videos.

"Any leads?"

"My money's on Allison." He gestures his head toward Uncle Jack's wife, who's downing another glass of champagne and has her other hand on the waiter's bicep for some reason.

"Well, it definitely won't be me."

He turns his head toward me and frowns. "You sound confident."

I down the last piece of bacon from the plate. "Can't cause a scene if you're not here."

"You're ditching Grandma's party early?"

"She won't even notice. Not with Wonder Boy over there." Landon follows my gaze toward Micah, who's now dancing to the restaurant's Christmas playlist with Grandma like she's the oldest contestant on *Dancing with the Stars* and he's trying to wow the judges by twirling her. To his credit, Grandma *does* seem to be enjoying it, but it doesn't mean I have to like him for it.

"Big date?" Landon was the first one to know about my companionship service. After some sketchy texts from strangers who got my number through the grapevine, I enlisted his help with creating a website where interested parties could fill out a form instead of contacting me personally.

"Not really. Just some guy who wants me to go to a party with him but wants to lay some groundwork first. Set up an ironclad backstory, or something. But hey, it's dinner."

Landon cocks an eyebrow. "This is dinner, too."

"Yes, but this is dinner with..." I gesture at all the family members milling about, and Landon gets it. He chuckles and runs a hand through his hair.

"Say no more." He stabs one of my discarded scallops with his fork, pops it into his mouth, and asks while chewing, "Where's he taking you?"

"We're meeting at O'Donnell's."

"Classy," he teases, his blue eyes sparkling.

I shove him with my shoulder. "Whatever. You know their burgers are better than this fancy stuff."

"Burgers? Where?" Ian, who falls between me and Landon in the birth order, drops himself into the chair on the other side of Landon, mussing our baby brother's hair in the process. He's already got a plate piled high with shrimp, so I'm not sure why he cares about my burgers.

"Holly has a date later," Landon says matter of factly.

"You bailing early?"

"I'm here now."

Ian snorts. "Do they know that?"

Ugh. I hate when little brothers are right. "Fine. I'll go mingle, and then I'll have a mysterious stomach ailment, probably scallop-induced, and then I'll bail for a big, juicy, greasy burger." I add a little dramatic flair and pantomiming to the end, just to rub it in to Ian that I get to chow down on real food and not dry buffet chicken for dinner. Also, I get to change out of my tights and heels, but I doubt that'd be a selling point for him.

I find Dad first, then Mom, and then rest a hand gently on Grandma's shoulder while she's talking to Uncle Jack. She looks up at me, and her eyes go bright and wide.

"Well, aren't you pretty as a picture?" She scans me like I'm dressed for prom and not just in a plum sweater dress I used to wear to the office this time of year.

"Thanks, Grandma." I bend and kiss her cheek. "Happy Birthday."

She squeezes my hand, and I notice how prominent her bones and veins are through her papery skin, and I feel bad for leaving her birthday party when I never know how many more she'll have.

"Thank you, dear," she replies, and then Aunt Beth swoops in and says dinner will be served shortly, and she whisks Grandma away to her table.

I retreat to my table where Micah has now joined the fun along with our cousin Scott, his wife Ali, and their ~~gremlins~~ children. Scotty Jr. and Joey are seven and five, and they're clearly unhappy about something. And instead of being sandwiched between their parents, they're right next to me. Technically Scotty, the older of the two, is next to me, but Joey is next to him, and they're arguing until Ali finally shushes them for a family prayer (during which Joey steals his mom's phone).

When the prayer's over, Ali readjusts the toddler on her lap and tries to beat the odds of parenting three children solo, since Scott is so engrossed in conversation with Micah next to him that he doesn't seem to realize that his children are also at the table and are, if we're being frank, tiny monsters.

Ali tells the boys to return the phone, but then her daughter nearly squirms out of her lap and she has to readjust, and then Scotty Jr. tries to steal the phone from his little brother. Joey puts up enough of a fight that Scotty has to yank hard, and suddenly I don't really need an excuse to sneak out of the party because Scotty Jr. pulls the phone from his brother with such force that his arm flies back, elbow first, and connects with my wine glass, tipping it over and flooding the white tablecloth—and my dress—with merlot.

You can't hear a pin drop, because most of the party is blissfully unaware of our table's mishap since they're engaged in conversation with other adults and they've got no idea anything out of the ordinary is happening in our little corner. But I'm a little shocked that more heads don't turn when Ali raises her voice at her sons, or when little

Madison on her lap startles and wails at the sudden change in her mom's demeanor.

Regardless, I'm drenched in wine, which actually isn't that bad, but which I'm going to play up to my advantage to get out of here without attracting negative attention from my family (read: Mom).

"Oh, no..." I say, rising and dabbing at my dress with my napkin. "Welp, looks like I need to go home and treat this stain. Bummer."

Landon deadpans, "Bummer," shaking his head. "It's so bad I can almost see it."

I shoot him a look and he smirks, and Ali apologizes from across the table, offering to pay for the dry cleaning or to replace the dress.

"It's fine," I promise, and it is. It's going to be fine, and if it's not, well, I needed to downsize my wardrobe anyway.

I tousle Landon's hair. "Tell Grandma I love her, and let Mom know why I left, okay?"

"If she even asks," Ian interjects.

"Oh, she'll ask," Landon and I reply in near-perfect unison.

I glance toward Mom, who's engrossed in conversation and unaware of anything I'm doing, which is the ideal scenario. I grab my phone and bag and quietly sneak out the back door thirty minutes earlier than I'd been hoping to.

To Christmas!
(The Drinking Song)
Nick

O'Donnell's is busy and loud, and the beer is cheap, and it's a good place to meet a stranger for an arrangement I'm not wholly comfortable with but that I need nevertheless.

I check my watch again, even though I checked it two minutes ago. She's late, which is not promising. Or she's here, and we haven't connected, or she came in and saw me and left, which would be terrible but par for the course. Come to think of it, maybe her being late is the exact thing I'm hoping for.

The door swings open, and a woman in ripped jeans, a black sweater, and an orange beanie bursts in on the draft of cold air that flows in from outside. She scans the tables, glances at her phone, and turns toward the bar. After another quick check of her phone, she sidles toward me and plops down on the stool next to mine.

"Sorry I'm late," she says without formalities like a handshake or eye contact. She rips the beanie off her head and exposes a mess of dark waves, which stick out in all directions, untamed, and flags down the bartender to order a whiskey sour.

"Holly?" I ask, just to confirm, and she finally meets my eyes. She looks at me like she has no idea why I need to ask, like 'isn't it obvious, considering I sent you my picture earlier today?', and there's something refreshing about the honesty written across her face.

She nods, taking a sip through the straw of the drink the bartender has set in front of her. "And I'd assume you're Nick, considering you know my name and look just like your photo?"

I feel my cheeks burn, but then she reaches over the bar, grabs a pen and a spare napkin, and turns her body toward mine.

"So, you need a date?"

None of this is what I expected when I heard about Holly and her—for lack of a better word—*services*. At first I pictured a leggy blonde with a designer bag, or a suit-wearing brunette with a briefcase: someone put-together and organized, not a woman who takes notes during our consultation on a spare cocktail napkin with a borrowed bar pen. It's simultaneously more unnerving and more comforting that she seems so normal, so casual about this arrangement.

"I do," I answer as she taps the blue Bic on the wooden bar top. "My office's holiday party is coming up soon, and I can't be the loser who shows up alone." I don't say *'again'* but I feel it's implied, and definitely assumed based on her reaction.

She cocks a brow at me, pausing before scribbling a note on the napkin. "Most guys would just take their cousin or something."

"Do you always try to discourage clients from hiring you?"

She shrugs and takes another sip of her drink. "I turn down clients if something feels off."

"And something feels off about me?" I readjust my glasses as Holly scans my face; she could be a detective with how she wordlessly analyzes me, investigating me with nothing more than her eyes.

"Most clients don't request a consult. Not an in-person, anyway."

I start to defend myself, but she cuts me off.

"This doesn't feel like a cousin-appropriate situation. What's really going on?"

I swallow, caught already, and if she can read me that easily I wonder if everyone at work has already figured out my secret. "I may have been talking about a new girlfriend for a few months."

"Why would you do that?"

That's the real kicker, isn't it? The why behind it all, the piece of the puzzle that makes me seem more desperate than the rest of the near-complete picture. "I was trying to impress one of my coworkers. I, um... She's really nice, and everyone else always had weekend plans and cool stories, and I just wanted to seem interesting." The confession is a relief to finally share. More relieving is that Holly doesn't seem fazed by it.

"Mmm," she hums. "So your plan to win over this girl was to make up an imaginary girlfriend and talk about her all the time?"

"I know it's stupid, but she was dating someone else when we started working together. They broke up about a month ago."

Holly purses her lips and picks at an invisible piece of lint on her jeans. "So you wanted a consultation to, what? Make sure we're on the same page regarding our fictional backstory?"

"Something like that."

"Ah, so there's more." She shifts in her seat and sucks down the last of her cocktail; I motion to the bartender for another round for each of us. I might need the whole keg to drown my shame.

"How good is your acting?"

She shrugs and taps a finger on the bar. "I had a couple small parts in high school musicals. And no one's called me out yet on my fake dates."

I croak out "Good," then clear my throat and drop the bomb: "I was thinking we could stage a break-up at the party, where Catherine could see it."

Holly perks up at this, like a dog who just heard the word *walk*. Not that I'm comparing her to a dog, it's just... she has that excited energy about her, like everyone loves her but sometimes she's maybe a lot to handle.

"I'll pay extra, of course, because I know that's not one of the services you advertise."

She just smiles and shakes her head. "This just got about two-hundred percent more interesting, Nicholas."

"Oh, uh—it's just Nick, actually."

"Ok, Just Nick. It would be an honor to be both your fake girl-friend and the catalyst to helping you find a real one." She pulls her hair over one shoulder and poises her pen over the napkin. "Tell me about her. What am I like?"

"I, um... I don't really know."

She peers up at me, her expression a marriage of confusion and amusement. "You've been dating this imaginary woman for months, and you don't know what she's like?"

"Well, when you put it that way, I sound pretty stupid, don't I?"

She smiles but doesn't laugh.

"Yeah, this was a terrible idea," I realize aloud. "I think I'm just going to skip the party."

"No." Holly grabs my forearm when I stand to pull out my wallet. Paying and getting out of here seems ideal at present. I wonder if I've embarrassed myself enough for one night, or if I'll end up tripping over a chair leg and wiping out on my way to the door. Bonus points if I take out a waiter with a full tray. But there's Holly, her grip loosening but her gaze still holding me.

"Don't skip it. We'll make it work, whatever you told them."

She glances at my seat, and I sit down. "I tried to be vague," I begin, though what she's about to see might not provide much confidence in that claim. With a sigh, I pull the folded papers from my coat pocket and present them to her.

Her eyes widen and flit between papers and my face. "Sorry," she says, pointing at the pages. "Are those your notes?" When I nod, she laughs and steals the papers from my hand. "I thought you said you were vague."

"I was. About her... er, you."

"But you created a whole backstory?"

My cheeks burn for the second time since she's been here, though, despite her gentle razzing, I don't feel embarrassed.

After a few moments of scanning my notes, she smacks my arm, laughing. "Oh my gosh—we take a ballroom dance class every other week?"

I don't know if it's the second beer on an empty stomach or if her casual ease is contagious, but I hear myself ask, "Doesn't everyone?" before I know what's coming out of my mouth.

Then she's tumbling—metaphorically—down, down, down a laughter rabbit hole, growing louder and laughing longer with each bullet point on the list.

"We went white water rafting for our three-month anniversary?"

"It sounded fun."

"I was bitten by a snake?"

"I couldn't tell everyone *I* was the one bitten."

"And you saved me?"

I shrug. "It wasn't a venomous snake, so you didn't really need to be saved, but since we didn't know that at the time, yes, I cleaned the affected area and made sure you got the help you needed."

She's holding her whiskey sour—her third, now—and she drinks while eyeing me. "And what help was that?"

I think for a moment, because no one really cared to ask about the aftermath before. I'm not sure what the right answer is here, because I feel like it should be 'we went to the hospital,' but that's incredibly boring. "If I said 'a snack', would that be..."

"Throw in a nap, too, and I think you've found yourself the right cure for a non-venomous, perfectly harmless, hypothetical snake bite."

"Done." I slap the bar like I'm a judge with a gavel, then pick at my fries that arrived twenty minutes ago when Holly was asking questions about the goat yoga session we attended together.

"You really thought of everything, didn't you?" she asks.

"It's not my fault everyone's first question on a Monday is 'What did you and your girlfriend do this weekend?'"

She snorts, choking a moment on her drink. "Are they really asking about our sex life?"

A fry is midway to my mouth, and I stop, mouth gaping, shell-shocked by the question. "What?"

Holly slides the paper toward me. "'The sex is great'?"

"Oh. That's, um... Sorry. I'm not trying to—"

"Yeah, no. 'Cause I don't— I mean, sex *is* great, but that's not part of the deal."

"Of course not. I wasn't expecting—"

"Good." And that's that. One syllable ends the entire conversation.

She flips through the remainder of the list, a log of every imagined memory between myself and some woman I made up on a whim so I didn't seem pathetic around my coworkers, and passes the pages back to me before returning to her burger. It's torturous, this silence between us now in this over-crowded bar, and I'm afraid I've blown the whole plan with four stupid words.

It's only after she finishes the last bite of her sandwich and slurps her whiskey sour dry that Holly speaks again. "I'm in."

DJ PLAY A CHRISTMAS SONG
Holly

THEY—SOME VAGUE, INDISTINCT, PROBABLY woefully under-quali-fied *they*—say a picture is worth a thousand words. But *they* must never have seen the photo Nick Goodman submitted with his client request form: nondescript, hastily cropped, truly unremarkable.

There. I summed it up in five.

But the man himself? Okay, at first glance, sort of the same. But with a little conversation, a little laughter, a little liquor? I'm intrigued. He's funny. Cute. Sort of scared-seeming, like he's perpetually afraid to offend or put off.

Obviously, I take him on as a client, because someone who has an entire timeline drafted for their fake relationship must really need the win. The cute browline glasses and just-shy-of-too-long hair don't hurt, but my reasons are truly strictly professional.

Nick, after all, is three jobs in one. He's requested a second meeting before the party, and then there's the party itself, which he advises will be "two to four hours of torturous forced mer-riment" followed by a manner-yet-to-be-determined breakup. It doesn't sound like even remotely the worst event I've been to with a client. The open bar is a plus, because this is the kind of job where drinking is not only allowed, but encouraged. (It's me. I encourage the drinking.)

A woman approaches my car, her face illuminated by her phone, and I roll down my window. "Holly?" she asks.

"I sure am. Kiki?"

"Close. Kik*o*," she replies, emphasizing the last vowel. Before I can say I'm sorry, Kiko is sliding into my back seat and fastening her shoulder belt. "I can tell you're about to apologize, but don't. It happens literally every day. My grandmother thought my name was Kiwi for the first two weeks of my life. That's only a fifty-percent accuracy rate, so by comparison, you nailed it."

I swipe my email and Nick's photo closed, and pull up the Pickup CARtist app instead. Kiko's name and photo greet me along with her destination and the early steps of the GPS guidance to get there, but I know this route by heart. "You're a fan of O'Donnell's?"

"Who isn't?" Her voice is bubbly, full of energy and warmth, like shaken champagne about to be uncorked. She's wearing black jeans with a highlighter-pink blazer over a shimmering silver tank top. It seems to suit her personality well. Our eyes meet in the rearview mirror, and she smiles. "I know it's a bit much for the venue, but my best friend's band is playing there tonight. Neon. You know them?"

"Of course!" You don't live in Songbird Springs without becoming a fan of Mia Montgomery. The band's been on a crazy tour, but playing at O'Donnell's is a tradition for them, since they're locals.

Kiko waves excitedly to some friends near the door. They're all in bright colors, like their dress code for the show was Fashionista Modern Mom but Make it '80s Cosplay. One of them is in a lime green dress and glittering boots, and I do a double take before I drive away, smiling at the thought of Ali enjoying a nice night out with her friends and laughing internally at the idea of Scott at home wrangling three kids on his own.

Not This Year
Holly

Kyle van der Mullen, of Fat Pig BBQ restaurant-owning van der Mullen family fame, is just as charming as the establishment's name might suggest. I was hesitant to take the job at first, because I once met his family eons ago at their restaurant and I have no desire to sit around a table with them, but apparently jerks with money are willing to pay double my regular rate for a little companionship. Also, added perk, I got a new dress out of the deal, because Kyle's "woman" would "never be caught dead in polyester." Instead, I might actually be caught dead in velvet, because this dress is so snug I'm not sure I'll be able to breathe throughout the evening.

Since getting dressed for tonight, I haven't been able to get "Black Velvet" out of my head—the four lines I know, anyway—and it silently plays on repeat in my brain as Kyle and I approach the front door of his parents' house.

Scratch that. It's a mansion. Or mansion-esque.

It's huge.

"Pretty nice, huh?"

My mom always told us 'Money can't buy taste,' and the van der Mullens are, I think, exactly who she had in mind when she said that.

Kyle puffs out his chest, apparently so proud of his *parents'* house, and admires it from the bricks of the horseshoe driveway.

"It's big," I answer, and he emits a low chuckle.

"Yeah," he sighs with a smile, like I just paid him the greatest compliment of his life.

He places a hand on the small of my back, which is a move we contractually agreed upon (for a fee), and guides me to the front door. It opens on our approach, and Mrs. van der Mullen greets us in a red satin dress with a deep sweetheart neckline. And here I was afraid the hip-hugging number Kyle bought for me was too much for dinner; I thought these overly dressy at-home family dinners were just part of made-for-TV movies.

I am relieved, three hours later and five-hundred dollars richer due to some un-agreed-upon cheek kisses from Kyle during dessert, when I am back in my car and on my way to Nick's apartment.

Am I positive the man isn't going to murder me when it's just the two of us alone? No. But could it be any worse than staring at Genevieve van der Mullen's UV-poisoned cleavage while trying to eat undercooked steak, or putting up with Gregory van der Mullen calling me 'honey' and 'sweetie' every thirty-seven seconds? Also no.

Still, it's nice that Nick answers the door in a pair of dark jeans and a green sweater over a button-down shirt and is dressed nothing like how I'd expect a murderer to be clothed.

"Thanks again for coming over." He gestures for me to enter, and I gladly do. His house smells like cranberries and vanilla and warmth, and I drop into an oversized armchair in his living room.

He props himself against the closed door and crosses his arms. "Rough day at the office?" Maybe it's the glare on his glasses, but I swear his eyes twinkle.

"Have you ever had to deal with someone so obnoxious you wish the Rapture would happen at that exact moment, just to make it end? Or, I don't know, that huge earthquake that would give California island status?"

"We're not in California, so I don't know if that would help, exactly..."

I sigh and roll my eyes, and he shifts his weight from one foot to the other. "But yes, I totally get the sentiment. There's this one guy at work who is a total jerk, thinks the world revolves around him. And, joy of joys, he's dating my sister."

"Ooh." I sit up a bit, slipping out of my heels and curling my legs up onto the chair. "Intriguing. Tell me more."

Nick shrugs—which, I've noticed, is a pretty regular state for him. His shoulders are probably the strongest part of him from all the reps they get in. "He's just a tool. One of those guys who knows he's better than everyone else and doesn't let them forget it, you know?"

Yeah. I know the type. "Sounds like a guy I dated about a year ago. He was a ten, looks-wise, but then averaged with his personality? Maybe a three overall. I don't know. Maybe a negative four. He was the worst."

"Worse than the date you just had?"

I'd love to say I haven't thought about Mark in the last ten months, but that would be a lie. Mark is, for better or worse, always in the back of my mind like this nagging mosquito I can swat at but never squash. And though Mark didn't have the same bank balance as Kyle van der Mullen, he had the same hubris, and I had the same disdain. "Yes. Worse than the date I just had."

Nick cocks an eyebrow like he's waiting for more of the story, but there are more pressing matters at hand. Things like, "Are you ready to plan our breakup?"

He answers with a nod, and it's the most certain I've seen him since we met last week. "Yes. Let's do it." He lowers himself into an armchair just inside the door and leans in, resting his elbows on his thighs. "I was hoping for nothing too crazy. Not, like, a big blow-up fight. How are you at crying on command?"

"Nicholas."

"Just Nick."

"Just Nick." I narrow my eyes at him. "Do you really think your best bet to win over Lady Coworker is to make your current girlfriend, who braves whitewater and wrestles deadly snakes—"

"The snake was harmless."

I wave off the interruption. "You think that making me, a total badass, leave in tears is the best way to attract someone else?"

He opens his mouth and quickly closes it, once, twice. "Crap. You're right."

"Your best bet is for me to dump you. How are *you* at crying on command? Or should I just go crazy and make you cry for real?"

Nick recoils and cringes. "Please don't."

"Why did you invite me here, anyway? If you wanted another consult, why not just meet at the bar again?"

He straightens and clasps his hands. "I promise I'm not a total creeper."

I snort at this, because Nick Goodman is adorable. Innocent and sweet, with his floppy mop of hair and his hipster-but-not-too-hipster glasses and his gentle smile and his self-doubt. "I never accused you of being one."

"It's just," he continues, suddenly—apparently—finding the toes of his shoes very interesting, "I thought that if we're as serious as I'd told them, you should probably know about my house. Like the layout, or the location, or..."

"Or where we have all of our 'great sex'?"

His head snaps up and I send a wink across the living room toward him. He smiles at this, at least a half-smile that creates the cutest divot of a dimple at the corner of his mouth. "Yes. You should absolutely know where we have all the sex."

"*Great* sex."

"Sure." He practically launches himself from his chair, striding past me toward the kitchen, motioning for me to follow him. "C'mon, I'll show you where the various types of magic happen."

I hop onto my feet and drop my heels just inside the front door. Then I hurry to catch up with Nick, who has disappeared down the hallway; the faint sound of the hummed melody of *Black Velvet* guides me to him.

THE CHRISTMAS SWEATER
Holly

"Wow."

Nick opens the door wider and steps out of the way so I can come in off his porch and escape the cold air outside. His gaze sweeps over me, over a black turtleneck sweater minidress with a row of red, green, and gold tassel garland across my décolletage, down over my legs and their black, gold-flecked tights, all the way to my red-and-green plaid stilettos.

I could have fun with this. I could give Nick the whole 'eyes up here' spiel, but if we're being honest, it's nice to have someone take me in, to have someone look without leering, to feel like someone notices the hard work that goes into dressing up for a date, doing my hair, shaving my legs in *winter*. Like, this is natural-insulation season, but I'm taking care of business so I don't look like one of those cartoon ads for a match game app that tricks you by making you think it's a makeover game.

"'Wow' you can't believe I'm on time? Or 'wow' you can't believe I showed up at all, or...?"

Nick's eyes find mine again all on their own. "You look nice," he says simply.

"Do I? In this old thing?" I'm joking, but he doesn't seem to be.

"I'm actually... surprised? I guess? That it's an ugly Christmas sweater party, but you somehow look..." He trails off like he's not sure how to finish that statement without deeply offending me or embarrassing himself.

"Nice?" I offer, repeating his own word.

He meets my gaze again and nods once. "Yes."

"You do, too." And he does. He's wearing dark jeans with a quarter-zip sweater, mostly Kelly green but with a red stripe across the chest and a pair of reindeer knit in with white thread. "I think you're a little misaligned with the theme. Your sweater doesn't seem *that* ugly."

"Au contraire, *mon ami*." He grins and presses a spot on his side, and little lights illuminate his shoulders and scrawl *Merry Christmas* across his torso. "How about now?"

I can't help but laugh. Nick responds in kind, boyish and charming and warm. If we'd met before he hired me, I think we would've become friends.

"You're right. It's hideous."

"Exactly what I was going for." He winks and grabs his coat, then locks the front door behind us. Nick drives because his car is significantly nicer than mine. It doesn't seem fair that he gets his own place and a car that doesn't have a few warning lights perennially illuminating the dash. I bet he's never been fired for the sake of golf outings.

The party is being held at a refurbished barn in Ferryton, and the drive is filled with pop Christmas songs and a review of some of the highlights of our fake relationship to make sure we're telling the same story, if asked.

"And if you talk to George," he says, "you've only heard great things about him and the job in general."

My head snaps toward him and I smack his shoulder. "Do you really think I'd tell your boss anything else? I'm not a monster."

In the glow of passing street lights I can see his smile. "No, you're just going to dump me in front of all my coworkers."

"What can I say?" I shrug this time and settle into my seat. "I take my job very seriously."

He hums along to a Michael Bublé song on the radio, quieting as we pull into the gravel parking lot for the barn. "Is this stupid?" he asks.

"Probably. But we're here now, and you've got to pay me either way." If the lack of any sort of snort, snicker, or smile is any indication, he's too nervous to appreciate my humor. "Don't worry." I rest what I hope is a comforting hand on his, which he hasn't moved from the PRNDL stick. "I'm going to break your heart so spectacularly that Catherine is going to take pity on you and drag you under the nearest mistletoe."

This earns a smile and that adorable dimple again, and his glasses frame his eyes as they shift to me. "Promise?"

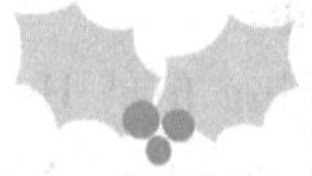

Nick and I, like any happy couple, cling to one another's side during the party. I remind him under my breath to wrap his arm around my waist, but I don't reciprocate the touch. We can't look *too* happy, after all—or at least I can't. But the happier Nick looks now, the more devastated he'll seem later.

Nick gets pulled into a conversation about golf, which I excuse myself from, and I'm at the dessert station eyeing up the sweets when an older man steps beside me and points out a tower of bite-size caramel-apple pies. "These are the absolute best," he says with the confidence of someone who has eaten a few in his day.

I glance sideways and do a double-take at his suit, which is black but printed to look like an ugly Christmas sweater, with rows of green trees and red ornaments and white snowflakes banding across the fabric.

"You like the suit?" He gives me a wink, more Santa Claus than seductive in execution and—I think—intent. Then he balances a napkin and bite-size pie over his beer bottle in one hand so he can extend his other toward me. "George. McGillis."

Ah, Nick's boss. I shake his hand and introduce myself, trying to make a good impression that will reflect positively on both myself and my faux beau. "Holly. I'm here with Nick."

"Holly." His smile falters as his forehead crinkles. "I thought—"

"Right. I forgot. Nick has probably called me Emily before, if he talks about me at all."

George's eyes light up and the grin returns to his face. "I've definitely heard talk of an Emily. Do you go by your middle name?"

"Nope." I shake my head, ready to tell another lie tonight, all in the name of getting paid by a nice guy so I can attend a wedding that makes me wish my best friend was Amish. Oh, the tangled webs we weave. "I know it's hard to believe, since Nick is normally so detail-oriented, but he totally forgot my name during our first date. I think he latched on to the 'l-y' at the end and started calling me Emily around the time our entrees were delivered."

I get a chuckle from George at that, which I think is a good sign that our story is, at the very least, plausible. "And he just kept doing it, even after you corrected him?"

"Who says I corrected him? If he asks you, my name is *definitely* Emily." I arch an eyebrow, then allow myself to smile when the joke lands. "I had to break it to him on our second date. I didn't want to make it awkward, and I wasn't sure what the statute of limitations was on that. But now he calls me Emily almost as a term of endearment. Recently 'Holly' has made people think of the Maharelle sisters, so it's kind of nice not to hear people sing 'and I'm Dooneese' every time they hear my name."

Nick chooses this moment to rejoin me, and he's greeted by more laughter from George. The man must be a fan of SNL.

"You've got a funny one here, Goodman," George says, shaking a finger toward me as he addresses Nick. "You have to hold on to the funny ones."

"Of course," Nick answers, glancing from his boss to me and back.

Someone rests a hand on George's shoulder and he turns, then apologizes to us over his shoulder, and takes off with the other attendee.

"Looks like someone made quite the impression." Nick passes me a glass of punch and takes a sip from his own, eyeing George discreetly as he does.

"What is it that you do, exactly? I feel like I should apply for a job here. The boss already loves me."

"And he bought the whole Emily story?"

I nod and take a drink. "Sure did."

"Great." Nick takes a step closer to me as a coworker approaches, and after another brief introduction, I help myself to a mini pie while they chat about a project they're collaborating on. It's then that I see him, from the corner of my eye. Tall, devilishly handsome, inconceivably charismatic. And headed this way.

I nearly choke on crumbs from the pie crust as I hurry to finish chewing, and I try not to let on that I've seen him as I rejoin Nick and wrap an arm around his waist. I force a smile onto my lips and rest my head against Nick's shoulder, feeling him tense under the touch. His coworker—Carter? I haven't needed to pay too much attention to people's names—nods his regards and wanders toward the bar.

"You okay?" Nick tilts his head down to check on me, but I place a hand on his chest and assure him I'm fine. I *will* be fine, if we can just hide somewhere. Where's that Apocalypse when you need it?

I'm about to sneak off to the restroom when Nick stretches an arm and waves, then lowers it with a grumble. "Well, I found my sister. And then I saw her idiot boyfriend."

"Oh! Great!" I'm grateful for the distraction and the opportunity to talk to someone—anyone—other than the man who just spotted me from across the room.

Nick's sister, Clara, might have the same curly hair and dimple as her big brother, but she rocks it in a cover-model way, exuding confidence in every step toward us and in the way she says his name, drawn out and cheerful, and in the way she hugs me. "Oh my gosh, Nicky! She's beautiful!"

I feel the heat rise to my cheeks; being called beautiful by some-one who is so stunning takes me back to the time my elementary school got a grant to have an artist visit us, and she looked at my fourth-grade self-portrait and said it was excellent work. I knew she was lying, and everyone else knew it, and I threw the portrait in the trash before I even left school that afternoon.

I can't throw myself in a trash can (I'm scanning the room but can't seem to find one, or I'd be there), so I half hug her back. It's not a full hug, since one arm is still clutching the back of Nick's sweater in a desperate attempt to stay rooted to the one person at this party who can save me from—

Nick clears his throat as Clara releases me. "Holly, this is my sister, Clara. Clara, this is Holly."

"A.k.a. Emily," I add, clinging again to Nick, who gestures to the tall figure who has moseyed up behind his girlfriend.

"And this is Clara's boyfriend," he starts, and we both finish his sentence.

"Mark."

LAST CHRISTMAS
Holly

THREE SETS OF EYES lock on me, then two pairs shift to Nick.

"You know Mark?" Clara's ruby lips curl in amusement as her gaze returns to me.

"Holly is... Emily?" Mark asks Nick.

"It's a long story," he and I both answer.

Clara's attention bounces between Nick and me like we're in the Wimbledon finals, but Mark's eyes stay locked on my face. I can feel it, even if I'm avoiding looking back.

"So... are you going to tell the story? Or are we supposed to guess?" Clara's bright voice breaks through the din of the party.

There are so many stories to tell here: the Emily-is-Really-Holly story. The How-I-Know-Mark story. The I-Want-to-Be-Anywhere-But-Here storyline that is rapidly developing. And then there's the story we came here to tell: We've Had a Few Great Months, But I'm Moving On.

Nick's telling the rehearsed story about our first date and the name mix-up, and he must be a pretty decent actor too, because it makes me feel all warm and fuzzy even though I know it's a lie. I drift more closely to him, and with his arm around my shoulder I feel safe, protected, like I'm on *Survivor* and he's a tiny shelter and Mark is a Fijian storm.

He finishes the retelling, then looks down at me. He gives that dimpled half-smile, and Clara asks how I know Mark, and Mark is *right there* and unbothered and smug, and I can't do it. I can't do the whole break-up thing, the whole thing I was hired to do, the whole look-pathetic-in-front-of-the-most-obnoxious-ex-ever thing.

Mark takes it upon himself to answer his girlfriend, which is great, because I've gone voiceless for—if you ask my family—the first time in my life. "Holly and I went on a few dates," he says.

I choke on the fortifying sip of punch I just took. Did Mark just say we went on 'a few' dates? That's a weird way to describe our relationship. Our year-long, wretched relationship.

"You okay?" Nick takes a step away as I cough, and concern and curiosity play on his features.

"I'm fine." The gasping for oxygen is contrary to my claim, but I recover, clear my throat, and finally meet Mark's eyes. "We dated for almost a year, actually." Even months ago, well after we were over, I wouldn't have dared to challenge him. But what's he going to do now, in front of his perfect girlfriend? Tell me I'm crazy again? Tell me I'm making too much out of it? Gaslight me again?

Turns out, yes.

"Off and on, nothing too serious." He's fully behind Clara and wraps his arms around her waist, less protective and more possessive. She's like a shield for him, like no assaults launched at him could land without collateral damage.

It makes sense, then, what happens next: the way I snuggle up into Nick's side, the way I squish my face against his chest, the way I challenge Mark with my eyebrows and my words. "And thank goodness it ended, or I never would've met and fallen in love with Nick."

Nick's whole body goes rigid, and I hear his *gulp* echo throughout his ribcage. Clara gives a little squeal of delight and reaches out to smack her brother's shoulder. "In *love*? You don't even let us meet her until after you're using the L-word?"

"Looks that way," Nick says. I toe the floor. "Anyway, we'll let you get back to the party. We've hardly spent any time together tonight, so..." He gives a little wave and turns, and his hand presses into the small of my back to guide me to a corner with an abandoned bench. "What the hell, Holly."

"I'm sorry. I know I went a little off-script..."

"A *little* off-script? You tell Mark and Clara we're in love, and it's supposed to be believable when you break up with me in thirty minutes?"

I drop my gaze to my empty punch cup and shift my weight from one foot to the other. "No."

"Are you serious?" He drops onto the bench. "You're not going to do it, are you?"

"I'm sorry," I answer, and I really am. "Obviously, I'll refund you in full for my fee. I know I screwed this up for you."

"I guess I just don't understand why. We were on track. You'd been perfectly and appropriately disinterested in me for most of the night. Why, all of a sudden..."

"Because Mark Thompson is an ass and I couldn't let him win."

Nick leans forward, resting his forearms on his thighs. He examines his own punch glass as I plop down next to him, then looks at me with genuine concern. Bless him. "Want to talk about it?"

I don't, but I owe Nick some sort of explanation here, now that I've blown up his whole plan with Catherine. "I mean, it's kind of what you said the other day. The guy's the absolute worst, and *you* just have to *work* with him."

"And see him at family functions."

"Oh, god, I didn't even think..."

He shrugs, softening a bit from just a few minutes ago. "So, what happened with you two?"

What happened was that Mark never made time for me but blamed me anyway for every rift in our relationship. What happened was that Mark didn't communicate, didn't respect me, didn't value me, didn't think I was worthy of him; that he thought I was too much and not enough, all at once. What happened was that Mark didn't even invite me to this same party last year because I 'wouldn't have fun' and 'wouldn't fit in.' And what happened was that Mark made me believe that all of these things were reflections of my faults and failings, and not projections of his own shortcomings. "There wasn't room in a relationship for three of us," I say simply, because the rest of it is hard to say and harder to explain.

"He cheated?"

"No." I shake my head. "But between me, him, and his ego..."

"Say no more," Nick chuckles.

I touch my fingertips to his forearm. "I really am sorry," I repeat.

He glances at the spot where our skin meets, then up to me. "I get it. I'll just have to fake a break-up on my own, I guess, in a few weeks."

"I know I have no right to ask you this, but when you do... Can you make me seem not pathetic? Like, I don't want Mark to think that seeing him again rattled me and made me realize that I wanted him again or something."

He sits up and smiles, and his expression doesn't scream *pity* but it certainly whispers it. "I'll be sure to preserve your dignity."

Because we're in love, according to our story, I scoot closer to him and rest my head on his shoulder again, though I do withdraw my hand and use both to hold my cup. "Is this okay, for now?"

I feel his nod. "It's good," he answers, which is not what I asked but is nicer to hear. "Do you want to get out of here soon?"

Seeing Mark always takes a toll on me, and at present I feel both emotionally and physically exhausted from our brief interaction. But I also feel terrible for screwing up the arrangement Nick and I had agreed upon, and that he had paid me for. "I'm here for as long as you want to be."

He pauses and surveys the room. "Are you up for a little more mingling?"

"Forced merriment? For you? Of course." I squeeze his hand and stand, pulling him up with me. "Let's go show everyone how awesome you are. I will tell anyone anything after what you just did for me. If you want me to tell anyone about how great you are in bed, I will. Point me toward Catherine and I'll go prime her for our breakup."

When Nick laughs, I feel like I matter. There's something about the way his head dips forward and his hair falls over his forehead and he has to adjust his glasses on his nose every time. He commits effort to the simple act of laughing, and warmth spreads from my chest to my fingertips and my toe knuckles at the sight and sound of it.

"Is it okay if I hold your hand?" he asks as he runs a hand through his hair, pushing back the tumble of curls. "Since we're in love, and everything."

"Sure." It was part of the contract, and even if I'm not charging him for the date, I need to uphold some part of our arrangement.

He slides his hand into mine, palm to palm, without lacing our fingers together. We look like we're crabs, linked at the claws, but I roll with it as he leads me toward one of his closest friends at work. I've heard plenty of stories about Garrett, but I'm still not quite prepared for the shock of meeting someone who is so unlike Nick but so close to him.

Garrett's wearing ripped black jeans and a green T-shirt that shows Santa holding a bag of gifts and text that includes some reference to a sack, though I'm unable to read the full phrase on account of the leather jacket that flaps with his animated arm gestures. His hair is pulled back in a messy bun I could only aspire to recreate myself. "Nicky, my maaaan," he says, clapping him on the back. "And you must be Emily," he adds, lifting me off the floor in a bear hug.

"Hey," Nick interjects. "Personal space, man."

Garrett releases me with a casual apology. "I'm just so excited to meet the famous Emily!"

"So, fun story," Nick begins, and he tells the name story again. I'm glad we prepared it in advance, or our Mark meeting would have been a challenge to navigate.

Garrett rubs his chin with a finger and furrows an eyebrow. "So Emily doesn't actually exist, but Emily is actually Holly?"

"Right," Nick confirms.

"And I *do* exist, turns out," I add.

There's an amused breathy snort from Nick, and I can't help but smile. Whenever we do break up, I'm running straight to Catherine and telling her to snatch him up, because he'll make her feel like a million bucks, even if he doesn't realize it.

Speaking of, we never find her during the party. Instead we chat with Garrett and excuse ourselves after Mr. McGillis passes out the envelopes with holiday bonus checks inside.

The ride back to Nick's house is much quieter than the ride to the party. I mostly sit and pick at my cuticles and wish for an alternate reality where I'd never even met Mark Thompson, or at least one where I hadn't dated him, or one where I acted like a professional and followed the contract I'd set up with my client.

Nick pulls into his driveway, but before he can put his car in park, I'm unbuckled and reaching for the door handle. "I'm so sorry again about tonight. I'll get your refund processed as soon as I get home."

"You really don't have to—"

"I do," I insist. "Just remember to make me not look like a loser or a lunatic when you get around to breaking us up."

He nods, forcing a smile that doesn't quite reach his eyes. "Of course. You'll thoroughly devastate me in the most compassionate way possible." Then he unbuckles himself, and we both exit the car.

As the doors close, Nick catches my eye above the roof. "Thank you, Holly."

I haven't done anything other than make a mess of things, but I give an appreciative smile anyway. "Merry Christmas, Nick. I hope everything works out just the way you want it to." And with that, I leave Nick Goodman standing in his driveway, alone in the cold.

JUST FOR NOW
Nick

I RETURN HOLLY'S MONEY as soon as she refunds me. Not because she didn't screw up my plan—she absolutely did. But by doing that, she still accomplished half of what we set out to do, which was to make people believe I actually have a girlfriend, and that she's awesome, and to make Catherine maybe a little jealous.

There are four of us waiting in a haphazard line for the single-cup coffee brewer in our break room when Garrett walks in and slaps my back. "Du-u-ude," he says, apparently already a few energy drinks into his morning. "You talked about Holly so much, but you never said how hot she was."

Catherine rolls her eyes from her spot in front of me in line. "Seriously, Garrett." Then she turns to me with an arched eyebrow. "Who's Holly? What happened to Emily?"

"Holly *is* Emily. It's a whole thing," my friend answers for me. "Anyway..." he makes sure Catherine's not watching him and mouths *H-O-T* to me. Sometimes I wonder why we're friends, but I feel like my choices in the office are Mark or Garrett, and it's not even a competition.

"Sorry that I missed out on meeting your girlfriend," Catherine says, once Garrett's across the room reorganizing things in the refrigerator so he can squeeze in his leftovers.

I shrug. "Not a big deal. Sorry you missed the party."

"Hurtful, Goodman. I heard there was karaoke. You'd rather I be subjected to that than sick at home?"

The woman in front of Catherine turns with a bit of a glare when her coffee is done, and Catherine steps up to use the machine.

"I must have missed that part. We left before it was over."

"Ah." There's a *wink-wink, nudge-nudge* quality to her 'ah.' Like 'Ah, you and your girlfriend snuck out early, eh?' and I want to tell her yes, but no. Yes, we left before it was over, but *no,* not like that, or for that, but I don't. Her mug fills quickly and she dunks a tea bag into the steaming water. "Well, Monday calls. Have a good day, Nick."

I *do* have a good day. It's a good day when Carter and I test the code we've been working on and it actually does what it's supposed to do; it's a good day when George calls me into his office for my end-of-year review; it's an even better day when he offers me a ten percent raise for the new year.

And then I get to the restaurant. Dinner out, just the four of us, is always our anniversary gift to our parents. But this year Clara's brought Mark, and for some reason my parents are thrilled to see him. He commandeers the conversation all throughout dinner, and his laugh is too big, and he's trying too hard, but it's all working: Mom and Dad are charmed by him.

We make it all the way to dessert until he acknowledges my presence, and even then he's more interested in my parents than in me. "So," he says, still chewing his steak (that Clara and I are paying for, so three cheers for that raise), "what do you guys think of Nick's girlfriend?"

My parents have heard bits and pieces, mostly from Clara. I've tried not to talk too much about the whole Emily situation around them because I figure the fewer people I lie to, the better.

Dad answers, "We haven't met her yet," matter-of-factly, like it's the most normal thing in the world.

"Nicholas!" Mark playfully chides. "You're in love with the woman and you haven't even introduced her to your family?"

Mom's fork clatters to her cheesecake plate. "In *love*, Nicky? I didn't realize it was so serious!"

"To clarify," I address Mark directly, "she's the one who said she's in love."

"Oh, brother, you're in love," Clara adds, rolling her eyes. "It was super obvious."

On one hand, Clara's absolutely lost it. On the other, it's a great testament to my acting skills, and I'll take any compliment I can get from this crowd.

"Well, that's wonderful, dear." Mom glances at Dad, who nods. "If it's so serious, you'll have to bring her around."

"It's really not." I stab a piece of pie with my fork and shove it into my mouth, trying to buy some time to come up with an excuse for why Holly definitely won't be coming around. "I feel like things are fizzling a little. I don't know. We'll probably break up soon."

If I was just having dinner with my family, I would be fine. But Mark is also here, and he snickers and stretches, putting an arm around the top of Clara's chair. "I'd like to say I'm surprised, but..." He lets his half-thought linger there as he takes a drink of his Manhattan.

"What's *that* supposed to mean?"

He takes another swig and swirls the amber liquid in his glass before setting it down. "Nothing. Just that between the two of you, I wasn't expecting things to last as long as they did. Especially after realizing you were dating *Holly*?" He cringes. "Yikes."

It's official. I hate Mark Thompson.

Mom frowns, confused. "I thought you were dating an Emily. Who's Holly?"

"It's a long story," Clara and I answer together.

"And for your information, Holly's great," I snap back at Mark. I mean, she seems great, and I did promise to preserve her dignity with this jerk.

"So great you're planning to dump her?"

"I didn't say I was planning to dump her. I said things are fizzling."

Mark rolls his eyes and smirks.

"You know what? I think I *will* bring her around a bit more."

"What about bringing her Christmas tree shopping?" Clara *loves* Christmas tree shopping day. Each year, we drive to Evermore Evergreens to find two perfectly good, healthy trees to chop down and haul home. Each year, I get a lecture about how I need a tree, too, even though no one really comes to visit to see it decorated so I've stopped wasting the money and time to buy and decorate one.

I lean toward Clara to ask more quietly, "You honestly don't have a problem with your boyfriend's ex-girlfriend hanging out with our family?"

Clara just shrugs and cozies up to Mark. "I don't mind it. Mark's moved on, and clearly Holly has, too."

Eight eyes watch me, waiting for an answer. For some inexplicable reason, I care most about the two across the table taunting me.

Fresh out of excuses, I sigh. "I'll see if she's free."

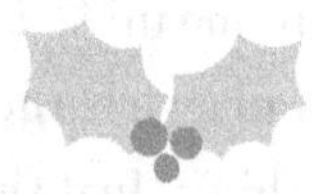

My phone vibrates in my pocket three times on my drive home, but I don't bother checking it until I'm in the house and have changed into sweatpants and an old college hoodie. I slip my feet into the rarely worn slippers Mom gave me for Christmas freshman year at Wilde Lake, and once I'm on the couch with my feet up, I finally read the notifications.

I got your repayment.

Which was totally unnecessary, btw. I should be the one paying you.

I'm not going to, because that would defeat the purpose of this whole little side hustle I've got going on. But know that's my current sentiment.

Thanks again.

Despite my frustrations with Mark and how the whole night played out—including the implication that I'm incapable of maintaining a relationship, apparently?—I find myself laughing at the texts from Holly. She texts like she talks: a little random and over-sharey and refreshingly honest. The fact that she's texting at all is promising, and I take a deep breath before I reply.

Keep it. You earned it.

He lives!

I thought you were ghosting me before you break up with me!

No—just got home from dinner.

Actually, you did such a great job pretending to be my girlfriend that my sister thinks we're madly in love.

No offense to your sister, or to you I guess, but we're not that good at acting.

I don't know if I acted differently at the party, or if it's because of the way Holly attached herself to my sweater, my side, my hand, but we must have been pretty convincing. I'm sure there's a large amount of wishful thinking on Clara's part, too, but somehow Holly and I planted a seed in her brain. And now my family wants to meet her.

> Is there any chance I can call you?

She types and deletes, types and deletes, types and deletes. And then she calls.

"What's up?" Her voice is cheery, if a little cautious, and she greets me before I can even say hello.

"Hi," I reply.

I can hear music in the background, jazzy and subdued, and I wonder if I've misread her. I wonder if 'jazzy and subdued' is a better descriptor than anything I've come up with so far; if she's home with an expensive bottle of wine and fancy cheese and maybe a boyfriend who likes those things, too. But then she speaks and I think I had it right before: There are many sides to Holly; *jazzy and subdued* might be one, just like *fun and upbeat* and *quirky and unique.* She's just *her.*

"Hi," she draws out. "What's up?"

"Oh." I didn't really practice this conversation in my head, mostly because I wasn't expecting to have it tonight, and partially because I spent my drive home from dinner internally bemoaning my sister's interest in the biggest jerk I know.

I bet Mark was the kind of guy who shoved kids into lockers in school, or who flirted with girls so they'd do his share of a group project, or who did the bare minimum at college but graduated with honors because his family's name is on some building somewhere on campus.

"If I'm interrupting, I can—"

"You're not. And I called you. Let me just—" She cuts herself off. I hear muffled talking and a shrill *beep,* and then the music is gone and she's back on the phone. "Sorry. Just doing some baking. Is that better?"

I nod and, realizing she can't hear it, verbally confirm. "Yes. It's good." We suffer through a brief awkward silence before I realize she's probably still expecting me to answer the question of 'what's up?'

"We have a problem." It's probably—no, definitely—not the best way to start my update, but Holly doesn't seem fazed. "Well, I guess, *I* have a problem."

She gives a drawn-out *"Okaaaaay,"* and I take a breath to collect my thoughts.

"I had dinner with my family tonight. And Mark." I know I said as much in my texts, and I appreciate that Holly doesn't interrupt or sigh or make any other indication that she's annoyed by the repetitiveness of my story. "He asked my parents about you, and the whole thing about you being in love with me came up..."

There's a sharp intake of breath on the other end of the call. "Yeah. Sorry about that. I got a little carried away, maybe."

"It's fine, but, long story short... How would you feel about going on a few more dates?"

I hope that Holly's silence can be attributed to her attention returning to baking, or to an accidental pressing of the mute button, and that she didn't just hang up on me when I asked.

"Holly?"

"Yeah?" she asks, her voice cheery.

"I'd pay, obviously, if you're worried about—"

"I'm not." It's not that Holly isn't typically bold, because I would definitely describe her that way after our three meetings. But Holly isn't normally—at least with me—curt.

I pause, and she pauses, and then she sighs. "How many more dates are we talking about?"

Clara only mentioned Christmas tree shopping, but I'm sure that'll lead to at least one other outing. It's a busy month, and my parents (and sister) are relentless. "It's not like we have to keep up the farce till death do us part, or anything. It's just a few dates. Just for now."

She's quiet again, though there's shuffling in the background that makes me immediately nostalgic for my grandma's secret-recipe Christmas cookies. But the warm and fuzzy feeling fades when Holly asks, less than enthusiastically, "What do you have in mind?"

CHRISTMAS TREE FARM
Holly

"YOU'RE WEARING *THAT* TO a farm?" Landon barely glances up from his laptop as I duck into the kitchen for a quick snack before I leave to meet Nick.

I peel a banana and answer, "It's a *Christmas tree* farm. It's not like I'm going to be traipsing through fields of manure. And besides, I didn't know you were so interested in my sartorial choices."

"It just looks like you're trying a little too hard to impress someone, considering the occasion. That's all," he says with a shrug. He goes back to speed-clacking at his keyboard, hard at work even on a weekend, because that's what you do when you're young and smart and ambitious and have prospects that will lead to things like home ownership and paid-off student loans.

"You're trying to impress someone?" There's a hopeful tone in Mom's voice as she hauls three bags of groceries through the door from the garage and plunks them down on the island where Landon's sitting. He rises to help, but Mom holds out a hand to tell him to stay, and closes the garage door.

I take another bite of my banana and try to catch Landon's gaze. When I told him about Nick—and, more importantly, Mark—we both thought it would be good to make this particular dating situation seem real when Mom found out about it. The last thing I need is for Mom and Mrs. Thompson to bump into each other at Della's Grocery and for Mom to blow my cover to Mark's mom. I can hear the conversation now:

Mrs. T: *Oh, Mark said Holly has finally moved on, found herself an entry-level chump!*

Mom: *Holly? No. Holly's just renting herself out to anyone slightly more desperate than herself, but with a greater net worth.*

Mrs. T, later, to Mark: *Honey, your intel is wrong! Holly's just as much of a pathetic loser as she's always been!*

So, yeah, Mom needs to think I'm out of the game when it comes to Nick.

"I have a date this morning."

She glances over my outfit, a quick, barely perceptible and yet somehow-still-very-obvious dip in her attention from my eyes to my feet and back. "You look nice. Where are you headed?"

I shrug and drop my banana peel in the trash. "Evermore Evergreens, out near Ferryton."

Mom pauses with a box of pasta halfway in the pantry. "Christmas tree shopping?"

I nod. "We're going to chop one down, apparently."

"Well, first, this sounds serious. Picking out a tree together? Normally home decor decisions don't involve a significant other until a little later on in a relationship."

"It's a tree. It's temporary."

Landon mouths *like your fake relationship* at me and I fork him the finger while Mom puts away the jar of sauce I've handed her.

"What's the second thing?" I ask. She looks at me like I have two heads. "You said 'first,' so I figure there's a second."

She closes the pantry and scans my outfit again. "Do you think the sweater's a little much? You're going to a farm, not a nightclub."

I'm not sure who she thinks is wearing a red cable-knit sweater to a nightclub. Sure, fine, it's an off-the-shoulder sweater. And yes, I have wriggled into the skinny jeans I was wearing months ago, back when I wasn't drowning out my sadness with Cool Ranch Doritos and reruns of *The Rookie* on a nightly basis. And if we want to be super particular, yes, the sweater has tiny glittery threads and the boots I pulled on are wedges and I learned how to do a fishtail braid just for this morning and... Okay, fine. They might have a point.

"I'll go change."

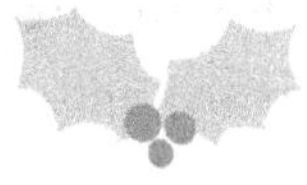

Turns out, my brother was right. Also, that's a private confession, and he is never to hear that I said those words.

The Goodman family (and Mark) are all decked out in red and black Buffalo plaid flannel, like they're auditioning to be the next Brawny Man. "You could've warned me about the dress code," I tell Nick as we unbuckle our seatbelts in the hay-strewn lot. My cream-colored oversized sweater (over straight-leg jeans and paired with more reasonable flat boots) makes me stand out against the coordinated family.

"It's tradition for the four of us. I didn't think you and I needed to be so matchy-matchy."

"And yet, Mark matches." I roll my eyes and climb out of the car. Of *course* Mark matches. Because he and Clara are real, and they would've talked about today beyond a hasty invitation in a nervous phone call.

Nick meets me at my side of the car, and I struggle to sync with his cadence and stride as we approach his family.

Even if Mark and Clara weren't with them, even if they weren't wearing the same outfit from the Family Matching portion of Old

Navy's website, I'd be able to pick Nick's parents out of a crowd. Mrs. Goodman has a mane of curls, thick and honey-colored, just like her son. And Mr. Goodman has a similar pair of fashion-frame glasses that he shoves up the bridge of his nose, and the same disarming, crooked smile as Nick.

"Hey, Holly!" Clara's the first to greet me, and she does so with an enthusiastic hug. Then she scolds her brother. "Nicky, I can't believe you didn't tell her about the shirts!"

"Yeah, man. Way to make her look like an outsider."

Leave it to Mark to always make me feel like I don't belong.

But then Nick's voice cuts through the brain noise. "Holly, these are my parents, Christina and Jonathan. Mom, Dad—this is Holly."

Jonathan greets me first, then Christina, who even compliments my sweater. There's something about each member of the Goodman family that feels comfortable and safe and known, right from the start. Even when one of them is holding a hatchet, another, a saw. Even when my ex is present and dead-set on making me look and feel as bad as possible.

"Shall we go find some trees to fell?" Mr. Goodman asks, shifting the saw from one hand to the other. Nick takes the hatchet from his mom.

"Let the merriment begin!" Clara shouts before taking Mark's hand in hers and marching toward the rows of trees.

I like her, save for her awful choice in men.

After a short hike up a dirt lane into the field, Clara and Mark take a turn down a long stretch with a sign marked *Blue Spruce*. I look up at Nick, wondering if we're supposed to follow them, but he continues straight ahead on our path. Christina and Jonathan slow until we've caught up to them, and Christina engages in conversation since her son seems unwilling to do so.

"So, what do you do, Holly?" she asks, and I'm relieved that Nick and I so thoroughly prepared for the Ugly Sweater Party that I can now confidently answer this question for anyone who asks.

"I work in hospitality. For now, at least." The nice thing is, it's not a complete lie.

Christina nods. "Is it something you could see yourself doing long term?"

Nick laughs the tiniest chuckle I've ever heard, and I elbow him as discreetly as possible. "It's something I enjoy, but it's not really where I envisioned myself." As a rule, I try to be as honest as possible, which might be hard to believe considering the whole fake-dating thing. But what I've just shared with Mrs. Goodman is one of the more truthful things I've said recently, or even allowed myself to consider. None of this—least of all being in the presence of Mark Thompson again—is where I imagined I would be when I looked forward to my life this past year.

Jonathan pauses next to a sign marked *Scotch Pines* and gestures with his head, like he's asking Christina if they should explore. She turns with him and Nick follows.

"Is this the kind you get, too?" I ask him.

He shoves his hands into his pockets and shakes his head. "I'm just here for the tradition. I don't get a tree."

I stop short and hear the record scratch sound in my head. "You don't get a tree?"

Nick shrugs. "I have a ceramic tree I set out on my coffee table."

"*Nicky*," I groan, borrowing his family's nickname for him. "You are absolutely killing me."

"I just don't see the point in spending a hundred bucks to put a dead tree in my living room for a month."

It's a fair point, I guess. I know I'm not in a position to blow that kind of money on something so temporary and trivial. Still, the idea of his house, or any home, being treeless for Christmas makes me feel like Buddy the Elf in a lackluster Gimbels toy department, and I have the sudden urge to fix it up with festive cheer.

Mr. and Mrs. Goodman stare at a behemoth tree before Mr. Goodman turns and asks Nick for the hatchet.

"I can get it, Dad." Nick steps up and gives a few good swings at the solid trunk before trading the hatchet for the saw; Jonathan steadies the tree as Nick works at its base, and Christina and I keep a safe distance. When it's down, Nick carries the heavier trunk end and Jonathan lifts toward the middle. Christina falls into step next to her husband and entwines her fingers with his, and I just kind of follow along.

"Your parents are cute," I tell Nick. "They seem happy."

He nods, looking straight ahead. "They are."

We're almost back to the hut they have set up for payment when we see Clara and Mark, already standing on the edge of the parking lot with a bundled-up tree. Clara's arms are wrapped around one of Mark's, and she throws her head back laughing before nuzzling up to him and snuggling into his shoulder. She waves when she sees us and I wave back, and it's not long until the Goodmans' tree is also wrapped in netting, both trees are secured on top of Mark's SUV, and we're standing in a small circle by the entrance to the farm.

Christina and Jonathan have resumed holding hands. Mark has his arm around Clara's back (I'm pretty sure his hand is in her back pocket). And in stark contrast, Nick and I stand side by side, not touching.

"Can we expect you at dinner, Holly?" Mrs. Goodman asks. I glance between her and Nick, because I'm pretty sure he's supposed to be the one answering the question. If not for his mother, then for me, because I don't know what answer he wants me to give. "I don't know if Nicky told you, but the other half of the tradition is that Jonathan and I make dinner and invite the kids over to unveil the decorated tree. Once, of course, Nick puts the star on top."

"And Clara plugs in the lights," Mr. Goodman finishes, proudly.

"It's a lot to expect someone to give up their full day—" Nick starts, before Mark cuts him off.

"I'll bring the wine," he says, and I instinctively lean into Nick, wrapping my arms around one of his, hoping it looks romantic and nothing like the panicked vise-like grip I know it is.

"I'm happy to bring dessert." I don't know exactly what time dinner is, but if we leave now I should have time to make something and have it ready to leave by five-something.

"Wonderful!" Christina's cheer is contagious. "We'll see you all at six, then."

We say our goodbyes and see-you-laters, and Nick and I are a mile down the road before he finally speaks. "You really didn't have to join us for dinner."

"I didn't want to risk blowing our cover."

"You could've just said you already had plans, or something, since this morning was a last-minute invitation."

I could have done that. Sure. But then Mark would be there, and I wouldn't be, and I don't need him to make me look bad in front of anyone—even if *anyone* is my fake boyfriend's family.

"If you're worried about payment, don't worry. I'll count tonight as part of this morning's fee."

"That's not—" Nick cuts himself off with a grunt. "It's fine. Do you want to meet at my place around five thirty?"

"Sure." I adjust the volume knob on his stereo; Taylor Swift has just come on the radio, and the song is festive and fun. It's a stark contrast to the drive home so far.

When we reach Nick's house, I head straight for my car. He stands outside, hands in pockets, waiting until I'm gone to go inside. Once I've adjusted the heat and the music to exactly where I want them to be, I put my window down and yell from the curb to the driveway, "I'll be here at five thirty. Is there anything special I should wear?"

Nick turns, but not before I swear I catch the hint of a dimple in his cheek.

Under the Mistletoe
Nick

As far as dinners with your fake girlfriend and her very real ex-boyfriend who is now your sister's actual boyfriend go, this one's not *terrible.*

It helps that Holly is naturally bubbly, and that my parents seem to love her. That's a fact *I* don't love, but I also can't blame them for enjoying her company, or her for doing exactly what I hired her to do.

Actually, I hired her to break up with me, but we're just glossing over that part of our history at this point.

Holly, in her ripped jeans and red sweater, looks like she stepped out of one of the made-for-TV movies Mom and Clara watch every year while stringing popcorn and cranberries into garland. I know she was being a smart-ass when she asked earlier if there is anything special she should wear, but I think she found the right combination. And she took out the braid from the Christmas tree farm, so now her hair is soft and wavy over her bare shoulders.

She's telling a story, gesturing with her wine glass in hand, but I'm only half listening. Instead my attention is focused on how Mom's smiling ear to ear, and how Dad's holding Mom's hand, and how Clara is relaxing into Mark's shoulder, and how Mark is—shockingly and thankfully—quiet. Everyone, myself included, seems to be at ease in Holly's orbit.

When our loungy dinner finally ends, I volunteer for cleanup duty and Holly sweet-talks Mom into letting her help me. Mom has a rule against guests cleaning up after anyone but themselves, but Holly can be pretty convincing, which I guess works in our favor.

"Your family's great," she says, rinsing off a dirty dish before placing it carefully in the dishwasher.

I open the cabinet where Mom's always kept her leftover containers, and it's nice to know that some things never change. I pull out two that should cover the remainder of the meal we didn't eat, since Mom's philosophy is that it's better to have too much than not enough. "They're pretty cool." For all the time we've spent together, we've mostly talked about my family, my needs, our plans. I'm not sure if that's avoidance, professionalism, or necessity.

"What's your family like?" I ask, setting an empty platter on the counter next to the sink. "And you don't have to do that, by the way."

"Do what?" She lifts the platter and rinses it, then holds it over the dishwasher like she's contemplating whether it should go in or not.

"It's safe," I tell her. "But you don't have to do the dishes. I can get them if you want to just relax."

Holly shuffles some dishes around in the bottom rack before adding the platter to the back row.

"I'm not paying you extra for that."

She freezes, hovering over the dishwasher, looking at me with a furrowed eyebrow.

I smile at her, rinsing the last of the dishes. "Relax. It's a joke."

She chuckles and hoists herself up onto the counter. "My family's kind of a lot. To answer your earlier question."

"How so?"

She shrugs, then readjusts her sweater so it sits higher on her arms. "I have three brothers. They're kind of like you, but also not."

"Should I be offended by that?" Mom and Dad's fridge is always organized and tidy, so I easily slide the stacked containers on a half-empty shelf.

"No."

I close the door, then lean back against the refrigerator. "Do I get more information about the ways I, your boyfriend and love of your life, am just like your brothers? Is this a weird *Cruel Intentions* kink?"

Holly whips a nearby hand towel at me and laughs. "Gross! No! It's just that you're ambitious, just like they are. And you're all adored by your parents. But one is a manipulative goody-two-shoes, one is basically a tech-bro, and the other is young and smart and kind and easily taken advantage of."

"Okay, so our ambition connects us, but I'm apparently not good at tech, not young, smart, or kind, and—and this is the big one—not manipulative?" I raise an eyebrow at my fake girlfriend, and she rolls her eyes in return.

"If you met them, you'd understand."

"Maybe I should."

"Should what?"

"Maybe I should meet them."

A loud *HA!* bursts through Holly's lips. Then, "Oh, you're serious?"

"Why not?" I abandon my post at the fridge, then close the dishwasher and rinse out the sink. "It would make sense, right? For me to have met your family? It's not like I can make up stories about them if Mark knows them and can call me out."

She seems to think about this for a moment, scrunching her features as she bites the corner of her lip. "You raise a valid argument."

"Unless that's weird for you. Like if you have a real boyfriend, or if this arrangement would freak them out."

Holly shakes her head. "It's fine. But I need you to pretend to be my real boyfriend at that meeting, too."

Interesting. Maybe Holly's family has no idea about her side-hustle, or maybe they do, and she's trying to convince them that she's not seeing serial killers. Or maybe there's something else, something personal that I have yet to scratch the surface of, that's driving her to want this.

"What's in it for me?" I ask, hoping she interprets the question with the same level of seriousness I intended, which is to say, not much.

She thinks for a minute, rubbing her chin like a local theatre's low-budget Hercule Poirot. "Well, I guess I could throw the meeting in for free," she finally says. "I bet we could even feed you."

"You don't have to—" I start, but she holds up a hand.

"It's fine. I'm benefiting from it, too, if we're being honest."

"Benefiting from what?" Clara asks, strolling into the kitchen to grab a fresh bottle of wine.

"Upcoming blood drive," I answer, just as Holly blurts out, "I'm buying Nick lingerie for Christmas."

Clara looks between us, shrugs, and leaves with the wine.

"Lingerie, huh?" I nudge Holly's knee. "That would benefit you?"

"Oh, sweetheart." She slides off the counter and picks up her nearly empty wineglass, then rests a steadying hand on my shoulder and pushes herself up on her tip-toes so her mouth is close to my ear. "That'd benefit both of us." She winks and laughs and drags me by the hand into the living room where my family is waiting around the darkened Christmas tree.

"There you are! We were afraid you two got lost," Dad says.

"Or distracted," Mom adds with a grin. There's no 'afraid' there—I can tell it's actually exactly what she was hoping had happened.

I've thought about the inevitable breakup with Holly, and I get the feeling Mom and Clara will be devastated. But maybe Holly would be open to remaining friends, after, just so my family gets to see her off and on and I don't have to hear about how I robbed them of her presence for all eternity.

"Sorry to hold up the grand unveiling." Holly plops herself onto the floor, cross-legged, in front of the empty third of the couch. I offer her the cushion, but she shakes her head. I sit next to her on the floor, my shoulder pressed to hers.

"For our newcomers, a history." Dad clears his throat and switches to his old-timey professor voice. "Four-score and seven—"

"One score and seven years ago, dear." Mom corrects him with a wink.

Dad begins again. "One score and seven years ago, we celebrated our first Christmas as a family of four." His tone turns sentimental, and he ditches the theatrical accent. "When Clara joined us on December thirteenth all those years ago, we knew our family was complete. Except, of course, future children-in-law and grandbabies. But I digress."

"The tree you see before you..." Mom takes over before Dad goes completely off-script in embarrassing ways, "...is the result of decades of love and creativity and memories. We've kept a few ornaments from our first Christmases as a couple, but the rest have been added from family vacations and traditions."

Clara rubs a hand along Mark's knee and explains, "Every year, Mom and Dad take us to pick out a new ornament that represents our year."

"That's why we have a burrito ornament," I offer to Holly. "Clara went through a pretty epic TexMex phase in twenty-two."

My sister swats at me, just as Mark asks her, "Are the ballet slippers yours, too?"

Clara guffaws and turns to me. "You want to take that one, bro?"

"It's not like they make dance shoe ornaments in any other style or color. And besides, I learned a lot of useful skills in my year at Miss Lisa's Dance Laboratory."

"Okay, you two." Mom scolds us with a smile. This playful arguing is a part of the unveiling tradition. Then she addresses Holly and Mark again. "Once upon a time, I dreamed I'd have a tree like you'd see in a magazine: matching glass balls, carefully hung tinsel, snow-white lights. But this tree has become my dream, mostly because of traditions that date back to—"

"One score and seven years ago?" Holly asks. There's reverence in her voice, like she's admiring a beloved classic Christmas film.

"Exactly!" With a single clap of his hands, Dad kicks off the festivities. "So, without further ado, dear firstborn, would you do the honors?" He lifts the star and hands it to me. The glittering gold star has adorned the top of every tree that's ever graced this living room. It's a relic so treasured (at least within these walls) that I'm surprised Indiana Jones isn't fighting snakes just to claim it as his own.

My parents must have cut at least a foot off the tree after getting it home from the farm, because I can reach the top *and* there's room for the star without it scratching the ceiling.

Once it's in place, Clara pops up from her seat on the couch. "My turn?" she asks, expectantly.

Dad replies by offering her the power cord in a deep bow. "My liege."

Clara shakes her head and orchestrates a count down from ten. When we hit one, she plugs the cord into the wall. Nothing happens.

"Oops," Dad says, then whispers in her ear.

With a goodnatured roll of her eyes, Clara says, "Alexa, turn on the Christmas tree lights," and the room glows with cozy colored lights. There's a chorus of *Oohs* from most people in attendance.

Holly leans in to rest her head on my shoulder. "It's lovely, Mr. and Mrs. Goodman."

It really is. The whole moment is, from the warm lights of the tree to the soft music playing in the background to the gentle touch of Holly's finger against mine on the rug.

"Shall we have dessert?" Mom asks, her eyes sweeping over the tree. "Holly brought a delicious-looking gingerbread roll."

As if on cue, Holly's stomach rumbles.

"Want some dessert?" I ask her. But she shakes her head.

"Can we sit here a few more minutes?"

"Sure." I stretch my legs and shift into a more comfortable posi-tion while the others head toward the kitchen, none faster than Mark.

"Do you like the tree?"

I feel her head nod. "I do. I'm a sucker for nostalgia. Especially at Christmas." Her finger drifts away from mine now that we're alone, but her temple and my shoulder are connected.

"Do you have any special traditions with your family?"

There's a pause, weighted with something unsaid. "Yes, but no. With four kids, we have chaos, mostly."

"Chaos can be good, though. I bet it made Christmas fun growing up."

She laughs, sits up, rolls her neck. "Christmas was full of three boys trying to orchestrate trades over Nerf guns because no one was happy with what they got."

"That doesn't seem so bad," I say, because I remember doing the same thing with my cousins years ago in my grandparents' basement.

"Just wait till you meet them."

"Looking forward to it," I answer. And I am, because I'm curious about what makes Holly *Holly*. I'm curious about the people and the moments that have shaped her into a gig economy-working, Pickup CARtist-driving, fake-dating, parent-pleasing, Christmas tree-lov-ing unicorn of a woman.

There's a commotion behind us, and Clara bursts in with Mark behind her, their fingers interlocked. "Are you guys coming?" Clara asks. Laughter seems to be bubbling beneath the surface, like Dad's telling jokes in the kitchen again.

"We're coming," Holly answers, and she jumps to her feet, offering me her hands and tugging to pull me up with her. We follow Mark and a giggling Clara through the living room, down the hallway, and into the kitchen.

My sister stops abruptly, just inside the kitchen, and erupts with laughter as she spins on her heels. "Gotcha!" she squeals.

Holly and I are in the entry to the room; everyone else is staring at us. Mom, grinning, shifts her eyes upward.

These sneaky bastards have trapped my fake girlfriend and me under mistletoe.

Christmas Wrapping
Holly

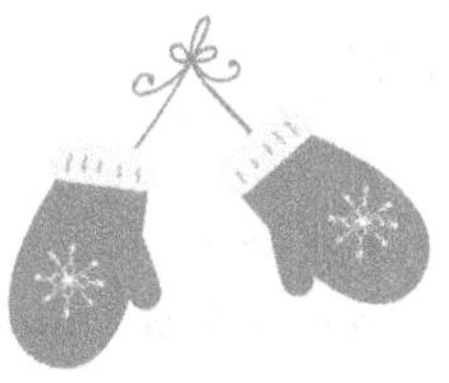

"We should talk about it, right?"

Nick's hands are stuck at ten and two on the wheel, his eyes glued to the road. He hasn't said a word in the five minutes since we left his parents' house, and he said maybe five words in the last twenty (painfully awkward) minutes of our visit.

"Do all your girlfriends get some weird hazing ritual? Or am I special?"

This gets a snort, at least. I'll take that tiny puff of nasal air as a win.

When Nick hired me, we agreed kissing wouldn't be necessary. Some hand holding, a little arm clinging, sure, but kissing was not on the table. Even after the ugly sweater party debacle, when he hired me for the Christmas tree farm and the "just for now" dates, we decided we could get through everything without needing to kiss. Until today, when his family choreographed a little moment for us under a sprig of mistletoe.

"This is definitely a first," he finally says.

"Ah."

"I'm sorry, by the way."

I shrug against my seatbelt. "It's okay. They can't all be great."

There's a pause, one where Nick's mouth opens and closes like a Big Mouth Billy Bass with no sound. "I meant, I'm sorry that they tricked us."

Heat rushes to my cheeks, which I know have to be as red as my sweater.

"Was it really so bad?" he asks a moment later.

"It was... forced? Stiff?"

"Unpracticed?"

"Unexpected. For both of us."

He shrugs. "Yeah, but you— Never mind." Nick's hands shift on the steering wheel, and he taps his index fingers against the vinyl.

I'm a naturally inquisitive person: I need to know who sings every song I hear. I need to hear full stories when I walk in halfway through a conversation. I read four biographies about founding fathers during the height of my *Hamilton* obsession. But I don't think I have ever wanted to know anything more than I want to know how Nick was planning to finish that sentence.

I don't dare ask him. I've already made this car ride awkward as hell.

We reach for the volume control at the same time. You can't hear the Spice Girls sing a Christmas song and *not* turn it up. Nick's fingers graze mine, and we both pull away quickly.

Yes, to the outside observer, we are clearly a normal, loving couple.

"Should we?" he asks when a commercial for a headache medicine comes on. It's kind of the perfect ad for a holiday station just a few weeks before Christmas.

"Should we... what?"

He stops at a red light and finally looks at me. "Should we practice? Nothing crazy, just... so we're prepared. Next time."

Next time. Next time is already on the calendar—Clara invited me to her birthday party next weekend. Actually, *invited* is too gentle a word, and it implies a choice was present. I am being forced to go, and I wouldn't have it any other way.

"You think they're going to try the mistletoe trick again at a party that has nothing to do with us?"

"You say 'the mistletoe trick' like it's a play in football. Right up there with The Brotherly Shove. The Philly Special."

"The Butt Fumble."

Nick's dimple graces us with its presence. "I was trying to list plays that actually benefited the team."

"It benefited the Pats, did it not?"

He shakes his head with a soft exhale. "Unfortunately." After a few quick taps on the steering wheel, he asks, "So, what do you think?"

I think he's maybe a little paranoid. I think his family's a little overzealous. But I think he's probably right: I think I'm going to practice making out with my fake boyfriend. "It's probably a good idea, just to look more convincing," I answer.

He's quiet a few more beats before he says, "I guess we should talk pricing..."

And he's right. We probably should. For anyone else, I would. But this whole arrangement is already more than Nick bargained or budgeted for, and it's my fault. Maybe that's what compels me to say, "Don't worry about it."

"If I'm going to torture you with having to kiss me, the least I can do is make sure you're compensated. For the therapy later, or stock in breath mints, or whatever you feel is appropriate."

I laugh as Nick pulls into his driveway and kills the engine. "It wasn't *torture*," I tell him. I swear he blushes, which makes me blush, and I wonder again how he was going to finish his sentence earlier.

"So, when do we start?"

The great philosophers have asked so many important questions. Marx wanted to know if social injustice could be overcome. Confucius wondered about the right way to rule. Nietzsche asked, 'Does it dance?' And yet all of them pale in comparison to Nick Goodman's innocent and nervous question: *'So, when do we start?'*

I glance between him and his front door. My parked car on the street. Isn't this the perfect setting for a goodnight kiss? Just something soft and simple before I get in my car and go home?

"What about now?" I shrug.

Nick's Adam's apple bobs with an audible swallow. "Oh." It's half grunt, half syllable.

"It's not, like, a full make-out session. Just a quick, little—" To demonstrate, I cup his cheek in my hand and press my lips to his. I pull away before he has a chance to recover from the surprise and kiss me back. "I'll see you," I tell him before unbuckling my seatbelt and leaving him alone in his car as I hurry to mine.

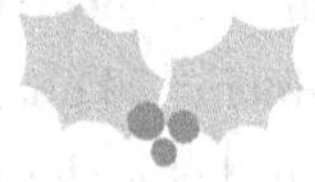

Mom's gift-wrapping station must be the envy of Santa's elves. She's pulled a folding banquet table into the living room, with bins of wrapping paper flanking each end. One bin is full of classic prints in red and black and gold, and the other holds her stash of special paper for my brothers and me. Baby Yoda for Ian. Batman for Micah. Penguins for Landon. Anything with Christmas light bulbs for me. A tote bag has capsized on the floor next to her, spilling out a heap of colorful bows. There's another bag for trash, two pairs of scissors, a stack of name tags, and I count three tape dispensers.

"How was your date?" she asks, looking up with a smile while she expertly curls ribbon on a package adorned with Grogu.

"It was good." I survey her progress. Mom does a great job of wrapping en masse, so she can make a huge mess and then clean it up and be done with it. When I left to meet Nick just a few hours ago, her station wasn't even set up. Now there are at least a dozen gorgeously wrapped packages on the floor, each one lovingly finished with coordinating bows, ribbons, and hanging tags. Mom has always thought the presentation of the package was just as important as what's inside.

She rises to add this newest present to a pile and pats the empty seat next to her. "I'm still going strong, if you want in."

Cheesy Christmas movies play on the TV at the front of the room. She's got a collection of candles from her favorite local candlemaker, Love + Kindness, burning on her mantle. A spot has been cleared out for a tree in the corner.

"Sounds good," I answer. "I have a few things upstairs for the guys."

"Great! I'll whip us up some cocoa."

I rush upstairs and change into leggings and a cozy Christmas sweatshirt with a giant penguin face on the front and the word *Chill* written in a blocky script, then rummage through my closet to find the things I bought for Ian and Micah earlier this year. I always get them the same thing: for Micah, his favorite cologne, and for Ian, something for his comic book collection. Then, if my budget allows, I try to get something to go with them. In the past it's been gift cards, or funny socks, or books from the little indie bookstore in town. This year, the budget definitely does *not* allow, partially because I lost my job the year I have to pay for the most expensive trip I've ever been on, and partially because I'm apparently giving complimentary upgrades to my Holly Dates clients.

"Still nothing for Landon?" Mom asks downstairs. Landon's the hardest one to shop for, but by far the most fun. I always try to find just the right gift, and nothing has spoken to me yet this year.

"No. Not yet." She doesn't need to know that I'm in the same predicament with her and Dad, and I just don't feel like another Texas Roadhouse gift card is the most sentimental choice for parents who have done nothing but rescue and support me when I needed it. Again.

"So," she starts, taking a sip of cocoa. "Just *good*?"

I look at her, a little puzzled, and she smiles.

"Your date."

"Oh." Heat rushes to my cheeks, and I silently curse myself for it. "Yeah. He's really sweet." I'm totally thinking about his demeanor, and not at all about the taste of his lips under mistletoe or in his car.

Mom's turned the volume nearly the whole way down on the television. Clearly, there is a greater potential for drama in this story than there is in her movie. "Do we get to meet him anytime soon?"

"Actually, yes," I start, and she's already biting her lip to hold back her obvious delight. "I thought maybe we could do dinner sometime this week."

"Absolutely!" She passes me a lingerie box, which is the perfect size for Ian's comic book. I find some candy cane-striped tissue paper from a bin on the floor. "Have you gotten his gift yet?" she asks.

The lingerie box in my hand sparks a memory from earlier that makes me smile. "No, but I have some ideas."

My phone chirps on the table next to me; there's a ride request in the CARtist app. I'd listed myself as available before I walked into the house, but completely forgot about it until now.

Mom doesn't ask anything else, just nods and kisses the top of my head before turning the volume up on the TV and settling back into a rhythm of cutting and curling and calligraphy. It would help my finances to be out driving on a Saturday night this close to Christmas, getting people to bars and home from parties and dinners, but it helps my heart to be right here, next to my mom, doing our favorite tradition together.

I update my status in the app and turn my phone upside down.

CHRISTMAS KISSES
Nick

"WHAT IS *THAT?*" Holly's on my porch, a giant pot in her arms.

"This," she says, blowing a stray chunk of hair from her face, "is a living Christmas tree. It lives inside all month and can be replanted outside after the holidays are over."

I move out of her way so she can come in out of the cold, and I close the door behind her. "Do you take that with you everywhere this time of year?"

She stares at me, blinking twice. "It's a gift. For you."

I feel a weightless feeling from my gut to my throat, and my mouth goes dry. "Oh," I manage to get out. "Thanks."

She turns and sets the pot on the floor at the edge of the living room before inspecting her hands and rubbing them together. "You're welcome. I was hoping it would be Nick Goodman approved."

"Yeah—it's good. Thanks." I know I'm repeating myself, but I'm just a little surprised, I guess, that between yesterday morning and now she had the idea to get me a tree, and that between last night and now she found one.

"So..." she starts. "Kissing practice?" She just dives right in, blowing right past the awkward ending to last night. The one where she kissed me and didn't even say goodbye after.

I laugh in reply, something that I know sounds nervous, and rub the back of my neck. "It's weird, right? To be an adult and have to practice basic kissing?"

Holly shrugs out of her coat and drops it over the arm of the sofa. "It's not so much that we have to practice *kissing*. We just need to practice making a few fake kisses look real. People literally go to acting school to do that, and since I can't afford Juilliard at the moment, we're going to have to be self-taught."

She sits on the couch and pats the cushion next to her. When I take a seat, she angles her knees toward mine.

"Should we set some rules, or something?" I ask.

Holly looks at me like I've sprouted two extra heads. "What, like no tongue? That kind of rule?"

Fire creeps up my neck and into my ears. "Something like that."

She cocks her head and stares at me for a moment. "I don't think we would need tongue in front of our parents."

"Great." I rub my clammy hands against my thighs, hoping the denim of my jeans will absorb some of my random, midwinter sweats before I'm supposed to touch Holly. *If* I'm supposed to touch Holly. I'm not sure why all of this is so hard or confusing. It's not like I've never kissed a woman before, but I guess I just haven't overthought it previously. Now I'm calculating angles in my head like I'm in tenth-grade geometry class, planning my face's approach to hers like a pilot plans a landing.

"So, we just do it, then?" I ask. When she answers with a shrug, I lean in, watching for cues from her.

"Stop right there," she says, a hand pressed against my chest. "Eyes open? Are you a sociopath?"

"I don't think so."

There's humor in her voice when she says, "Let's try again, but better."

"You're really good at making me feel less self-conscious about this." I'm joking, but serious.

"Okay, how about this... What if I take the lead for the first one?"

The first one. My stomach drops at the phrase, but I try to play it cool. "Sure."

Holly clears her throat and shoves her sleeves up her forearms. I think I see a spot of ink there, on the inside of her forearm, but I don't have a chance to ask about it before she cups my cheek in her palm and presses a kiss to my lips.

It's brief, and when she pulls away my lips tingle like I just shuffled along the carpet in socks and touched my finger to my mouth.

"Okay, not a terrible start." Holly's head nods along with her words. "You want to own the next one?"

With a great deal of effort, I keep my fingers from touching my lips, even as the tingling fades like the last embers of a fireworks display that I'm desperate to hold on to. Curious, I guess, even though it might burn me.

"Nick?"

"Hmm?" The buzz of the hum reignites that feeling, but only fleetingly.

"I feel like we had a fine first round, but we should probably do it again. Right?"

I shrug. "I guess?"

"Do you have a spreadsheet? Checklist?"

"For...?"

Holly wriggles in her seat. "For all the kiss categories we should practice."

Maybe I was actually shocked by something and my brain was fried, because I have absolutely no idea what she's talking about.

"You know—all the reasons we may need to kiss in front of people. Mistletoe, goodbye kisses, 'just because' stuff..."

"Obligatory 'everybody-else-is-making-out-so-we-should, too' kissing?"

She shoves my knee with hers. "Exactly. Smooching scenarios. I figured, based on our first two meetings, you'd be ultra prepared for today."

"Ha. Yeah." I rub the back of my neck, feeling tension knotting between my shoulder blades, just out of reach. I thought I was prepared for today; it's not my fault there are so many kinds of kisses, and Holly thinks we need to be well-versed in a variety of them. Except the ones 'with tongue,' I guess, which is fine.

"How about this..." Holly pulls a scrunchie off her wrist. I hadn't noticed before, but it's black and covered in tiny holly leaves. She holds it high overhead. "This," she says, glancing up at the scrunchie, "is mistletoe. So we're at your sister's party, and someone's floating around the room holding this over us like it's one of those toys they tease cats with." She looks up again, then at me, and shrugs. "So, kiss me."

And I do. With minimal hesitation. With closed eyes and closed lips and a hand that tucks her hair behind her ear before tracing the smooth line of her jaw. And then I swallow and pull away and open my eyes in time to catch Holly's smile.

"That was great!" She swats my arm and pulls her hair into a messy bun. "Next up, maybe just a casual 'oh no, everybody's watching us on the D.L.' kiss?"

"That seems very specific. What does that even look like?"

"Kind of like yesterday, at your parents' house, when we were alone in the living room? But maybe we noticed someone was watching, and we wanted to make it look like we were caught up in a sweet little moment, so we just kind of..." She trails off, and her gaze moves between my eyes and my mouth. Then she leans in, her hand braced against my chest, and whispers a kiss across my lips.

It's like time stops. If this is Holly in practice mode—untrained, apparently, by Juilliard, but practiced, I'm assuming, through her former clients—I can't imagine what a kiss with actual feeling from her might be like. It takes every ounce of restraint in me to swallow the *'wow'* that sits just behind my teeth.

She clears her throat with a tiny cough and slaps her thighs. "Well, that covers most of it, I guess. Everything except the goodbye kiss, which—" She jumps up from the couch; her eyes dart around the room. "Where's my coat?" She spots it, finally, behind me, and steps toward it.

"Wait—" I reach out, my hand connecting with the soft skin near her wrist. "Do you want to stay for dinner?"

Her lips pull to one side, like she's biting the inside of her cheek, and her eyes fall to the places where fingertips meet forearm. "I, um..." She slips her arm away. "Do you want to go out somewhere?"

It's a great idea, honestly, to get out of the house and maybe try to convince someone somewhere that we're a couple before trying to convince even more people who know us that we're in love.

I still don't fully understand why Holly had to go *there* in her description of us, but since she's used the L-word, I feel like we need to live up to the expectation. Just for a few more weeks.

"Yes," I answer. "We should go out."

"Great." She sighs out the word, like she's relieved I said yes, and I wonder if we're both thinking the same thing: at the very least, it delays our final kiss, if we don't skip it altogether. And we probably should skip it, considering the other kisses seemed pretty convincing already.

Holly fixes the sleeves of her sweater and slips into her coat. "Where do you want to go?"

"Did you want O'Donnell's again, or..."

"O'Donnell's is great," she answers. "Want to drive separately so we can go our own way after?"

"Oh. Uh, sure?" I'm pretty sure my house is somewhere between the bar and her place, but maybe she has plans after and she's not just trying to avoid spending extra time with me.

"Great! I'll see you there." With that, Holly lets herself out the front door. I'm close behind, and I stand for a moment in the brisk air of the evening as I watch her taillights shrink in the distance.

Heartbreak Holiday
Holly

PEPPER & POUR IS bustling, but the activity and the noise of the other patrons' conversations does nothing to mask Jasmine's incredulousness.

"I'm sorry. You *what*, now?"

I tap the glass of my Christmas sangria. Jasmine just asked about my weekend, and I told her that I spent all day Sunday kissing Nick. If we're going to make this believable, my best friend should probably be able to corroborate my story. Not that I said we were actually dating, because I hate lying to her, but if she wants to draw her own conclusions, that works for me.

"And?"

"And, what?" I ask, taking a drink.

Which is a mistake, of course, because the next thing out of Jasmine's mouth is, "And... was it incredible?"

And now I'm choking on sangria, in that my-throat-is-burning-with-alcohol way, and I sputter and cough.

Jasmine's relentless, and she barely waits until I've taken a breath before she raises an eyebrow at me. "Well? Was it good?"

I nod, avoiding her gaze. "It was..." It was nice. And unexpected. And unexpectedly nice. And was it good? "It was," I say again, this time an answer all on its own.

She reaches a hand across the table and sets it on mine. "Finally," she sighs, using her other hand to feed herself a sweet potato fry. "It's about time."

"Thanks?"

She holds both hands up in mock surrender. "All I'm saying is, I'm glad you're moving on after Mark."

"Mhmm." I take another drink of sangria, making eye contact with the cranberries floating in the drink instead of with my friend.

"Holly..."

A few more gulps.

"Tell me you're not still hung up on that dumbass."

"Absolutely not." I cross my arms, still clinging to the glass for dear life.

"Then why did you get weird when I said his name?"

My face might be passable as my most-used emoji: grimace. "It's possible that Mark is maybe Nick's coworker."

"Okay," Jasmine says, drawn out like she's crunching the numbers. "So we just need to make sure he isn't being toxic about you at work."

"And it's also possible that Mark is maybe dating Nick's sister."

"No!" Jasmine smacks the table, rattling our silverware and dishes. "So you—"

"Have to see him sometimes. I know."

She rolls her eyes with an exasperated sigh. "Is this guy worth it? Having to see the devil himself just for some guy who's good at kissing?"

"It's worth it," I answer quickly. Maybe too quickly. Jasmine, of course, has no idea about what this arrangement is financially worth to me. She would be on board with the Holly Dates site if she knew about it, if she thought I was just an enterprising mind who found a way to get paid to dress up and charm parents and maybe meet a nice guy along the way. But if she knew *why* I had to do it, she would absolutely demand I shut it down and offer to pay my way for the whole wedding. And that is out of the question.

So Jasmine hears a hesitationless *it's worth it* and double-raises her perfect brows at me. "Girl, you must have it bad for this guy."

Heat creeps into my cheeks and all the way up to the top of my ears, just as our server brings the bill. "It's not—"

"Oh, *shoot!*" Jasmine's rummaging through her purse. It's designer. Or a really good knock-off. But judging by the rock that's roughly the size of Pluto (R.I.P., planet status) that sparkles blindingly even in the dim dinner-shift lighting, I'd say it's very real and very expensive. "I left my wallet in my old bag."

This one, she explained at the start of dinner, was an early Christmas gift from Bradford that just looked perfect with her outfit tonight, so she decided at the last minute to use it. And, of course, even though she's got a stockpile of lip gloss and breath mints and gum and who knows what else in there, she apparently doesn't have any methods of payment.

"I got it." I pull my Amex out of my cross-body bag and pass it and the receipt to our server.

"Thanks," she says, taking a sip of her wine. "You're the best, Jolly Holly."

Not *I'll Venmo you* or *I'll get it next time,* but *You're the best.* Cool. As much as I love Jasmine, and as much as I love being 'the best,' we're from very different worlds. This is just how she is: She's used to getting everything, and she's unaware of the phenomenon of living paycheck to paycheck.

"Sure."

I finish my sangria while Jasmine tells me about the vacation Bradford's planning for the holidays: something epic and luxurious and expensive-sounding. Shocker.

Our server returns and passes the little leather folio with my card and our receipt to me. I open the cover and try not to react to the total of our bill. In the future, I've got to remember to stick to ordering just water and not a pitcher of sangria. Or I could pretend to forget *my* wallet so Jasmine can call Bradford to come to our rescue and bring his fancy Platinum Card to cover the bill.

But for now I sign the receipt, biting my lip when Jasmine says to "Tip him well; he was great!"

If I hadn't had a pitcher of sangria, I'd set myself as available in the CARtist app to try to earn that money back tonight.

And if I hadn't had a pitcher of sangria, I wouldn't feel so tingly when I drop my card back in my bag and see a text illuminating my phone from *Just Nick*.

Any chance you're free?

Right?

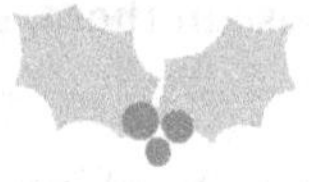

"Hey." Headlights from Nick's car cast a ghostly glow over the otherwise darkened, drizzly parking lot.

"You really didn't have to come all the way out here." It's not much of a greeting, and it would probably be more convincing if it wasn't punctuated with a traitorous hiccup.

Nick's dimple appears with a half smile, and I imagine myself finding which fingertip is the right fit for it. Like that little indentation is Cinderella's glass slipper and my phalanges are all the women in the kingdom.

Okay, fine. It's a very good thing that Nick came all the way out here.

"Why don't I get you home?"

I'm tipsy enough to let my mind create an image of him sweeping me off my feet and carrying me threshold-style from my car to his.

But I'm realistic enough, even when tipsy, to know that fairytales are not my future, and I shut and lock my door behind me.

Once I'm safely buckled in his front seat, he unzips a small cooler bag and passes me a bottle of chilled water. "You should probably drink this."

He's right, but I can't. Just on principle, really. I can't let him rescue me from a parking lot *and* ensure I don't get a hangover. It's too much. Especially considering our last interaction, two nights ago.

A few minutes down the road, against the gentle cadence of windshield wipers and soft Christmas music on the radio, I ask, "Why are you being so nice to me?"

His answering chuckle is a balm to the soul. "Should I *not* be nice to you?"

"Not after Sunday."

Ah, Sunday. The day of our smoochfest, the make-out mini-marathon. The day I maybe didn't exactly end the night the way I should have.

"What? Just because you lured me to a restaurant with a promise of dinner and then didn't show up to said restaurant, you think I should be a jerk to you?"

Okay, I *definitely* didn't end the night the way I should have.

"I get it," he says. "I think. Why you didn't show up."

"You do?" If he gets it, I hope he fills me in, because I'm still trying to name the reason behind my ghosting him at O'Donnell's.

"Look, Holly." He pulls up to the white line at a red light, and his turn signal flashes against wet asphalt. I try not to read too much into the way he massages his forehead or scrubs a hand down his face. "I was thinking, maybe we should call it. I'll pay you now, for Saturday and all the family stuff we had planned coming up, and I'll be the pathetic loser who gets dumped three weeks before Christmas..."

"It sounds like I'm the one getting dumped." What I wouldn't give to go back in time two days and do things differently; to get out of my car instead of watching, slouched down in my seat, from a well-hidden spot in the back corner of the lot; to not let him stand there, waiting, going inside the bar and reemerging on the stoop in the cold, looking for me; to not absolutely freak out at a simple, meaningless kiss. To answer one phone call; to return one text message. Maybe, if I'd done any of those things, I'd see that dimple right now, instead of the hard crease of a frown. "You'd be totally justified, by the way."

The light changes to green, and Nick turns left. "I know," he says on an exhale.

We ride wordlessly for a few more minutes; the only interruptions to the '90s Pop Holiday Classics station are the robotic-sounding navigation instructions from his phone.

When we're a minute from my house, I ask, "Why'd you come pick me up?"

Nick takes the last turn onto my street.

"You could've just told me on the phone that you wanted to be done."

"I don't *want* to be—" he starts, then shakes his head. He pulls over to the curb in front of my house, one with a lawn littered with inflatable Santas and penguins and nutcrackers, and puts the car in park. "I picked you up because you FaceTimed me from your car, and you'd been drinking. I needed to make sure you got home safe."

"You really live up to your name, Nicholas Goodman."

He doesn't bother to correct me with his usual 'it's just Nick.'

"Saint Nick," I call him.

"Holly." If it was possible to hear an eye roll, it would be exactly the tone with which Nick says my name. It sobers me.

"So, this is it, then?" I wish I could ignore the bile in my throat, the weight in my gut, but I can't just deactivate every emotional and physiological receptor in my body. The ending to this make-believe relationship kind of sucks, and I feel it all over.

At the very least, Nick Goodman could give me the courtesy of eye contact. Instead, he stares at the road ahead of him. There's a metaphor in there somewhere, but I'm too upset to appreciate the poetry in it. "Don't you think it should be?"

No, I want to say. *I'm sorry*, I probably should say. "Whatever you want," is what comes out.

His answering silence is the push I need to swing open my door and march myself inside my house.

ALL I WANT FOR CHRISTMAS IS YOU

Holly

I REALLY, *REALLY* WANT to place Nick Goodman at the top of my Defecation Directory, but there's a near-empty bottle of water on my nightstand that reminds me that he's the only reason I'm not cursing the daylight when my alarm blares the bridge of *All Too Well (Sad Girl Autumn Version)* at 7 A.M.

Outside, the day is gray, and I let myself have a few more minutes in the fetal position before I brush my teeth and take a shower that sets records for heat and speed.

The irony is not lost on me that I need to book a Pickup CARtist to get me to my car so that I can work today, because everyone in my house has better things to do than to drive my mopey self to a bar's parking lot and hear my tale of woe along the way.

Downstairs, my phone in hand, I'm drawn through the living room and toward the kitchen by the scent of coffee and the sound of a pair of voices. And there, in an oversized sweater and a pair of overalls, is my mother, pouring coffee for a man who sits with hunched shoulders at the kitchen island. He tousles his caramel curls and adjusts the temple of his glasses behind his ear. My heart leaps into my throat.

"There you are!" Mom grabs my empty travel mug from the drying mat and fills it with coffee, emptying the pot.

Nick turns, unsmiling, and avoids my eyes. "Hey."

"Hi?" The one-word question is a greeting and a 'What are you doing here?' all in one.

Mom answers for him. She rounds the island to hand me my mug and says, "It's so sweet of him to return your car for you." She gives an on-brand wink, one that says she's already pegged Nick as a Hallmark-movie-hero kind of guy.

"It was very nice," I agree, though a whole mental gymnastics meet fails to yield an answer to how he could have brought it home.

"You left your key in my car last night."

My cheeks burn. It's wild, feeling humiliated for two completely different reasons, with two completely different audiences, simultaneously. Mom raises an eyebrow like I've neglected to fill her in on some of the spicier, not-quite-Hallmark-friendly aspects of our relationship, and Nick probably thinks I'm some idiot who was so tipsy off a little sangria that I was probably five seconds away from giving him my Social Security number. Or that I was so devastated by the breakup of our pretend relationship that I totally forgot about my things.

"Thanks for bringing it back." The key is on the corner of the island, and I swipe it and pocket it before I lose it again.

"Sure." Nick takes a final drink of coffee, but he's intercepted by Mom when he attempts to rinse the mug. "Thanks for the coffee, Mrs. Christopher. It was nice to meet you," he tells her, before telling me, "I should head out."

"I'll walk you." I slip into my shoes on the mat inside the front door and follow Nick to the porch. There's my car, perfectly parked on the street, right between the driveway and the mailbox. "Thanks for bringing my car all this way."

Nick shrugs and adjusts his glasses. "No problem." He swipes at his phone, then stands with his free hand shoved in his pocket, rocking back and forth on his heels.

"Wait a second—" there's *my* car, but... "How are you getting home?"

He shrugs again, that signature move of his. "I just requested a Pickup CARtist."

I don't mean to laugh, but it erupts out of me. "I'm happy to drive you."

"I'm good," he answers. He's met my gaze for all of three seconds since I found him in my kitchen. I know he's avoiding me, and while the self-preservation parts of me are screaming and begging me to avoid him, too, the stubborn, easily offended parts of me want to rumble. Two can play his stupid game, so I unlock my phone, open the Pickup CARtist app, set myself to available, and quickly find his ride request. With one click, I hear a notification *ding* on his phone.

He gives the device a quick glance and scoffs. "Holly—"

"It's the least I can do. And if giving me a one-star rating at the end would make you feel better, I'd totally understand."

He rocks back on his heels again and squints against the sunlight toward the road.

"I'll even comp the ride. And I don't expect a tip."

Finally, a laugh. His dimple is still in hiding, but at least he gives me *something*. "That's good. You shouldn't."

"C'mon." I nudge his arm with my elbow, and he follows me down the stairs to the street.

The ride back to his car, still in the Pepper & Pour parking lot, feels like a rewind of last night. And if our car is taking the same path in the opposite direction, maybe that's a sign for us, too. "I shouldn't have ghosted you."

"I know."

"I'm really sorry."

"Sure."

This conversation is going so well it could be the inspiration for the bluesy, moody, woeful Christmas song on the radio.

Morning commuters navigate the roads, but with no one behind me I take a long stop at the intersection of Finch and Blackbird. "Why did you bring my car back?"

He shifts in his seat. "You needed it for work. I had the key. How else would you have gotten it?"

"You could've dropped the key off at my house. You could've left it on your porch and told me to pick it up whenever. You could've thrown it into the river and laughed about the karma."

Finally, though I suspect it's more a signal of *you have the right-of-way* than a desire to engage with me, Nick turns his head and looks at me.

"You're really nice, Nick. And I know this is no excuse, but I think that freaks me out a little."

I appreciate that when he rolls his eyes, he does so without malice. "You've never interacted with a nice person before?"

"Not as nice as you." It's true; Nick Goodman is as good as they come, based on our limited interactions. "And I think that's why I bailed on Sunday. I was afraid all the lying would affect you."

Do I get credit for half-truths? Because sure, this is part of the reason I skipped out on dinner. The other reason is because I'm starting to worry that this lie feels like an inconvenient truth—but, like, one that just has an impact on me and not a catastrophic impact on the planet.

Nick turns forward again, watching the Songbird Springs geography pass us by on our route to Pepper & Pour. "So, to recap here: You said you'd meet me for dinner, left me stranded alone in a parking lot, and purposely neglected to return my calls for two days because I'm too nice?"

When he puts it that way, it doesn't sound great, I guess.

Nick's car is backed into a spot along the edge of the Pepper & Pour parking lot, right by where I'd parked last night. I cross the empty lot and park in front of his car.

"I'm sorry for being such a jerk. On more than one occasion."

Nick unbuckles his seatbelt. "You don't have to apologize—"

"I do! And I want to. You deserve so much better..."

This time, Nick's laughter activates his dimple. "Now you're starting to sound like a real girlfriend. One who's about to break up with me."

"I'd love to be given another chance to break up with you. If you'll let me."

With one hand on the door handle and the other holding his keys, he seems to at least consider the idea.

"I promise not to screw it all up again."

"Well, that sounds like a deal if I ever heard one," he says, but sarcasm taints his voice like fish taints a break room refrigerator.

"Will you at least think about it?"

Maybe I sound desperate, but he nods.

"I'll think about it." He climbs out of the car and bends down for a final goodbye before closing the door. "Have a good day, Holly."

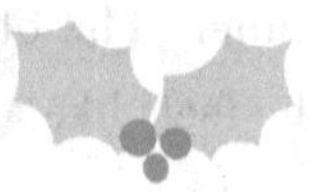

My 'good day' begins at the gas station where I pull up to the pump and realize I don't need to be here at all: My quarter-full tank from last night is somehow fully full now.

It continues when I go inside the gas station for a soft pretzel and a Coke Zero, treat myself to a Holly Jolly Holiday one-dollar scratcher, and win a hundred bucks.

Which I then use to get a blowout, and because my hair looks better than it ever has, I decide to treat Nick to lunch that is equal parts 'thank you' and 'I'm sorry.'

I think tacos are a universally loved food. At the very least, they're a litmus test for the trustworthiness of any human being: You don't like tacos? I can't trust your opinion on anything. That's why I show up at Nick's office with a bag from Tacodilla just before noon.

The young guy at the desk just inside the front door glances up from his computer. "Can I help you?" His name tag says *Donovan,* but his haircut says *I'm an intern and I come from money.*

"Hi! Yes. I brought these for Nick Goodman?"

Donovan's eyes shift to the corner of his oversized desk. "All deliveries can go there."

The thought of leaving the perfection that is Tacodilla with the generic pizza box already perched on the corner is horrifying. One does not simply abandon Tacodilla with mediocrity; one hand-delivers this gloriousness to its recipient directly. Donovan doesn't strike me as the kind of person who has been told 'no' very often, but here goes nothing.

"Actually, I was hoping to give this to Nick myself. I'm... um... we're kind of..."

"Holly?"

I should be grateful for the interruption, but the voice that says my name is too familiar, and it makes the tiny hairs on my neck stand up.

"What are you doing here?" Mark asks, and Donovan turns back to his computer. Apparently he's satisfied with handing responsibility for me over to his coworker.

"Just bringing lunch for Nick."

"Oh." Mark's brow furrows, and I wonder if Nick has already started telling people we've broken up. "I can take it for him, if you want."

I reactively pull the bag back, like I'm a mangy stray protecting a bone. It's a miracle I don't growl and bare my teeth, but I guess this is a sign of my personal growth when it comes to dealing with Mark Thompson.

"I'm good. If you could just point me in the direction of his desk..."

But it's not necessary. A flood of business casual pours out of what must be the clown car of meeting rooms. I recognize a few faces from the party, but most are so engrossed in conversation that they walk right past Mark and me. I spot Nick pretty easily—his hair is more unkempt than his coworkers, his sweater a special brand of *department store chic*—and my heart sinks as the pretty blonde next to him touches his bicep and laughs. Then he laughs, and I consider admitting defeat to Donovan and slinking out the front door after dropping my bag of tacos on the desk with pizza that definitely can't be hot anymore.

And then Mark shouts, "Hey, Nicholas! Your girlfriend's here!" at the crowd, and despite holding my breath I mutter "It's just Nick."

And then a miracle happens. Nick's head pops up. His serious face—I'm assuming the gut reaction anytime Mark talks to him—brightens when we make eye contact, and he cuts through the sea of his coworkers to find me.

"Hey, Holly." He ignores Mark altogether, which is a skill I wish I possessed.

"I brought you lunch," I say by way of greeting. I hold up the Tacodilla bag and his smile grows. Mr. Dimple even arrives (yes, I have named it), and I feel like this is the best idea I've had all day.

That is, until Nick says, "Your hair looks really nice," and I blush.

"Thanks!" I raise the bag higher. "Tacos?"

"Sure. Thank you." He takes the bag and turns, taking a few steps behind the crowd.

Okay, this was not necessarily the plan, and I can feel Mark silently gloating next to me. I'm not sure what it is about him, but

I feel like he's always wanted me to lose, to be embarrassed, to feel ashamed.

But then Nick stops, looks back, and asks, "Are you coming?"—all of which is great. But when he extends his free hand to me and my fingers wind into his, nothing could be better.

BRING ON THE CHEER
Nick

I WOULDN'T TYPICALLY DESCRIBE myself as high-maintenance, but the pile of button-downs and sweaters that's rapidly accumulating on my bed might suggest otherwise.

Who would have guessed that dinner with Holly's family would make me second-guess and overanalyze every article of clothing I own.

My alarm sounds. I should be getting in my car right now, but I'm half-dressed in a pair of dark-wash jeans (maybe they're the problem with every outfit I try on?) and no closer to a decision than I was twenty minutes ago. I call Clara, because *desperate times* and all that.

"What's up, Bro?" she greets me on speaker.

"I'm staring at my closet wondering how all the shirts I wear on a regular basis with no qualms are suddenly all awful."

"Dinner with Holly?" she guesses.

"Her whole family," I answer.

"Oof."

"Not exactly helping with the nerves there, Sis."

She laughs. "Restaurant or house?"

"Their house."

"Oh."

"What's *that* supposed to mean?" If I was desperate a minute ago, I'm hopeless now.

"It just means there's a larger range of what could be acceptable. A restaurant has vibes; you know how to dress if you're going to a steakhouse or a place like O'Donnell's. But an in-home dinner really keeps the door open. You risk going too fancy or too casual."

I press the heel of my hand to my forehead, trying to push back the painful knot that's forming just behind the bone. "I've been spiraling for twenty minutes because of that. So what's the magic outfit?"

"Let me ask Mark."

I roll my eyes over her muffled voice.

"Mark says he would wear dark jeans, but not too dark, and a nice sweater. No collared shirt though."

"Perfect. Thanks."

"Sure! Good luck!"

Clara is notorious for getting distracted between a conversation and the red circle that disconnects the call, so I hear an added "He's got it so bad—" before the call ends.

I don't have it bad. I have a bad case of *my closet is boring*. That's it.

With a sigh and the realization that I only have three minutes to finish getting ready or I'll officially be late, I decide the jeans are fine. And there's a sweater in a gift box, its tags still on, that I figure will be perfect to wear.

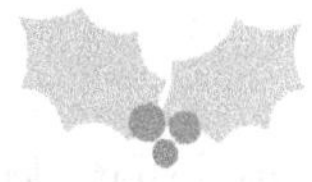

Holly's family's house is crowded, bustling with the kind of activity and energy that I'd expect to see in a feel-good Christmas movie set in a small town.

Mr. Christopher is outside repairing a lawn ornament, but he escorts me to the door where Holly's mom greets me and apologizes that Holly isn't the one to do it. "Between you and me, she's agonizing over her outfit choice," she says as she hangs my coat on the rack by the door. "But you didn't hear that from me."

"Mum's the word."

There's a commotion in the kitchen, a Premier League game on the living room TV.

"You must be Nick!" Two of Holly's brothers, each with a beer bottle in hand, one in a pair of ripped jeans and a Henley and the other in a pair of dress pants with a shirt and tie, emerge into the living room. "You want a beer?" The more casually dressed brother seems to be the talkative one.

"I'm okay," I say.

"Cool. Grab a seat, if you want. Chelsea's kicking ass."

"Language," Mrs. Christopher says.

The brothers roll their eyes, smiling, and drop into lived-in cushions on a pair of armchairs.

Instead, I follow Holly's mom into the kitchen, offering assistance, mentally scolding myself for forgetting the bottle of wine I'd planned to bring. But I guess that's what happens when you're distracted by your uninspired wardrobe offerings.

"Hey, Nick," another brother says. He looks younger than the others, with messy hair and a cool nerd vibe. He's paired khaki cargo shorts with a Christmas sweater that appears to have Santa eating computer-shaped gingerbread treats and the words *'Got Cookies?'* on it.

"You must be Landon."

He smiles, like he's impressed that I know him based on his attire alone. "Good guess."

"Holly's told me a lot about you." If I had to guess, I'd say the brother in the tie is Micah, and the one in ripped jeans is Ian. But Landon required no guessing; he's exactly as Holly described.

"I heard a lot about you, too," he says with a half grin that makes him look a little like the Grinch when he gets an evil idea.

Though I'd love to know more about the meaning of his words and his smile, I don't get the chance to ask, because Holly bursts through the door and nearly collides with the open refrigerator door.

She's wearing a black dress, and there's a white sweater encircling the crown of her head. "Help, Mom—I'm stuck."

There's a fair amount of watching awkwardly as Holly and her mom tag team the removal of cable-knit thread from the jaws of a decorative hair pin, made even more awkward when Holly—head still obscured by yarn—says, "I'm just glad Nick's not here to see this. He'd think I'm such a—" which is immediately followed by her head poking through the neckline, red cheeks, and a sheepish "Hi."

"Hi," I answer, just as Landon replies, "Nice, Sis," with a laugh.

"I'll give you two a minute," Mrs. Christopher says with a look at Holly, a smile at me, and a clear 'give them some privacy' look toward Landon. The youngest Christopher's head rolls with his eyes, but he follows his mom out of the kitchen.

"Hi," Holly says again, once they're gone.

"Hi." There's a small section of her hair that's stuck on the front of the pin—a fancy-looking Holly leaf on antiqued gold—and I smooth it back into place.

"Thanks."

Standing less than an arm's length away, with her gazing up at me with those bright eyes—blue with flecks of amber—it's hard not to think about last weekend, all the kissing, all the craziness that's happened since then. The ghosting. The breakup. The taco date. The decision to stick it out and carry out this charade as planned.

Okay, I guess it's not a *lot* of craziness, but for six days? It feels like more than enough.

I uncurl my fingers, which have been lingering in her hair a breath too long, and cross my arms instead. "So... I'd think you're such a what?"

"Hmm?" Holly hums, taking a step backward.

"Earlier, when you were trapped in your sweater. You said you were glad I wasn't here to see this because I'd think you were such a... what?"

"Oh." She shrugs and laughs. "Pretty much anything terrible. Moron. Child. Dumbass. Take your pick."

"Did you just say children are terrible?"

Holly slaps my arm with the back of her hand and smirks. "Jerk. You know what I mean." Her hand does a quick sweep down my bicep. "Okay, sir, is this cashmere? Did you dress up for me tonight?"

I give a quick shrug and say, "At least I was dressed upon arrival."

Smiling, she hits me again before turning and sliding two wine glasses from their under-the-cabinet rack. "Rosé okay?"

"Sure. And for the record—" I take the glass of wine she passes toward me— "it was kind of adorable, the whole head-stuck-in-your-sweater thing."

Her cheeks take on the same color as her wine, and I follow her into the living room with the rest of her family. There, Micah and Ian are arguing about whether Chelsea paid off the refs or just outplayed Aston Villa. Mr. and Mrs. Christopher are adding fuel to the proverbial fire by throwing out 'what about' questions that may or may not be relevant to the game they just watched. Landon sits, seemingly unconcerned with everything around him, in the corner of the room, focused intently on the screen of his laptop.

"Are you a sports fan, Nicholas?"

"It's just Nick, Dad." Holly glances up at me and winks.

"Yeah, a little," I answer. "Mostly hockey, tennis... a little basket-ball."

"Those are three really different sports, man," the dressy brother says.

And Holly confirms my earlier suspicions. "Have you officially met Micah and Ian?" she asks, pointing first to the dressy brother and then to the casual one.

"In passing."

They raise their beer bottles to me as a greeting, but before they can open their mouths to argue again, their mom jumps from her seat and summons them toward the kitchen. "Dinner's about ready, boys. Help me set the table, would you?"

Everyone leaves but Holly, Landon, and me. "You're exempt from helping?" Holly asks her brother.

"I'm on call. Have to solve this problem." Landon taps the keys on his keyboard, but Holly snorts.

"You're playing Minesweeper."

Landon slams his laptop closed. "Am not."

"You are, too. I could see the reflection in the window." Then she drops her voice and whispers conspiratorially, "Don't worry, I won't tell."

"Hey," he says, setting his laptop aside and shrugging. "We've all got our little secrets, right?"

It would feel ominous if it wasn't for Holly's laughter and the suspicion that Landon helped her set up her website. "So, he knows?" I ask when Landon leaves for the kitchen to help his brothers.

She nods. "Yeah. He helped me design the Holly Dates site, which Mom also knows about. But Landon's the only one who knows you're a client." As if she's reading my mind, she adds, "Don't worry, he wouldn't tell."

At times during dinner I wonder if Holly's right, but those moments are sprinkled into an otherwise lively conversation about everything from work to soccer to education to our mutual hatred of Mark Thompson.

"I don't know, I always liked him," Micah says, eliciting a groan from everyone else at the table.

"Et tu, *bro*-té?" Holly rolls her eyes and slouches back on our shared bench, leaning toward me until her cheek rests on my shoulder. "Micah *loves* Mark. He's still mad he got stuck with me in the breakup."

"Not true," Micah protests, but Ian snickers from the seat next to him.

"Dude, it's so true. You wish you could *be* him."

"Me? I'm not the one who showed up in something straight out of the Mark Thompson fall line."

All eyes fall on me, though most look away just as quickly. Holly's cheek still warms my shoulder; she drags her fingers along my ribs. "I think it's a nice sweater," she says. I won't tell her that it's a birthday gift from Clara and Mark and that I know he picked it out.

"Thanks." Not that I can afford cashmere, but if I could I'd buy thirty more of these sweaters and wear one every day I'm with Holly. I'm already heady from a few heavy pours of wine, and her rhythmic stroking over my bones makes me jelly. I wrap an arm around her and tilt my head to rest on hers, feeling her nestle in closer to my side.

It's funny, the way she blended so perfectly into my family and I seem to fit in pretty well right here, in a small kitchen crowded with big personalities and loud conversation and cheer and Christmas music and love.

Okay—the love is sometimes hard to see. The Christopher family is *ruthless* when it comes to board games. We play a few once the table is cleared from dinner, and then Holly presents two cinnamon roll apple pies that she put in the oven to bake after dinner. She drizzles cream cheese frosting over the still-warm cinnamon roll crust, and my mouth waters. It somehow tastes even more incredible than it smells, and we demolish a pie and a quarter in no time.

When we're all in carbohydrate comas, Micah checks his gold watch. "I should probably head out." Ian doesn't seem to have the same urgency, because he grabs another beer from the fridge.

"I should go, too," I whisper to Holly, whose head has found my shoulder and whose fingertips have found my sweater again.

"Are you sure?"

I stifle a yawn. "Yeah, it's getting late. And we have Clara's party tomorrow."

"Right." Holly yawns and slowly gets up. "I'll walk you out."

I say my *thank you*s and *goodbye*s, and then Holly and I are on her parents' front porch. We're alone, save for the audience not-so-covertly watching through the living room window.

"Thanks for a great time tonight."

"Sure," she replies. "Thanks for coming. And for everything, I guess, since Sunday."

"Sure."

Holly shivers—she came outside with nothing warmer than her sweater on—and I pull her in against me, rubbing her arms as her fingers investigate the cashmere under my coat. "Speaking of Sunday..."

There are few things guaranteed in this world. We all know about death and taxes, and *I* know that Holly's about to mention the kiss that wasn't.

"Should we finish up that final scenario?" she asks.

Warmth spreads through my chest at the thought. "It would be weird if we didn't, right?"

"Definitely." The word is a breath, and she's already on her toes, her eyes already on my mouth. They flutter shut as I brush the back of my knuckles over her cheek, tucking a stray wisp of hair behind her ear, and let my hand linger at the nape of her neck. Her palms go flat against my chest as my lips greet hers, gentle and soft and only for a moment. A perfect goodbye kiss.

"I'll pick you up tomorrow at six for the party?" she asks with a half smile when it ends.

I clear my throat before answering. "That sounds good. Thanks again for tonight." I kiss her forehead once and turn down the porch steps, heading for my car.

"Hey, Nick!" Holly calls as I open my door. She drops her voice when I turn toward her. "Think that was convincing?"

I chuckle and answer through tingling lips, "I would say yes."

THE BEST TIME OF THE YEAR
Holly

ON A TYPICAL DAY, if a date was treating me to brunch in a restored barn with floor-to-ceiling windows that reflected the lights of a dozen illuminated Christmas trees and at least three times as many flickering candles, I might start a wedding registry. I might propose with a napkin ring. I might beg him to run away and elope with me.

But today is not a typical day. Today is the day of Clara's party. It's also the day after Nick kissed me goodbye, and at this particular moment, sandwiched between those two events, I'm feeling traitorous for being here with someone other than Nick.

It was apparent from the moment we arrived that I was supposed to be mostly arm candy and not participate much in conversation, which feels traitorous to myself. But I'm being paid, and there's French toast, and the bartender is apparently doubling the correct portion of champagne in her Christmas mimosas.

What I'm trying to say is, I have coping mechanisms.

This date, Alexander, sent his request on Tuesday. At first I ignored it, but after the pitcher-of-sangria-and-subsequent-fake-but-real-breakup situation, I accepted the job. Nick didn't ask for an exclusivity clause, even after we changed the plan. Still, the fear of being seen by someone I know, or who knows Nick, pounds in my chest. But since I'm mostly arm candy, no one cares or even notices if I'm distracted by scanning the restaurant for anyone I should promptly hide from.

Alexander and his parents are talking about money; from what I've been able to piece together, his parents have a lot of it, and Alexander is trying to prove that he is worthy of having some of it, and I am supposed to be proof of that, somehow. Words and phrases like "responsibility" and "entrepreneur" and "settling down" volley across the table while I sip on champagne-infused cranberry juice and do my best to mind my own business.

I smile when I'm spoken about, nod when I think I'm supposed to, rub his knuckles with my thumb when he reaches over to hold my hand.

On a typical day, I would love a job like this.

But today I hate nearly every second of it.

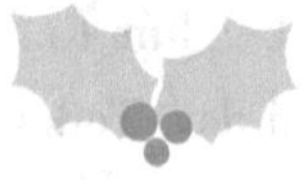

I arrive at Nick's about ten minutes early, which is impressive considering my propensity for tardiness. Nick is always on time, but it's still a little surprising when he's bounding down his porch steps before I even put the car in park.

"You look nice." His greeting comes as he buckles his seat belt, on the heels of a wide smile as he opened the passenger-side door.

Vines of heat creep up my neck, some stretching as far as my ears. I'm flattered and appreciative that he's taken notice of the extra time I put into my outfit, my makeup, my hair.

He looks nice, too, with his hair tamed and styled; his tan slacks with not a wrinkle in sight, glossy shoes that make me think of a musical we performed in college, and a sweater that looks expensive like the one he wore yesterday, this time in a deep shade of olive that just works for him. With his glasses, too, he looks like he could be a professor whose evening job is playing the role of Mark in regional theater performances of *Rent*.

"Thanks," I answer, awkwardly delayed. "You look nice, too. You've really upped your sweater game since your company party."

And then it happens. Without thinking or prompting or reason, I reach across the armrest that's doing a terrible job of separating us, and I... well. There's just no other way to say it. I *caress* his shoulder. Just to feel that crazy soft knit. But still.

Our eyes move to the point of contact and when his rise to meet mine, there's a spark there. A flash of something I can't name. And a smile.

I apologize and pull my hand away, matching his smile with one of my own.

"No need to apologize; it's the cashmere's fault. I can't stop touching myself, either."

His eyes widen when he processes what he's just said, and we both cackle a laugh that breaks any awkwardness there might be after last night's kiss or the random arm caress. Nick adjusts the volume knob, turning up my Christmas playlist, while I back out of the driveway. Once we're on the road, my hands lock at ten and two on the wheel and Nick navigates me to his sister's party.

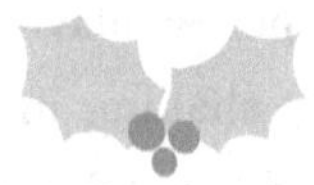

"Is this weird for you?"

Nick passes me a bottle of beer as I stand in the hallway surrounded by pictures of his sister in various affectionate poses with my ex-boyfriend. There's one of the two of them hiking part of the Appalachian Trail, another of them dancing in formal attire, likely at a wedding.

I shake my head *no* and take a swig of beer. It's artisan, and hoppy, and I don't really like it. I take another sip.

"I should have warned you—"

"What? That there would be pictures of Mark at Clara's apartment?" I turn toward Nick and meet his eyes. "I've been around them together. The pictures don't bother me. I'm just—" I catch myself before I say what I really want to say, what's honest and raw and what has been bothering me ever since I saw the two of them together at the Ugly Christmas Sweater party, what has been bothering me ever since I met Clara and immediately liked her.

"Tell me."

I shake my head again.

"Holly—" He leans in, shoving a hand in his pocket and digging a toe into the floorboards. "This is my sister we're talking about. If there's something I should know about Mark—"

"You work with him. You know what he's like."

"I know he's an ass. But from a relationship standpoint... Was he—? Did he ever—?"

My heart cracks in half at the concern in Nick's voice, the unasked questions I fully understand. "No. Never."

The tension in his body eases only a little. "That's good."

"Yeah." He and Clara seem happy together, and she has the confidence and radiance of someone who isn't made to feel small by someone who claims to love her, so maybe Mark has changed.

"Anyway," I say to Nick, shaking my past with Mark from my mind, "he is not the boyfriend I am focused on tonight." I slip an arm around his waist, and he does the same to me before we meander back to the living room crowded with Mark and Clara's friends.

It's easy, standing here like this on the outskirts, taking it all in, with cashmere at my fingertips and comfort at my hip. Clara flits through the room, mingling and laughing with each guest, with Mark close behind her.

I don't know if Clara was ever taught how to greet someone without invading their personal space. It's oddly comforting, after spending decades with three brothers whose favorite sign of affection is body checking everyone into a wall, to be greeted with an enthusiastic hug and a warm smile. Like the body checks, Clara's hug knocks me off balance, but she also steadies me, righting me when the impact sends me stumbling. And Nick's hand on the small of my back doesn't hurt.

"I'm so glad you're here!" Clara shrieks. Her cheeks are tinted rosé pink, almost the same color of the mauve velvet dress she's wearing. She scans my outfit and massages one of my curls between her fingers. "You're so pretty, Holly."

"Thanks," I answer, feeling myself blush. "And you look fantastic, birthday girl." Fantastic *and* a little disheveled, like she had a glass too much of champagne and maybe engaged in a pretty serious make-out session in a closet ten minutes ago. And honestly, good for her.

She squishes my cheeks between her palms and looks at her brother. "Don't let this one get away," she stage whispers. "I really like her."

"Yeah. Me too." Nick's fingers glide across my back until his hand comes to rest curled loosely around the top of my hip bone.

I know I shouldn't feel anything, that it's all for show. But I melt into Nick's touch and enjoy it anyway through a second beer, some gift opening, and casual conversation with some of Clara's friends who have known Nick since they were kids.

Mr. and Mrs. Goodman have decided to skip tonight's party in favor of brunch with Clara and Mark tomorrow, and when Nick asks if I want to join them via an invitation breathed into my hair, I don't hesitate to say yes.

I spend so much of the night with my head against his shoulder that I'm half expecting to see the texture of his sweater imprinted on my cheek when I excuse myself to the restroom. Instead, all I find on my face is a smile that stretches from ear to ear.

One that flickers, I'm sure, when I step back into the hallway and almost collide with Mark.

"Having fun?" he asks. For a moment I ruminate on all the ways he could mean it, all the comments it could lead to. But I'm sure it's innocent; I have to stop assuming the worst about him.

"Of course. It's a great party."

"Yeah." He nods and slides out of the way so I can pass him and return to the rest of the crowd.

It's an unremarkable interaction, but one that still feels off.

"You okay?" Nick asks when he finds me in the kitchen. I'm torn between a glass of punch or a plate filled with crackers. He wraps an arm around my shoulder and kisses my temple.

"I'm fine. Just weighing my options at the carb smorgasbord here."

The partygoers who had been refilling their own plates leave the kitchen, and I expect Nick to put some space between us now that we don't have an audience. Instead, he hoists himself onto the countertop and wedges me between his knees.

"I really appreciate you for being here." He fidgets with his amber bottle, his thumbnail mindlessly picking at the label.

I shrug. "It's fun. Clara's great."

"She really likes you." His voice softens. "I do, too."

My heart flutters, light and free. It's so nice to hear it, but I can't ignore the glassy sheen in Nick's eyes.

"Do you, now?" I grin up at him, ostensibly flirty.

"We all do," he says, and I'm surprised by the sincerity in his tone.

"Well, I like you, too," I confess to both of us. "You're pretty great, Just Nick Goodman."

Nick straightens at that, setting his bottle on the counter next to him and reeling me in by my hips.

It's not that my *whole* life flashes before my eyes, but there are definitely moments that do. Like my very first kiss ever. My very last fight with Mark. The day Nick and I practiced kissing and he leaned in with his eyes open, mistletoe, and Nick's face in the O'Donnell's parking lot a week ago.

It's like all these memories are woven together by a common thread, and this moment gets stitched into the series because Nick startles at Clara's shrill "You guys are so freakin' cute!" as she enters the kitchen. He springs off the counter, toppling his bottle with the movement, like he got caught with his hand in the cookie jar.

Everything from his physical response to the expression on his face to the way Clara's smile grows as her eyes dart between her brother and me screams *'you just walked in on something you weren't meant to see,'* which is a weird reaction from someone who's supposed to be madly in love with me and who I'm supposedly making out with on a regular basis.

"Thanks, Sis." Nick runs a hand through his hair and picks up his bottle before dropping it in the recycling bin.

If I thought the kiss I could sense nearly happened was the biggest shocker of the night, I'd be very wrong. Because before he leaves the room, Nick Goodman whispers a kiss onto my forehead and a "love you" into my hair.

SHAKE UP CHRISTMAS

Nick

MY TEXTS ARE STILL unanswered at 9 A.M., just as they were at midnight when I sent them and 2 A.M. when I woke up looking for Advil and a glass of water.

It's either an answer that yes, it was too much, or it's just a sign that Holly has healthy boundaries when it comes to her cell phone and she's not checking it every hour of every day.

The real test is whether or not she shows up at brunch, I guess.

Our server shows us to a round table when we arrive, which means I'm in full view of my family when I anxiously check my watch and phone to see if she's officially late or if she's responded yet.

"You okay over there, Nicky?" Clara asks, cocking her head over a mimosa that has already appeared at our table. Cranberries float and bubbles fizz, and a sprig of pine garnishes the glass.

"I'm good."

"You worried Holly's going to flake on you?" Mark asks. He's not known for his useful contributions to conversation. Not at work, not last night, and definitely not now.

"No."

As if on cue, Holly appears in the doorway and finds us via the hostess's open-palmed point. "Good morning everyone. Sorry I'm late," she says to a chorus of greetings from the table. I rise and pull her chair out for her, feeling better when she squeezes my arm and kisses my cheek before sitting down.

Mom passes her a menu.

"You have to try this Christmas mimosa." Clara swirls her glass, sending cranberries careening into crystal.

"That sounds delicious." She smiles, but it doesn't reach her eyes. Instead, her head is on a swivel before she buries her face in the menu.

Conversation turns to what everyone plans to order, and I take the opportunity to lean behind Holly's menu with her. "Are you alright?"

One side of her mouth turns upward. "I'm good."

Now, obviously, is not the time to start the whole 'Are you sure I didn't screw things up by saying *I love you*' conversation, so I take her at her word and return to my own menu. "I wonder if their French toast is any good here."

"It's delicious," comes the quick reply from my right.

"You've been here before?"

Our server arrives, ready to take our orders. I'm not a fan of the whole I-can-memorize-the-entire-table's-order-with-great-ac-curacy mindset, but apparently that's the style here.

Mark orders first, followed by Clara, and when it's Holly's turn the server cocks her head. "Did you want a Christmas mimosa again, hun?"

Holly swallows before clearing the panic from her eyes and smiling. "I'd love to try one. Thank you."

The server's brows furrow, but she nods and takes Holly's food order, followed by mine and my parents'.

"It's really beautiful here," Holly says, her eyes scanning the wall of windows and miles of woods in the distance. She nudges my knee with hers and weaves her fingers into mine. "Want to look around with me?"

There's no joy in her voice, no flirtation, no excitement. It feels more like duty, fear, or something that ties the two together. Either way, I let her lead me to one of the dozen or so decorated trees in the restaurant, tucked into a corner near the bathrooms. She drops my hand and glances around nervously, biting her thumbnail.

"What's going on with you today?" I keep my voice low and try to look like we're a couple in love and not one in the middle of a fight. Which we're not. We're neither of those things.

She peers up at me, her eyes wide. She says through teeth still clenched around her thumbnail, "I was just here yesterday."

"Okay." I shrug. "Did you have a bad experience? Did someone get sick from the food?"

"No." She shakes her head and looks around again, making sure we're still alone. "I was here yesterday. With a... with a client." She practically whispers the last word.

"Oh." I rock backward like I'm avoiding a jab, even though it's already landed. "Should I be worried?"

Holly's eyes soften as they meet mine. "No. It was a once-and-done thing."

"I meant," I start, hoping I don't betray the sudden swell of feeling in my chest, "do you think anyone here will say anything?"

"Other than our server? No, I don't think so." Pink blossoms in her cheeks, and if we were anywhere else, alone, I would ask her about her previous comment. But we're here, and we're slightly in damage control territory, and there's something more pressing that comes to mind.

"Did you kiss him?"

Her mouth opens like she wants to argue, but she can't find the words. "That's not really—"

"I need to know, Holly. If not, if anyone asks, we can say you were here with one of your brothers or something."

She gnaws at her bottom lip. "No, we didn't kiss. But I still don't think anyone would buy the brother storyline."

I have no right to be jealous, and yet the feeling courses through my veins to every extremity. My toes tighten, my fists clench, my shoulders tense, the tips of my ears burn.

"It's fine," Holly promises, but I'm not convinced. She takes my hands in hers and gives a firm but gentle squeeze. "I'll take care of it." Then she kisses my cheek and turns toward the bathroom.

She's back barely a minute later, an actual smile on her face this time. "I swear, the women's room is the next best thing to the boardroom." She wraps her arm around mine, and we rejoin my family.

Our server swings by our table a few minutes later, refilling glasses of water and goblets of wine. She nods toward Holly, and I swear she winks. "How's the mimosa, hun? Do you like it?"

Holly takes a sip and smiles. "Delicious. Thanks for the recommendation."

"Of course."

Holly holds her glass out to me. "Would you like to try some?"

It seems like something a couple would do, so I take a sip just as Clara asks, "So, should we expect to see you at the cabin, Holly?"

Four sets of eyes dart from Holly to me as I sputter and try to swallow my drink before I end up wearing cranberry juice.

"A cabin? Tell me more." Holly rests an elbow on the table and perches her chin on one hand while she rubs my back with the other.

Clara looks at Holly, then back again at me. "Did you seriously not even invite her?" My sister shakes her head as though I have shamed our entire family in a public square, and she takes matters into her own hands.

"Every year, we spend a long weekend up north at Hope's Knoll. It's this gorgeous resort in the sweetest town, and there's ice skating and the best hot cocoa ever. Plus it's super romantic, which is why I can't fathom why my brother has failed to mention it to you."

"Because it's a little last minute, and it's a big time commitment." It's not a great defense, but it's something. Obviously I can't divulge the real reason why Holly shouldn't come along, which leaves me with not much to work with.

"I might have the time," Holly replies. "When's the trip?"

"We leave Wednesday after work and get back Sunday night," Mom chimes in. I swear my family is conspiring to make sure I die of embarrassment.

"Have I mentioned there's a spa?" Mom, Dad, and Holly let out a collective sigh.

"A couple's massage sounds good," Mark says, and I try to hide the disgust I feel when I imagine him, naked, with my sister.

"This Wednesday?" Holly asks, tapping an index finger against the table.

"Mhmm." Clara nods. "Please say yes. As a birthday gift to me."

"She gave you a scarf last night, Clar," I remind her. "One I'm pretty sure she made herself."

But Clara shakes her head and grins. "So clearly we're best friends, which is all the more reason why she should come along with us."

"I'll see what I can do." Holly wraps her fingers around the inside of my arm. "Maybe we can discuss the details later?"

I nod, because *sure,* we can discuss them. But I can't imagine she'd be willing to come along with us for four nights for what is fast turning into a couple's getaway instead of a family trip.

Conversation continues around the table, and the food is amazing, and the company's pretty great too. Holly laughs along with the rest of us when Dad tells old stories about Clara and me when we were kids, even harder when Mom corrects his memories for him. She seems especially entertained by a story about me in my potty-training years.

And when brunch is over, we've paid our bill, and Holly has bought two lemon blueberry muffins to go, she and I are the last to reach the parking lot. We're hand-in-hand, just like the couples ahead of us.

Clara and Mark are the first to leave, with Clara waving goodbye as Mark peels out of the parking lot in his ostentatious sports car, which screams that his Christmas bonus last year must have been significantly higher than mine.

Mom and Dad give both of us hugs and make me promise to call them later with an update about the weekend getaway once Holly and I get a chance to talk.

"So good to see you again, Mr. and Mrs. Goodman," Holly says, sliding her hand into mine as my parents climb into their car. She's cementing her status as their favorite person with every little gesture.

We wave as they drive away, and then it's just the two of us in a sea of cars in the restored barn's parking lot.

"Well, that was exciting," she says. "Sorry for the little scare in there."

I'm pretty sure that when most guys hear "little scare" on a date, it has to do with a little blue plus sign on a stick, and not a date-for-hire that threatens to expose you as a liar to your parents, sister, and workplace archnemesis.

"How did you know it would all work out?"

Holly shrugs. "I saw the server go into the bathroom and slipped her a twenty to act like she'd never seen me before."

"Not gonna lie, I'm a little disappointed at the lack of creativity there."

We share a laugh, and it's not until her fingers squeeze mine that I realize we've been holding hands since my parents left.

"So, this cabin..." Holly takes a step back and crosses her arms, rocking backward and forward between her heels and toes. The sun illuminates one side of her face; strands of hair turn golden.

"I couldn't ask you to go. It's—"

"But what if I *want* to go?"

Could Holly actually want to spend five days and four nights with me and my family? And *Mark?* "Do you want to?"

She shrugs one shoulder, tilting her head to meet it as it rises. "It sounds like fun. And there's a spa."

"And it's a three-bedroom cabin," I add. "Though our room would at least have two doubles in it."

"Oh, how dreadfully romantic." She speaks with a bend toward the dramatic, pressing the back of her hand to her forehead.

It wouldn't be the worst thing, having Holly along on this trip. At the very least it would ensure that I don't have to spend the whole weekend locked up in my room alone or forced to watch my sister make out with someone I can't stand. Some might actually think it would be fun, to have someone to hang out with, visit the little antique shops with, grab hot cocoa with.

"Unless you don't want me there." Holly tucks her hair behind her ears and peers up at me through thick lashes.

"No, you should come. If you want to."

She nods. "I think it sounds great."

"Great," I repeat. Look at me, planning my first romantic getaway with my fake girlfriend. Is this one of the relationship goals everyone talks about on social media?

"Great." Holly presses the button on the side of her phone to check the time; the screen lights up with a photo of a sunset on the beach. "I should probably be going."

"Of course. I'll text you the details for the trip."

"Great."

I lean in to kiss her cheek until I remember we're alone, and there's an awkward pause where we completely forget how to say goodbye without an audience.

"I'll just..." She hooks a thumb over her shoulder in the direction of her car. "See ya," she says.

"Bye, Holly."

I saunter toward my own car, glancing back as I go. Holly's still sitting in her driver's seat when I reach my own car a few rows away. My phone buzzes once I start the ignition, and Holly drives off, waving.

Finally, twelve hours later, I have a response to my midnight text messages:

> It definitely helps make things more convincing.

> So not too much at all.

Christmas Cookies
Holly

MOM IS POSITIVELY GIDDY about the idea of me going away with Nick and his family for the weekend.

"Are you sure you don't care that I'd miss lunch on Sunday?" Mom started a tradition years ago of inviting my dad's side of the family over for lunch the weekend before Christmas since so many of them travel for the holiday.

She waves a hand and purses her lips. "Sweetie, if you're going away with that hunky young man, you could miss my funeral."

"Mother!" I throw an aptly named pillow across the couch at her, and she catches it, laughing.

"I'm just saying, you've been working so hard, and if you have the opportunity to take a little vacation *and* enjoy a little romance, you should absolutely take it."

It has been a lot, managing my Pickup CARtist schedule and my social calendar recently, now that I've got so many events with the Goodmans added in there. I always thought of Christmas as being a relaxing time, full of fireside hot cocoas and old movies. Now I'm learning that managing the holiday parties and events is anxiety-inducing, and if you're sitting down and enjoying a quiet night in, you're probably doing it wrong.

"Okay, then. I guess I'm going away for the weekend." I text Nick with the news, sure to include a row of smiley face emojis. He texts back seconds later with a gif that makes me snort.

We go back and forth for a few minutes until Mom finally asks, "He makes you pretty happy, huh?"

I bite my lip, unsure how to answer. After a moment, I decide on, "He's a great guy." It's true. Nick Goodman has been absolutely wonderful since our first meeting. And he's starting to relax a lot more, which makes him even easier to be around. I'm getting comfortable, which is probably very wrong, just like giving my mom hope about our future.

"Finally. You deserve to have a good one." Then she scoots a cushion closer and says, "Show me where this man of yours is whisking you off to this weekend."

I've been browsing the Hope's Knoll website since Nick sent me the link five minutes ago, catching glimpses of cabins and fireplaces between message notifications and replies, so it's easy to give Mom a quick virtual tour. "There's a skating rink, which is open year-round. Then they have hot chocolate bars, and there are, like, a million and four fireplaces around this place." It seems like every picture features couples or families sipping cocktails or cocoa in front of a cozy, crackling fire. "And Clara said there's a lot of shopping, so maybe I can finally finish my Christmas list."

"Is there room for two more?"

"Mmm, maybe not on this particular trip, but I can report back in case you want to plan a weekend away with Dad." The last thing I need on my fake-romantic weekend with my fake boyfriend and his very real, very enthusiastic family and my very real ex-boyfriend, is for my parents to tag along, uninvited. Not that I don't love them, because I do, and our vacations as a family have always been pretty enjoyable, but they're kind of... a lot. And I can't imagine all the wedding and baby plans that would be made for us if Mom and Mrs. Goodman and

Clara were able to sit around with cocktails and talk about Nick and me.

Mom pats my knee and rises with effort, like our old, sunken couch could use a few extra inches of stiff padding. "Well, I'm going to go decorate some cookies I made earlier. Any chance you want to join me?"

"Sugar cookies?"

Mom smirks; her eyes sparkle. "Ninja-bread men."

"I'm in."

DECK THE MALLS
Holly

MY HEART IS NOT in Pickup CARtistry in the three days before the cabin getaway. I have a fair number of jobs Sunday night after a cookie-decorating marathon with Mom, and throughout the day on Monday thanks to a double-header concert from a well-known group that tours exclusively at Christmastime. They've got shows at the Ferryton Falcons' arena, which I am extra well-acquainted with on Tuesday after driving guests to and from a rare Tuesday-night game. There's also a Tuesday matinee performance of the local theater's Christmas show, which I provide transport to and from but also enjoy from the balcony with Mom.

It's a busy week, and my bank account appreciates it (feel free to hate surge pricing, but it's going to help pay for the bachelorette weekend of my best friend's dreams), but what really brings a smile to my face is opening a suitcase Tuesday night and preparing to pack for a dream vacation that I've been told in no uncertain terms I am not paying a cent for.

And that's followed by an immediate sense of dread, because I have no idea what to pack.

Cue an emergency call with Jasmine, which is not helpful due to her recommendation of "a few cute sweaters, leggings, and some great lingerie." I text Nick, and he delivers exactly what I need: Clara's phone number.

When she answers the FaceTime call, I am panicked and pacing. "S.O.S. How do I have a closet full of clothes and yet nothing to pack for this trip?"

She laughs, crystalline and bright. "I was just about to call you!"

"Me?" How would I know what to pack for the trip she's been on a dozen times?

"Yeah..." she starts, and I can tell she's moving down the hallway of her apartment that's lined with pictures of her and Mark. A moment later she closes the door, and her voice quiets. "So, this might be a little weird, but I was hoping you could give me some advice."

"I'm not sure I have anything helpful—"

"It's about Mark." Clara bites her lip, and I already dread the conversation we're about to have. "If it's weird, tell me to shut up. But I figured since you and Nick are so happy, and you and Mark seem to be good as far as exes are concerned... maybe you could help me?"

I gulp. Comically loudly, except not quite so comically, because I really hate where this seems to be going. "Sure?" I choke out.

"Okay, so. I'm also packing, and it's our first super romantic trip—and yes, I know that sounds weird considering you guys and my parents are all going to be there. No offense. And I just wanted to make it a little more exciting, I guess. So anyway, I was wondering, is he a fan of—"

"I don't really know," I answer before I even hear the end of the question. "Things with Mark were always kind of..."

"Boring?"

I sigh. "Yes." It's refreshing to know it wasn't just me. It's even more refreshing to hear such straightforward honesty coming from someone I've known barely two weeks and who I view as a friend, even if our entire relationship is based on a lie.

"Well, that's a bummer." She sighs too, then chuckles. "I guess some things from my packing list will just live in my nightstand drawer."

The really fun (insert sarcasm here) thing about living in your childhood home with your parents and little brother is that sometimes people just barge into your room without knocking. Growing up it was Micah, who acted like he owned the place. But right now it's Landon who bursts through the door.

"You talking to Jasmine?" he asks, rushing toward the camera to say hi. Sometimes I'm surprised Jasmine asked me to be in her bridal party instead of my brother. They connected over a shared love of horror films the first time Jasmine came here for a visit, when Landon was supposed to be at a soccer tournament in New Jersey that was cancelled at the last minute.

"No." I pull the phone away, but the damage is done.

"Hi!" Clara waves, and Landon tries to swipe the phone from my hand. "I'm Clara, Nick's sister."

"Ahh," Landon replies, settling for resting his chin on my head to stay on the screen. "Are you the one I have to thank for getting this one out of my hair this weekend?"

I angle the phone downward to cut him out of the camera's view and elbow him in the ribcage. He clutches his side like he's Lin-Manuel in the Hamilton duel scene and begins his retreat, but not without shouting "Bye, Clara!" and waving obnoxiously on his way out the door.

"Which brother was that?" She's sprawled face-down on her bed, with her chin cupped in her palm.

"That was Landon. He's the youngest of the four of us."

"He's cute," Clara says with more enthusiasm than I'd like.

"He's an overgrown toddler."

I hip-check my door closed, but it doesn't keep out Landon's "I heard that!" from his room next door.

"Anyway. Packing. What do I need for this trip?"

"Hopefully more exciting things than I do." She rolls her eyes, and I feel my cheeks burn. "But seriously... Some casual but cozy things for ice skating and shopping. Dinner could be dress pants or nice jeans. Oh! That outfit you wore to my party was great, if you wanted to bring something like that."

I take a mental note of all the pieces I already have and what I might need to pick up at the mall tomorrow morning. Which is to say, probably everything, because I feel like nothing I own is cute or fancy enough for the resort.

"And then, for—oh wait. Hang on one sec." Clara's brows furrow, and she sits up. "Sorry, Holly. I have to go. I hope that helped!"

"Yeah. Thanks, Clara."

She's off the phone before I can say goodbye, or ask what the 'and then' was going to lead to. With a healthy dose of curiosity but an awareness that time is running out, I pack two oversized sweaters and two pairs of leggings, then two pairs of jeans and the black skirt I wore to Clara's party on Saturday. Just in case, I throw in the Ugly Christmas Sweater dress I wore to Nick's party on our first official date.

I know I screwed up that night. A lot. But I smile at the memory anyway.

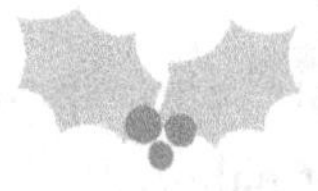

For a Wednesday, the mall is packed. Like people-are-lined-up-four-deep-at-each-entrance-five-minutes-before-the-place-opens packed. I have a vaguely specific list of things to purchase, which really amounts to 'whatever speaks to me comes home with me,' and about four department stores and eight boutiques to browse. And maybe some blue-haired old ladies with walkers that I might need to dodge.

When the doors open and we funnel through, I decide to bypass everyone by power-walking to the far end of the store and to the boutiques first. Which is a terrible idea, because the first three stores have great clothes, but only if I'm hoping to spend a day's worth of CARtist money on one outfit. So it's back to the department store I go, where I pick up a basic black dress and a glittering red wrap sweater from a rack marked 50% off. I pay for the outfit and a new pair of shoes, and I consider purchasing a matching hat, glove, and scarf set that feels more polished than the amateur beanie and scarf I crocheted for myself two years ago until I see my total. Homemade is making a comeback anyway.

The only thing that stands between me and the door is the lingerie department. I brace myself for the arduous journey of crossing through that silky terrain, dotted with men like landmines, who are fondling boa trims and lace with their grubby fingers and wondering which size is least likely to insult their wives. All I need to do is make it through eight aisles, and—

"Holly?"

Shit.

I pause on instinct, and then realize, *if I keep moving, maybe I can pretend I didn't hear him.* Because nothing screams *PERSONAL HELL* like being trapped in a place as vulnerable as the lingerie department with a guy who has seen every dimple of fat and every stretch mark on my body and who felt the need to offer "fixes" for all of them.

"Nice try." Mark's smug face greets me when I pivot on my heels.

"What are you doing here?"

He smirks, and I make a note to kick myself later. "Just picking up a little something for the weekend." It looks like he's got a black lace bustier, a black satin robe, and a red chemise with white boa trim dangling from the hangers hooked over his index finger. How original.

"Cool. See you later, I guess."

"You're not going to pick out something for Nick?"

Oh, I hate that: the idea that women's lingerie is for their partners' enjoyment. Sirs, I would spoil myself with anything lace, satin, mesh, or PVC, even without you around, and check myself out from all angles, thank you very much. Take all the seats.

"Who says I don't have a whole bag packed just for my bedroom wardrobe?"

Mark crosses his arms, power posing, with lingerie still hanging from his hand. "Please. You probably have one of Micah's hand-me-down sweatshirts and a pair of flannel pajama pants."

"*Pshuh,* yeah, right." It's *Landon's* old sweatshirt, and a pair of flannel *shorts*. But he's still technically wrong, and I'm going to embrace that.

"That's what I thought. Anyway." Mark looks at his watch. "I should get going, but I'll see you at dinner, I guess." He doesn't wait for a goodbye, because Mark does whatever he wants, whenever he wants, and he doesn't account for common courtesy.

Once he's meandered away from lingerie, through footwear and then menswear, I decide a cute set of silky pajamas wouldn't be the worst thing in the world, and I browse the racks.

SOMEWHERE IN MY MEMORY
Holly

AS A CHRONIC UNDER-PLANNER and over-packer, I'm pretty pleased that I've managed to squeeze everything I need into my full-size suitcase and a small weekender tote, the latter of which is used almost exclusively for footwear.

Nick seems equally impressed when I open the trunk of my car and he realizes I have space for all of his things, including a duffle, garment bag, and a large suitcase that he carries out flat and insists on transporting that way, too.

"You promise it's not a body?" I ask before I close the trunk.

"I promise."

"Good." We buckle in and start driving. Nick has okayed a detour I requested since I had to go on my shopping excursion this morning, and twenty minutes later I'm parking in front of a massive brick retirement home.

"You can wait here if you want. I'll leave the engine running."

But he doesn't want that. Nick follows me across the parking lot and past the welcome desk, holding doors open for me as I carry my haul, offering three times to carry at least the balloon bouquet.

"And let you take all the credit? Ha!"

He shakes his head, smiling.

When we finally reach her room, Grandma's playing solitaire on her armchair table and muttering about a wrong answer given on a game show rerun.

"Well, hi there, birthday girl!"

Grandma looks up and grins as I enter with arms overflowing with goodies. Nick pokes the balloons through the doorway when they get stuck, then lingers just outside in the hallway.

I set everything on the small two-person dining table in her kitchen, then kneel next to her for a hug and a quick kiss on the cheek. "How are you?"

"I'm much better now!" Her eyes light up with the Grandma Glisten. We started using the phrase when we were tweens to describe that misty look that Grandma gets whenever she's excited. It's part sparkle, part teary, and all joy. "But what are you doing? We already celebrated my birthday."

I shrug. "Yeah, but that wasn't your actual birthday." Back at her party, when I put the reminder on my calendar to do something special for her today, I'd planned to spend a full day celebrating her: painting her nails, taking her out to lunch, going to the movies—doing whatever she wanted to do. But instead I've been stress-shopping for a getaway with a fake boyfriend and his family, and all I've got for her is a cake, a present, and a measly fifteen minutes before we really should get back on the road.

"But," I start, reaching for a large lavender gift bag decorated with pastel rainbows and glittering unicorns, "if you don't want presents, I guess I can take them back to the store."

I am blessed to have a grandmother at all. So many friends of mine grew up without theirs, or they've lost them on the cusp of adulthood. But not only do I have a healthy grandmother, she is lively. Spirited. Capable and opinionated and wonderful.

And now she yanks the present from my hands and pushes sparkling tissue paper aside until she pulls out the gift: a vase I found that perfectly matches the pattern on the china set she lost in a fire, back when Grandpa was still alive. Her eyes well with tears as she turns it carefully in her hands.

"Oh, Holly. I don't know what to say."

"My grandmother once taught me that 'thank you' is a good place to start," I tell her with a wink.

She passes me the vase, which I set on the deep mantle of her electric fireplace, next to a lesser vase holding a bouquet of pastel ranunculus. I touch a pink petal and breathe in the faint, sweet scent of the flowers, which are Grandma's favorites, and mine, too.

"Don't be alarmed, dear, but there is a handsome young man watching you from the hallway."

I turn from the fireplace to see Nick propped against the wall outside the open door, his feet crossed at the ankles and his hands shoved deep in his pockets. When Grandma draws attention to him, he shifts.

"He *is* pretty cute. Think we should invite him in? Maybe he can help us eat some of this cake."

Grandma glances between me and Nick and waves for him to come in. "I'm assuming you're the boyfriend I've hardly heard anything about?"

"Grandma!" I shouldn't be embarrassed, considering he's not actually my boyfriend, but I still feel heat prickle my ears.

Nick, for his part, chuckles like the good-humored saint that he is. "I'm the very lucky guy, yes." He holds out a hand to shake Grandma's, but she motions for a hug instead. He bends and acquiesces, because again... *saint*.

And then he kisses my cheek and has me sit down in the armchair opposite Grandma's so I can keep talking with her while he cuts the cake, finding plates and forks with little trouble and even offering us drinks when he delivers our slices to us.

"Where'd you find this one?" she asks, talking about him like he's not standing a foot behind me.

"The internet."

Grandma rolls her eyes—she's always believed in finding love "the old-fashioned way"—but she's starting to open up to the idea that people have to look outside of church, work, and their siblings' friends to find relationships. Not that she branched out too far—she and Grandpa were middle-school sweethearts who got married at twenty and stayed married for fifty years, until Grandpa passed.

We carry on a bit more, with Grandma and Nick laughing and joking as much as she and I are, until her old grandfather clock chimes and reminds me that we are far behind schedule to make it to the resort in time for dinner tonight.

"We should head out," I say.

I start to collect our dishes, but Nick takes them from me, quickly hand-washes and dries them, and puts them away. Then Grandma rises from her chair for a real hug. "I meant to ask," she starts, pointing a wrinkled, bony finger at the balloons. "Why all the unicorns?"

"Do you like them?" I ask.

Her confusion turns to a smile, and she pokes at the three-foot tall, helium-filled masterpiece. "They're rather delightful."

"Then that's why." I wrap her in a hug and kiss her cheek before she ditches me for Nick.

Once goodbyes are finished, Nick takes my hand in his, and we mosey toward the hallway. "I love you, Grandma," I call to her as I close the door behind us.

We retrace our steps through three hallways, the welcome area, and the parking lot before he pulls his hand from mine to open the driver's side door.

CHRISTMAS C'MON
Holly

"CAN I ASK A weird question?"

We left Grandma's an hour ago. It's dark out, and my maps app—which is one of three sources of light on the winding roads that will lead us to a weekend of relaxation—tells me we still have two hours to go until we reach the resort. Which is not ideal, since we have a dinner reservation in an hour.

"It would be weird if there was no weirdness in our regular interactions, so go for it," Nick answers, mid-text conversation (the second source of light) with his mom, apologizing that we're going to miss the aforementioned dinner with them.

"Do you think, when this is all over, we could—"

"Still be friends?" He shifts to face me from the passenger seat. "Not weird at all, if that's what you were thinking."

I nod, keeping my eyes glued to the swath of road illuminated by my headlights. "It's just that... I think my family likes you, and they'd probably kill me if I didn't bring you around anymore after the holidays."

"Are you sure it's not because you think I'm cute?"

I can hear the wink in his voice, that gentle teasing, that knowing *I-heard-what-you-said-in-there* taunting. A quick peripheral glance reveals that he is smirking but looking straight ahead, which is somehow more annoying. The hubris, to be so certain he's affected me that he doesn't even need visual confirmation of the blush in my cheeks.

But then he tucks his phone into his back pocket and re-settles himself into his seat. "I was thinking the same thing, actually. Plus it's been fun, hanging out."

It *has* been fun hanging out. And not just the making out parts, either, but those moments we steal away during family dinners and birthday parties, and moments like this one, driving down back roads and listening to music and just talking.

"Maybe I'll take you out for dinner once we break up. As friends, of course," I add, when I realize it sounds like I'm asking him out on a date. Which I'm not.

"Dinner sounds great."

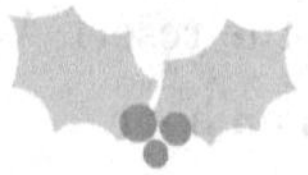

I may have spent part of the drive trying to mentally calculate how many days are left until Nick and I mutually break up, and how many days we have left until our non-date dinner, which may have led to my missing our exit, which led us to Rosie's Burger Shack. If we have to miss dinner at a swanky resort, at least we can shovel greasy smash patties bedecked in sautéed onions and hot honey BBQ sauce into our mouths.

"This is delicious." Nick backs up his words with a moan that I'm trying to convince myself doesn't sound sexual, even though it does, in fact, sound like a bedroom noise.

I steal another cheese fry from the plastic basket between us and chase it with a sip of the most perfect chocolate milkshake that has ever existed.

Nick also takes a cheese fry, because—if we're being honest—they're technically his. "I'm half tempted to ask if we can stop here on the way home on Sunday."

"I'm sorry, do we not need lunch and dinner between now and then?"

He laughs and adjusts his glasses with the heel of his hand, careful not to let his BBQ- and melty-cheese-covered fingers touch the lenses. "I promise, the food at the resort is actually quite good. It's just..." He trails off and surveys the table.

"It's just not Rosie's-Burger-Shack good?" For emphasis, and not because I'm a starved bridge troll who steals people's food, I eat another fry.

Nick clears his throat. "I was going to say, the company there versus here..."

Right on cue, a child wails from across the room. "I don't know; it kind of sounds like Mark's found us."

There's a snort, a chuckle, then that precious, perfect dimple, before he wipes a napkin over his fingers. "I'm sorry. That you were basically rid of him, and now you have to spend all this extra time with him, because of me."

"More accurately, it's because of *me.* And you don't need to apologize for anything. Mark's..." What *is* Mark? An afterthought? A blip on an otherwise great time every time I hang out with the Goodman family? "Mark is tolerable." And he is, with the buffer of the Goodmans.

"That's generous of you."

"Well," I say, pointing one last cheese fry at Nick, "I'm not stuck dating him anymore. I've moved on to better things."

He rests his elbows on the table and leans in, raising an eyebrow over the rim of his glasses at me. "Such as?"

If he were still alive, I'm positive Sigmund Freud would insist on studying my stupid brain. Why do phrases like *'Such as this,'* and

'Such as you,' and *'Such as that one day when we practiced making out'* keep running through my mind?

"Such as an all-expenses paid trip to a beautiful resort," is what I decide to say.

"Speaking of which." Nick pushes himself back from the table. His smile has faded, his dimple is gone. "We should probably get back on the road."

"Yeah. We should."

And other than the sound of carols and Bing Crosby and Mariah Carey, we spend the last half hour of our drive to Hope's Knoll in silence.

FEEL LIKE THE HOLIDAYS
Nick

"ARE YOU FREAKING *KIDDING* me?"

"For the third time, no."

"Well then, Nick Goodman, for the *fourth* time, I ask... Are. You. *Freaking. Kidding*. Me? Because you have *got* to be kidding me."

"Do you need me to pinch you?"

Holly backhands my arm. "Shut up. Let me take it in."

We're barely inside the front door of the resort's lobby. The valet has taken Holly's car, and the bellmen have taken most of our luggage. Holly rotates slowly, now on at least her third three-sixty of the four-story space rimmed by rooms with wooden balconies. Decorated Christmas trees fill every corner of the expansive lobby, and green garlands wrapped in yellow-white lights twist around the staircase and walkway railings.

"It's like a Hallmark movie on steroids," she mutters with awe and admiration coloring her voice.

"Well, when you're done gawking at the roided-out wannabe made-for-TV backdrop, would you like to make our way to our cabin?"

It's actually adorable, the way she stands here like she's Kevin McCallister entering The Plaza's lobby for the first time. She hooks her thumb through the strap of the tote on her shoulder and nods, still turning, still taking it in.

"I promise, if you move past the lobby, it gets even better."

Her head snaps in my direction, and her lips curl into a smile. "I doubt it, but okay."

Because we're supposed to be a couple, and because the staff here is famous for how they remember nearly every guest and interaction, I hold out my hand to Holly. She slips her fingers into mine easily, like it's natural and practiced.

She's so focused on what's behind us as we leave the lobby that she doesn't see the excitement that lies ahead: an old-timey trolley that acts as the resort's shuttle, transporting guests from the main building to their cabins and back again. When she notices, her fingers clench mine and she grips my arm with her free hand. "Are you kidding me?"

"We've established that I am not."

The shuttle is cozy, bordering on too warm, but that doesn't stop Holly from resting her head on my shoulder on the short ride to our cabin. Gray smoke billows out of the chimney, and the first floor is awash in golden light from the soft bulbs in the kitchen and dining room. No doubt, my family is sitting around the living room fire, at least two bottles deep into their wine supply for the weekend, which is fine, because Clara and Mark have a tasting planned at the vineyard tomorrow and can restock there.

"Any final words of wisdom or warning?" Holly asks as she takes my hand in hers again. The brick pathway to the front door is lined with lights that project snowflakes onto the ground, a feature that feels especially fitting when considering the dusting of snow predicted in our Saturday-morning forecast.

"Fake it good, I guess?" I answer, and she laughs, and I laugh, and then the door swings open and Mom stands with arms outstretched to welcome us to the cabin.

Clara's close behind her, sliding across the hardwood inside in a pair of fuzzy socks. It's tradition for one of us to supply everyone with a pair upon arrival; the responsibility rotates each year. Dad likes to find funny socks that match each individual's personality; Mom is a fan of matching socks for everyone. Clara's in charge this year, and I'm curious what she's whipped up for Holly and me.

"You guys missed the best dinner," Mark says, entirely unhelpfully and irrelevant to our conversation, which is very simply, *'hello.'*

Anyway. Clara pushes past Mom to hug Holly, and I feel a little slighted, because hello, I'm her actual flesh and blood.

Dad's asking about the drive up and Mom's offering to cook for us despite our confirmation that yes, we did stop for dinner, which I also told her via text message as we pulled into the Rosie's Burger Shack parking lot.

"I might take some of the hot chocolate I've heard so much about, if anyone else was planning to have some," Holly says, solidifying herself as Mom's Favorite.

Mom's love language is acts of service. The woman loves to be needed and loves to help others. I think that's why she's kept her hot chocolate recipe a secret: so that anyone who wants a mug will have to recruit her for help.

Mom's face lights up, and she tugs Holly through the front door and toward the kitchen island, where Mark, Dad, and Holly take a seat around the slab of granite as Clara and I take orders and prep Mom's work station.

We need whipped cream, crushed peppermint, mini chocolate chips, sprinkles, and five mugs (Mark has declined the cocoa, which is a faux pas the magnitude of which he has not reached before in Mom's eyes), and then we distract ourselves while Mom stirs the cocoa in the saucepan on the stove.

"What's everyone planning on doing tomorrow?" I ask, once we're back in the living room around the fire. "Aside from the wine tasting." I shoot Clara a look and a mild rolling of my eyes, as if to say, *'yes, I've heard you talk about this for months.'*

"You guys should come with us," she says, more to Holly than to me.

But Holly's eyes meet mine over her mug of cocoa, and I know that as much as she enjoys Clara and wine, she probably would rather spend an hour army crawling through a landfill in the summer than spend an hour playing nice at a wine tasting with her ex.

"I was hoping for some alone time with my girlfriend," I intervene.

"Not *too* alone though. I heard there's shopping, and ice skating, and a really cute bookstore?" Holly tucks her legs underneath her and shifts her mug from one hand to the other.

"There's a lot to do." It's funny that Dad recognizes that, because most days I find him taking a midday nap on the same recliner where he sits right now.

"And you should take time to enjoy Hope's Knoll itself," Mom adds, because Mom very rarely leaves the property when we come here. She's all about sitting in the lobby with a good book and enjoying one of the many tours or Dickens-themed events they host here.

"And also, some alone time." I swear Clara winks at Holly.

Two beams of light that are very distinctly headlights illuminate the room, and a gentle chiming fills the air. Saved by the bellmen.

"I'll get it." Mom takes my mug when I stand, and Holly's close behind me.

"Mr. Goodman," the bellman says, standing next to his brassy cart. "Shall I take these to your room directly, sir?"

I shake my head. "No, I can get them, but thank you." I help him unload the cart; Holly slips him a ten-dollar bill.

"Which room is ours?" I ask my parents. Typically we stay in the neighboring cabin, which has a layout I could walk in my sleep. But apparently its turn in the renovation cycle has come, and it's out of commission for a month.

"Third door on your left," Mom answers.

"Great."

"It was lovely seeing everyone tonight." Holly's cheerful, but she punctuates her words with a yawn. "Sorry to have missed dinner, but I'm looking forward to spending the weekend with the Great Goodman Family."

It's not lost on me that she excluded Mark in her declaration.

A chorus of *'good night'* follows, and then Holly and I climb the stairs toward our bedroom.

"So far so good?" She hoists her suitcase over the final step and leads the way down the hallway.

"Very good." My body is exhausted from hours in the car, and I could use a few minutes of alone time. "Once we get settled, do you want to use the bathroom first? I was hoping to take a shower before bed."

"Sure," she says. She reaches the third door on the left, swings it open, and stops. "Is this the right room?"

I count the doors we just passed. "Third door on the left. Should be ours."

Holly curses under her breath. *"Shit."*

"What's wrong?" I park my suitcases in the hallway so I have room to get behind her suitcase and peek in. I'm expecting a taxidermied moose head or an infestation of bees, but what I find is much, much worse. "Are you freaking kidding me?"

Cozy Little Christmas
Holly

"I THOUGHT YOU SAID—"

"I know."

"This is—"

"Less than ideal. I know."

"Ouch, Goodman."

Nick sighs. "You know what I mean."

"Are we sure your mom said it was the third door on the left? Should we double check? I mean, maybe we're supposed to be in a different room."

"Sadly, I think this is us." Nick reaches through the doorway and feels the wall for the switch before flipping the lights on and bathing the room in dim white from a series of recessed bulbs overhead.

Any hope I'd been holding onto that there was a twin bed or a couch or, I don't know, a fluffy dog bed hiding elsewhere in the room disappears with the darkness, and my initial fear about the room is confirmed. There, sandwiched between two wooden nightstands, is one singular bed.

Nick exhales, and I echo him. "Think there's any chance your family won't notice if I get a room in the actual hotel?"

"Not a chance. Plus, those rooms are probably six hundred a night, if there are even any left."

"So, do I sleep in my car? Fake a medical emergency and go home?"

He wheels my suitcase into the room, parking it next to the bed. "You're overthinking it. I'll just sleep on the floor."

The floor is hardwood and the rug is a firm, braided style. Maybe I'm a worse person than I ever thought, but I'm relieved by his plan and content to let him sleep there. "You can have most of the pillows, if you want. The blanket, too."

"Let's just unpack, and then we'll figure it out."

It doesn't take long to unpack my things; a few pairs of shoes line the closet floor, and I utilize barely a handful of hangers and the dresser's bottom drawer. Nick is still emptying his first suitcase, so I help myself to the attached bathroom where I organize the handful of hair and makeup products I've packed before changing into pajamas, brushing my teeth, and washing my face.

"Your turn." When I reemerge into the bedroom, Nick's sitting on the corner of his still-upright suitcase in front of the closet, like he's too afraid to sit on the corner of the bed like a normal person would. Like just hanging out there for five minutes while I'm in the bathroom will get me pregnant or something. But he rises and saunters wordlessly to the bathroom, a change of clothes in hand.

I hear the shower start, securing me a good ten or more minutes of alone time. Which is too much, really, because without distractions, my mind spirals. Instead of allowing my brain to doomscroll through all the possibilities of what could go wrong this weekend, I busy myself with reorganizing my dresser drawer, then head to my half of the closet.

"I thought you unpacked," I say to no one in particular as I move Nick's still flat-lying suitcase aside to make room for the upright one. It's not terribly heavy, but it's still definitely full.

The bathroom door creaks open and Nick asks, "Did you say something?" At least, I think that's what he's asking, because words are formed around his electric toothbrush, and because I'm not really paying attention to his words because his bare torso has entered the conversation.

Full disclosure: I've seen a fair number of naked torsos in my day. I have three brothers, and they have friends, and some dudes just don't like to wear shirts. I get it. I've seen six packs and keg bellies, tan skin and freckled skin, smooth and hairy and all the things in between. Some have been normal, and some have been... I think the technical term is *hubba-hubba.*

But seeing Nick Goodman's torso was not on my Bingo card for this year. He's still in a pair of dark jeans and nothing else but his glasses, with a section of hair tumbling over his forehead like he's been stressfully finger-combing it all night and it's fallen out of place.

You guys. It's *hot.*

"Holly?" He retreats, spits, and returns, sans toothbrush. "Did you say something?"

"Oh. No, yeah—just that—" I pat his suitcase. "You didn't unpack."

He runs a hand through his hair and eases his glasses off his face, and I pray he's got a nearsighted prescription strong enough that he can't see my face clearly—either the expression or the beet-red shade. "I unpacked all my clothes. Those are just presents in there."

"Presents?"

Nick cocks his head at me like I'm a Martian just learning human languages. "Yeah, we like to exchange gifts while we're here since we're normally traveling to visit family on Christmas Day."

"Okay, I get that. But you didn't tell me to bring any presents."

He shrugs, and without anything masking his movement I can appreciate how his muscles work together to form the gesture, how his skin glides over bone and sinew. "Why would you need to bring anything?"

Sometimes I just see gifs and memes in my head, and right now it's that blondish guy with the "really?" look on his face and the disbelieving blinks. "Is it not customary for a couple in the 'I love you' stage to purchase presents for each other's family at their gift-giving holiday of choice?"

He scrubs a hand down his face. "I can just add your name to the tags on my presents."

"No." I don't know what Nick bought for his family members, but I will not accept responsibility for a toaster or a sweater I did not painstakingly select myself.

"Okay." He shrugs again. "Maybe we can find something in town tomorrow?"

"Sure."

"Great. I'm gonna..." Nick hooks a thumb over his shoulder. "Shower."

"Okay."

And then he's gone, and I flop across the bed with my phone, hoping a little actual doomscrolling will keep me from the internal type. It must pass the time pretty effectively, because I feel like I've just started when the bathroom door opens and Nick strolls out in a cloud of steam like he's a rockstar on a foggy stage, and he's toweling off his hair.

And he's wearing an old baseball-style tee, and those browline glasses, and—

Shit. Are those *gray sweatpants?*

"What?" He pauses his hair drying and follows my gaze, giving himself a quick scan. "Oh, because I didn't wear the matching pajama pants my mom picked out for all of us? I can't stand the fleece. It's too hot when I'm sleeping."

"I won't tell a soul."

This brings a crooked smile to his face, and he straightens his glasses. "When we finish this whole thing and are just friends, can we maybe not have so many secrets and lies?"

I make a face. "I dunno. It's kind of our thing."

Nick's answering chuckle and dimple should calm me, let me know that we're good, and everything's fine. But no, they have the opposite effect, and I pull my sleeves over my clammy hands.

"No secrets. No lies." I give a firm, single nod to confirm.

"Great." He rocks back on his heels and twists his towel in his hands. "So... were you wanting to get to sleep now? Or...?"

"Yeah. Now's good, I guess."

"Cool. I, uh—" He clears his throat. "I think I might go hang out downstairs for a little while and join you later. I mean, not, like, *join* you, but—"

"Cool," I interject. The man needed saving. "Whatever. I'll be here." I might need saving, too.

He disappears into the bathroom to hang up his towel, then grabs a book off the dresser, slides his feet into a pair of fuzzy slippers, and opens the door to leave. "Oh, hey, Mark," he says.

Everything in me tenses and sweats—somehow—even more at the thought of Mark just outside the room, probably because of his too-close-for-comfort prediction of my sleepwear and the fact that I am not dressed like a sexy girlfriend on a romantic getaway.

There's chatter, and then Nick says "Yeah, man, I'll be right there," to the hallway and "Bye babe, love you," to me and flicks a wave goodbye from the doorway.

In the musical *Wicked*, Elphaba wonders aloud '*Did that really just happen?*' I am neither green, nor magical, nor beautifully tragic, but I've never related so much to a character in all my life.

Once the hallway creaking has subsided and I'm confident I'm alone upstairs, I roll onto my stomach with a groan and whisper-scream into a pillow.

It's Beginning to Look a Lot Like Christmas

Holly

NICK KNOCKS—*KNOCKS!*—ON THE DOOR at 6 A.M.

"Hey," he whispers. "Sorry if I woke you."

He *did* wake me, and I rub the sleep from my eyes and sit up. "Two things," I say through a yawn. "First, don't you think it's a bit suspicious to knock on the door of your lascivious love den instead of—and stay with me here—just walking in?"

"I'm a gentleman," he says with a half, dimple-inducing smile. "What if you'd been changing? Or doing naked yoga?"

"Um, hi, most boyfriends would *want* to walk in on either of those things."

"Um, hi." He mocks my tone almost perfectly. "Most boyfriends don't care about anything else. That's not who I am."

I am far too close to drooling, but I'll blame it on the sleep.

He shuffles to the closet, asking, "So what's the second thing?"

The second thing is that it's 6 A.M. and he's sneaking in from somewhere, and I never heard him come in last night, and there are no pillows or blankets or soft things of any kind on the floor. "Where were you?"

He shrugs. "I slept on the couch."

"You did *what*?" There's a beautiful irony in him sleeping on the couch *before* we have our first big fight—which is now—because normally people have to sleep on couches *after* big fights. I think that's irony, anyway, but to be honest Alanis Morissette has really gotten me confused about the term and I am too worked up at the moment to think too critically about it. "Why would you sleep on the couch?"

"Because it's more comfortable than the floor."

"What if someone had seen you?"

Armed with a fresh outfit, Nick swings by the dresser on his way to the bathroom. "I set an early alarm and came up here so I wouldn't run into anyone. And besides," he says from behind the closed door, "people in comfortable, healthy relationships are allowed to fall asleep on the couch while watching TV or reading or just because. That's why I took a book down last night—it's like a trusty alibi, just in case. Aren't I so sweet, for not wanting to disturb your sleep with my reading light?" He winks at me as he comes back into the bedroom, now fully dressed in a flannel shirt over a Christmas-themed graphic tee and faded jeans.

My breath hitches. There's something about the outfit that so perfectly embodies Nick Goodman: Easy. Comfortable. Stress-free. Cozy. I know I shouldn't be this affected by—checks notes—flannel and denim, but I'm going to do a little self-psychoanalysis and say that I'm more affected by his thoughtfulness and relieved by his foresight, and also still so tired that I'm being extra sensitive to a little thing like him pretending to want to not disturb me with a reading light.

"You okay?" He sets his folded pajamas inside the top dresser drawer and shuts it with his hip, leaning against it with his arms crossed.

"I'm fine."

His brow furrows and he scratches his chin where a five-o'clock shadow is thinking of forming. "Okay. Good. I'm going to walk up to the lodge and get some coffee. Did you want me to grab you anything?"

Coffee sounds incredible. "Yes, please. Can I get a latte? Something flavored?"

"Sure. Any preference?"

No particular flavor stands out in my mind, so I ask him to do what he's been doing since we arrived at Hope's Knoll: "Surprise me."

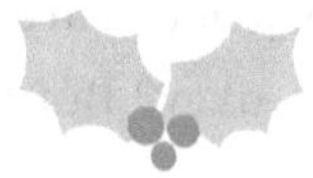

As beautiful and perfect as the resort is, I'm sure the downtown streets are straight from a Christmas movie. There's a bite to the late-morning air, but the sun shines down, warming my cheeks and nose. I'm on my second latte of the day, and I've already found one Christmas gift for Nick's family. Sort of.

In a startling betrayal to myself, the first and only gift I've found so far is an oven mitt set with a marshmallow bunny saying "What's up, my Gnomie?" on one and—you guessed it—a gnome asking "What's up, my Peep?" on the other. It's stupid, but practical, and Mark will find it hilarious.

I hate that I still know that about him.

"Any thoughts on the others?" Nick asks. He tightens his arm around my waist as we pass an elderly couple on the sidewalk, giving them extra room to pass. And if you're wondering why his arm is around my waist in the first place, don't get too excited: His parents are approximately ten steps behind us, and this is all for show.

I shake my head, because I still have no idea what the rest of his family might like, and even if I did, I am at the mercy of what I can find along this lovely but limited little street. "The only thought I had so far was a bottle of wine for Clara, but that doesn't feel super personal."

"It doesn't have to be personal," he answers quietly. "You don't even have to buy anyone anything."

Not that I actually bought Mark's gift, since Nick insisted on paying since it's all for his family and my spending money on presents was not part of our arrangement, but still.

"I want to. I really like them, and if we're going to stay friends—"

"Hey, buddy?" I'm interrupted by Nick's dad, who has paused by the blue door of Tubble, a body care and bath store. "Mom and I are going to head in here, okay? But you two can keep walking. We'll catch up."

"Sure!" Nick answers, performatively pecking my temple before we turn and continue down the sidewalk. A few seconds pass, and he looks back over his shoulder before dropping his arm to his side. "So. Where to next?"

Festive flags hang from streetlights, and swags and wreaths adorn storefronts. Half the window displays have inflatable Christmas decorations inside, which makes it hard to tell what each store is at a glance. Like the kitchen store So Fresh, where we bought Mark's oven mitt, could easily have been mistaken for a boutique with its window display of festively dressed mannequins holding an assortment of seasonal mugs and wine glasses.

"Is there a bookstore?"

"Yeah." Nick nods toward the far end of the line of shops. "Did you have an idea?"

"Maybe. But you're probably not gonna like it."

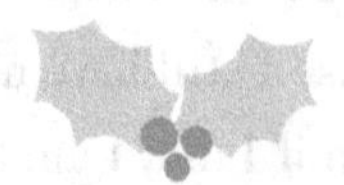

"How was shopping?" Clara and Mark are snuggled on the couch, her head in his lap and his hand stroking her hair, with a fire raging in the hearth. Her eyes are glassy, her speech a little slurred.

"Not too bad," I answer, dropping my bags quickly so I can strip out of my coat and cold-weather gear. I'm already sweating and I've been inside for eight seconds. "Picked up a few necessities."

She purses her lips at my collection of bags, but then apparently decides to ignore them and eases herself upright. "Hey, I wanted to ask you... Did you want to go to the spa for a manicure tomorrow? Or a blow-out Saturday? I was thinking we could have a bit of girl time before the ball."

"Before the what now?" I'm hoping the wine smorgasbord she sampled this afternoon has affected her speech more than I realized.

But Clara looks at Nick, and I look at Nick, and Clara sighs. "Oh, big brother, did you seriously not tell her?"

Nick is hanging our coats and scarves on the rack by the door, and he seems oblivious to the severity of his omission. "I told you there was a fancy dinner. And you brought that velvet dress," he says, and his eyes dip away from mine like he's appraising my body or imagining that dress on me again. "You'll be fine."

Clara lets out an exasperated groan and smacks her palm against her forehead as she flops backward against the cushions. "Nicky. You're such an idiot."

"What?" Nick shrugs and looks to Mark for help, but Mark just matches his gesture, like neither of them can understand how a 'fancy dinner' and a freaking *ball* are not remotely the same thing.

Clara's eyes narrow, and I would hate to be on the receiving end of that glare. But when her gaze turns to me, she brightens. "Shopping. Tomorrow. I know the perfect place."

I have plans already tomorrow—ice skating, hot cocoa, wrapping presents—but this seems more pressing. Because there's apparently a ball that I am ill-prepared for, and this isn't a fairytale where some magical woman floats in with a wand and *abracadabras* me into the dress to end all dresses. This is real. Well, some of it is. The *ball* part is.

"It's a date."

Clara shrieks and claps her hands. "Yay!"

As someone who never had the pleasure of having a sister, I feel like Nick has really struck gold with his. She's so energetic and bubbly and warm, like a bottle of champagne that's been sitting in a patch of sun, but more enticing.

It stings, knowing I'm lying to someone so sweet.

"Are Mom and Dad back?"

I only realize their absence when Nick brings it up, but their coats and shoes aren't by the door.

"They left town about an hour before us," he says, worry shaping his brow.

"Oh, right." Clara pushes herself off the couch and reaches out to Mark to pull him up with her. "They were hanging out in the lobby and told us to come and meet them for dinner as soon as you got back."

Nick and I exchange a look, and he rolls his eyes even as his dimple appears. And then he passes me my coat and scarf that he just hung up.

PLEASE SANTA
Nick

"HOW DO YOU KNOW so much about so much?" The words leave my mouth on a visible cloud, illuminated by the warm glow of vintage street lights and a sliver of moon that looks like it was meant to hang a hat on, or a coat, or a hope.

Holly laughs. "You knew, what? Two answers?"

"Four, thank you." We enjoyed post-dinner ornament making—and Christmas trivia after that—with my family, but we decided to walk back to the cabin while they rode the trolley because we've spent a lot of time with everyone else today and Holly deserves a bit of a break.

Holly coils her arms around mine, but I pull free and wrap my arm around her shoulders instead. My chest is still warm from the bourbon in the eggnog, and that warmth radiates out to my fingertips.

Yes, it's got to be the bourbon.

More into the fluffy ball on top of her beanie than to her actual face, I say, "I had no idea you had such a wealth of knowledge about Saint Lucia Day."

"You don't grow up reading American Girl books and *not* learn about Swedish traditions. Kirsten's series has *nothing* on Molly's, though. I mean, the girl's dad was kicking Nazis' asses and she got to hear his voice over the radio on Christmas?" She thumps a fist against her heart. "It gets me right here, every time."

"You seem very invested in the lives of fictional historical children."

"You have no idea. Can you imagine being told that because you have stick-straight hair you can't be the lead dancer? Even though you're the best?"

"I cannot."

"And then—" she hiccups, but it doesn't slow her down. "Then, the girl does the whole wet-pin-curl thing and gets the part, only to get sick right before the show and miss it altogether."

I can't help but to chuckle. "That's rough."

"It *is!*" Holly insists with an elbow to my ribcage, like she's defending a real person and not a child whose misfortunes were made up to serve a plot. "Bright side? That meant she was at home when her dad got back from the war, so I guess things turned out okay for her."

"Can I ask you something?"

A car passes, momentarily blinding us in the blue hue of its headlights. "Sure," she says, squinting.

"Do you ever stop?"

Question answered, I guess, because she cements her feet to the sidewalk and slides out of my reach. "What? Is it a problem that I'm a little energetic?"

"I didn't say that at all."

"Sure sounded like it," she grumbles.

"Let me rephrase."

Holly crosses her arms and glares at me.

"I just mean, do you ever get exhausted? Because you *do* have a lot of energy—which I love, don't get me wrong. But is it ever too much for you? Trying to act so happy and carefree all the time? Do you ever just have to take a break for *you*?"

Her eyes narrow, but the rest of her face softens. "It's not an act."

"Oh. No, I—"

She holds up a hand to cut me off, and I yield. "I've been told all my life that I'm 'a lot' or 'too much' or *blah blah blah*, and I always thought I needed to rein it in. But this really cool thing happened in the last few years where I stopped caring. Because life is short and I can't just live my life to make other people happy, because no one is living theirs to make *me* happy. That's *my* job. So it may be a lot of energy, and it may be too happy and carefree, but it's real, and it's me, and I'm not apologizing."

"I'd never ask or expect you to apologize."

"Good."

"I like who you are." I hold out my hand, palm up. An offering, a sign of peace.

"Good." She slides her palm into mine, lacing our fingers together. Acceptance.

I tug her closer to me and tuck a piece of hair back behind her ear, pulling her beanie down further. "I'm sorry that it came across as an insult. I promise..."

And then her free hand slides along my jaw, her thumb along my cheek, and her eyes lift to meet mine. "I know."

A moment passes, a smile is shared, and then she shivers in the cold and we resume our walk back to the cabin. It's in sight in the distance, a beacon calling us closer with its square patches of light along the first floor.

Neither of us says anything at first, but after two or three minutes Holly breaks the silence. "Can I ask *you* something?"

"Anything."

She glances down to the spot where our skin meets, then forward again at the sidewalk. "Why are we holding hands?"

It feels like an accusation—a gentle, unbothered one—but the instinct to drop her hand rushes through my mind. Stronger, though, is the instinct to hold on. The whole way back to the house, and even once we're inside. If I'm truthful with myself, which I normally am but am finding increasingly challenging in recent weeks, I answered her question a few moments ago, when I told her I like who she is.

But this is just a job to Holly. I'm just a client; this is just an act. "I figured we should be in character in case they saw us from the trolley."

"Mhmm." After a few more paces, she asks, "Nick?"

"Yeah?"

"Their trolley left the lobby when we did, and it looks like they're back in the cabin."

"Right. It's just—what if they left something behind? Or wanted to get another cocktail?"

She doesn't hesitate before saying "Good point" and shifting closer, pulling my arm around her shoulder again.

When we finally reach the cabin, I push the door open and we walk in, still connected, still in character.

Holly pushes up on her tip toes and kisses my cheek for the audience scattered around the living room. If they knew it was just for show, they'd be showering us with uproarious applause for the award-winning performance we're giving of Couple In Love.

But they have no idea, and my sister lets out an "*Aww*" from the couch, and Mom smiles from her recliner as Dad snores softly from his.

"I'm going to get P.J.'s on, but then do you want to watch a movie?" Holly asks, her palm pressed against my chest, her fingers absently brushing it.

"That sounds good to me," I answer before conducting a visual survey of the room to see if anyone plans to join us.

Clara turns to Mark. "You want to watch something?"

He shrugs, which feels like a pretty universal gesture for 'I'd rather go up to bed with you than watch a movie with my ex and your brother, but I can't say that because your parents are here.'

God, that man has a punchable personality.

"We might watch for a little," Clara says, likely interpreting Mark's preference and blending it with her own. Good for her, for not fully losing herself.

"I think your dad's done for the day." Mom's voice seems to startle Dad awake, and he seems perplexed; when he closed his eyes there were three other people in the room, but now when he opens them there are suddenly five. Though he'd rather confess a belief in sorcery than admit to dozing off.

"Come on, dear," Mom urges with a pat on his knee. "Let's head up. I want to finish that new Gwen Dolan-Pierce novel."

Holly falls into step next to her. "Aren't her books the best? And her own life—geez. It's like her love story with her husband was ripped straight from a romance novel itself."

"Jammies actually sound so comfy right now." Clara yawns and stretches, then kisses the top of Mark's head. "Be back in a jiffy," she says, then bounds after Mom and Holly like she didn't just complete the 'let's go to bed' trifecta.

Mark must be fluent in the language because he jumps up and follows closely behind with a hurried "Night, buddy" and a slap on my back.

On an unrelated note, I'll be wearing my noise-canceling head-phones to bed.

Dad, who has had the good fortune to have once again dozed off and therefore missed the implication that my mortal enemy is mere moments from defiling his only daughter, opens his eyes and does a double take at the now empty room.

"They're all upstairs," I inform him before flopping onto the couch's corner cushion.

He nods, but he doesn't move from his seat. "It's nice, you know." The only way to explain the lack of context is to attribute his words to the continuation of a conversation in a dream he just woke from. I look at him, waiting, and he answers my stare like I'm the densest idiot on the planet. "You and Holly," he says matter-of-factly. "It's nice to see you so happy. I wasn't sure you'd ever actually find it."

"Find what?"

My parents are sentimental. They met in their freshman year in college. My dad proposed to my mom at graduation. They've kept photo albums about and for Clara and me, even in the digital age. They've saved report cards and newspaper clippings and old dance costumes and sports jerseys and roughly eight million Christmas ornaments. *That's* how sentimental they are. Which is why it's so jarring to hear my dad choke up even as he smiles when he answers me:

"Love, of course."

IN LOVE (?!) ON CHRISTMAS
Nick

I DON'T LOVE HER. I can't love her. We are not actually in love.

Three sentences. For the duration of *Love Hard,* those three sentences run through my head.

"Was that a little... too close to home?" Holly asks.

Her voice startles me as the credits roll.

"You okay over there?" She nudges my foot with hers.

"Yeah. Fine."

She tugs on the blanket that doesn't quite cover us both, pulling it nearly to her shoulders as she sits up on her end of the couch. "I feel like we were supposed to learn a lesson from the movie."

"You do?" It would help if I had paid attention to anything other than *I don't love her. I can't love her. We are not actually in love.*

"Mhmm. Like, fake dating is bad, fake dating around the holidays never works, and we should be totally honest with everyone?"

I choke on my own spit and sputter a cough.

"Geez, Just Nick, you're really rattled tonight. What's going on with you?"

"Nothing."

"Sure," she says, yawning.

"You should go up to bed."

She nods slowly, like she's mulling it over, but then pauses. "Or should I stay down here with you?"

Does she know? Does she have a hunch about how I've spent the past hour and forty-five minutes, and now she's offering to stay close, as if to prove my mantra wrong? "Why would you do that?"

"Isn't it weird," she starts with a shrug, "for us to be sleeping apart all the time? If we sleep at our respective ends of the couch, then it just looks like we both fell asleep during the movie."

It's not a terrible idea, in theory. But in practice, well. I just don't think we should be spending the night together upstairs, down here, or anywhere else.

"Do you know what I think is weirder?"

She shakes her head. "No."

"That you wear some other dude's sweatshirt to bed."

"He's not some other dude. He's my brother."

"I don't think that argument helps your case the way you think it does."

Holly has a variety of laughs. I heard my favorite a few hours ago on the walk back from the lobby, that boisterous, full-joy laugh. There's a polite laugh, a less polite laugh, and this little thing she's doing now, which is like a Shirley Temple giggle with her hands covering her mouth to quiet herself.

This. This is my second-favorite.

I relax at the sound of it, easing into the comfort of her presence and her ability to make everything—somehow—fine.

"Are you sure you're okay?" she asks.

"Except for the sweatshirt thing."

She rolls her eyes at me. "Want me to ask Mark for his?"

"No." There's force behind it, like if it were in an email it would be bold, or capitalized, or at the very least italicized. "You should wear mine." Without thinking, I lean forward and peel off my sweatshirt, offering it to her with an extended arm.

She rises and grips the bottom hem of her own sweatshirt, wriggling it up over her waist, her shoulders. It's a slow, not-quite-sensual striptease.

Except for the slice of stomach exposed just between the waistband of her shorts and the bottom of her tank top. That part is, unfortunately, entirely and tantalizingly sensual.

And when she slips my sweatshirt over her head, gathering her hair in a fist to pull it through the neckline, I imagine what it would be like to have her in my sweatshirt, or a T-shirt in the summer, curling up on the couch or crawling into bed with me.

"*Now* are you good?"

"Yeah," I choke out before clearing my throat. "I'm good."

"Cool." The sweatshirt's slightly large on me, but more oversized on Holly, and her fingertips barely escape the sleeves. Still, she curls them around the blanket and pulls it over me, tucking it over and behind my shoulder. Her fingers trace the stubble on my jaw, and I swallow a moan that threatens to betray me.

"Good night, Nick," she says. Then she leans down, kisses my forehead, and has the nerve to walk away.

Santa, Can't You Hear Me

Holly

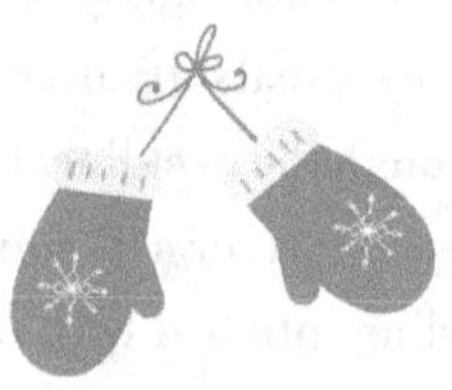

IF MY SMART WATCH hadn't died three months ago, I'd be able to confirm just how far I have paced across the bedroom since the long, slow climb up the stairs. Instead, I can only wager a guess—with great certainty that is almost certainly misplaced due to my terrible judgment with time and distance—that I have traversed two miles across the hardwood.

And then there's the gnawing at my cuticles and nails, and yes, I think I will get that manicure with Clara.

I cross my arms over the faded Wilde Lake crest on my chest to keep myself from consuming an entire knuckle.

Damn, this sweatshirt is cozy. And it smells nice, like pine and vanilla and the crisp air of forthcoming snow.

And Nick. It smells just like Nick.

His last name is embroidered in a gentle arc across my back, and with his alma mater emblazoned on the front and the scent of him wound in every thread and fiber, I feel like he's here, holding me.

Which is ridiculous, really, because he could actually be holding me right now, or at least on the same couch, or at the *very* least in the same room, and he's decided to sleep alone on a lumpy sofa.

All the pacing, all the stressing, the whole fingernail buffet—it was all for nothing. Because while I've been up here freaking out about the way Nick held my hand when he didn't need to, the way he said he likes who I am, the way he seemed so rigid and uncomfortably nervous while we watched that movie—he's been downstairs, alone, with every chance to be neither of those things.

And that tells me everything I need to know.

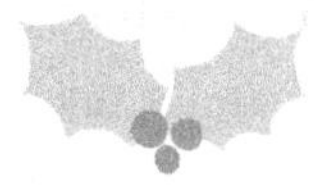

In a turn of events that shocks absolutely no one, I've slept like shit.

So at 6:23 A.M, still wearing tiny flannel shorts and my fake boyfriend's really comfy sweatshirt, I sneak downstairs for a glass of water and, I don't know, yoga or something. (I've never done yoga, but I'm sure the internet will tell me everything I need to know.)

I open the refrigerator as quietly as possible, and a voice emerges from the living room. "You don't have to worry about being quiet. I've been up for a while."

Hints of sunlight peek through curtains, and I can just make out Nick's shape on the couch, right where I left him.

"Do you want anything while I'm out here?"

"No, I'm okay."

I nod. "Great. Then I'll get out of your hair."

"Holly."

The yearning, the pleading in the tone. They stop me in my tracks.

"Stay," he says.

"Sure," I agree.

Nick curls up his legs to free half the couch for me. I set my glass on a coaster on the end table and lower myself onto the far cushion, and we sit in silence for a few moments.

"Did you sleep well?" he finally asks, and it's so laughable I almost snort.

"I think the fact that I'm awake before dawn is all the answer you need."

"Oh," he says thoughtfully. "Same."

I wonder if he lay there last night ruminating over every interaction, every word, every touch, just like I did, analyzing it all in his head just to come to the same conclusion I did. "You could probably get another hour in before anyone else wakes up." As I learned yesterday, Nick's family takes both R&R very seriously when on vacation.

He nods slowly, his gaze set on his knees. "I could," he says, before his eyes meet mine. "Or, we both could."

I feel as though I've just been propositioned by a rapscallion Bridgerton brother. "What?"

"I was using my non-sleeping time to think, and I realized you were right."

I cock my head and deadpan, "About what? There are just so many possibilities."

"*Hmph.*" Nick snorts like he doesn't really want to tell me that I was right, but he knows that he has to. "In all my non-sleeping thinking time, I decided I think your idea of us falling asleep on the couch together is great. It really helps to solidify the storyline."

Solidify the storyline. Because we're actors, and this is our show, and everything is for the plot.

"What if we just curl up here for another hour or two?" he asks.

"So, what if we do exactly what I suggested last night?"

He shrugs. "I told you, I had a lot of time to think, and I realized that your idea was superior to mine. Bright side, we still get to look like we fell asleep on the couch together, but with the added benefit of you sleeping on a real bed for most of the night."

"*Trying* to sleep on a real bed," I correct him. But it doesn't take much convincing to slip my legs under the blanket and pull myself into a relaxed fetal position.

I'm warmed by the proximity of him, and it takes almost no time at all to drift off to sleep, where I dream until Clara's shrill "Oh my *gawd* aren't they *so cute*?!?" wakes me.

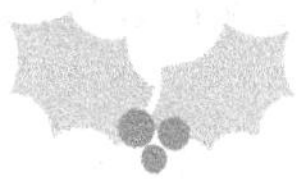

"So how adorable were you and Nicky all snuggled up on the couch this morning?" Clara asks from the fitting room next to mine.

I shrug as I slip the strap of a midnight blue gown over my shoulder. "Were we?"

"Only the *cutest*. Literally. So cute."

I look at myself in the mirror and wish I would've spent more time on my hair this morning instead of throwing it up into a messy bun. This look doesn't really help any of the gowns look formal and special.

"Are you ready?" A door creaks open.

I open my own door, and there's Clara in a body-con midi dress with ruching and a scandalous slit up her thigh. We say "Wow" simultaneously, and she purses her lips.

"I like it," she says, absently swiping her hands over the folds of fabric in her own dress. "What do you think?"

"I think it reminds me of what I wore to my tenth-grade homecoming dance."

"Ew." She scrunches her face like she's imagining '80s hair and poofy taffeta sleeves, and not the understated navy dress with a black mesh overlay that I actually wore.

Maybe I'd like this dress more if it didn't make me feel like a dorky sophomore standing next to the hottest senior at school, dressed in a modest A-line gown when she's wearing something with far greater sex appeal. "Were you thinking of wearing that for the ball? Or..."

"Oh. No. I was actually thinking of booking a room with Mark on Sunday, just the two of us. There's this cute hotel on the way home with heart-shaped Jacuzzis, and—" She trails off, and pink tints her cheeks.

"Oh." *Oh.* "I mean, this should make him think less-boring thoughts, that's for sure."

Her answering laugh is like a miniature wind chime on a breezy day: light and tinny and bright.

"It looks great on you, Clara. You should totally get it."

She gives herself a once-over in the collection of mirrors just across from our fitting rooms and nods to herself before turning back to me. "Now, you, on the other hand..."

"I know. It's not quite right."

"And you didn't like the gold one?"

Ah, the gold lamé dress that made me feel like I was auditioning for a Muse in a '70s disco version of Hercules. "No, I did not like the gold one."

"Hmm, okay, one sec. Go take that off, and I'll pass one to you over the door." Clara bounds off like she's Stacy London hosting a discount-designer store version of Supermarket Sweep. And just as I zip the blue dress onto its hanger, a sea of crimson cascades over the fitting room door. "Try this," Clara commands with the air of someone who knows with great certainty that what they're recommending is undoubtedly perfect.

There are dresses that spark cultural movements, that are iconic and breathtaking and special. My mom's generation had Princess Di's wedding gown. We had a swan gown and a meat dress on the red carpet (I didn't say they were all breathtaking in a *good* way). We had the green dress in *Atonement*, SJP's Vivienne Westwood masterpiece in the *Sex and the City* movie, and, my personal favorite, the yellow gown in *How to Lose a Guy in 10 Days*.

It's as if Santa's elves knew exactly what I've always wanted, switched jobs from assembly line workers to fashion designers, and handcrafted a red version of that dress—with the slight modification of a higher neckline and a giant, Christmas-appropriate bow on the lower back replacing the criss-crossed straps—then delivered it here, just for me.

There's no way I can pull it off.

"Do you have it on yet?" Clara has changed back into her street clothes and is standing outside my door, waiting, while I examine the dress on its hanger.

"Almost," I lie.

"Hurry! We need to get back in time for ice skating!"

I *have* been looking forward to ice skating—despite the fact that I am terrible at it—and I know Clara won't leave until I show off the red dress. I slip it off its hanger and over my body, then attach the bow's hook-and-eye closure at the small of my back. I open the door before I even look in the mirror, but I can tell by Clara's reaction exactly how it looks.

"Question." Her eyes scan over me and she taps a finger against her lips.

"Sure."

"In nine months, do I get to be a godmother? Will you eventually tell your soon-to-be child that I, beloved Auntie Clara, have orchestrated their conception by way of selecting the most *va-va-voom* dress for their mother?"

I roll my eyes even as heat rushes up my neck to the tips of my ears.

"Okay, fine. New question."

"I'm scared to hear it."

She nods, like *'that's fair,'* and asks, "Should I purchase earplugs for Saturday night?" Then she laughs and flips her hair over her shoulder. "Okay, you should change so we can check out and get back to the cabin."

"You really think I should get this one?"

Her eyes widen. "I would never forgive you if you didn't."

She shoos me back into my fitting room, and the last glimpse I get before closing the door is her browsing the accessories just beside the register.

Alone in the tiny room, I exhale, then turn and finally confront myself in the mirror, and—*wow*. Even with my messy bun, my washed-but-not-made-up face, the dress is stunning. It's simple in the front, understated and classic, but it sure makes an impression in the back.

I don't know if the whole I-sleep-in-a-hand-me-up-sweatshirt-from-my-brother thing is proof enough of this, but I don't generally consider myself a vain person. Not, that is, until I'm in this dress, apparently.

Clara comes back mid-ogle, asking if I'm ready, and of course I'm not because how can I be expected to take off something so perfect so soon?

But I must, and I change quickly and follow her to the register.

"Your total is—" starts the cashier, and my heart sinks.

I may have mentioned this before, but I'm kind of on a budget.

And this dress...

Well, somehow it's affordable. Like, I-don't-have-to-drive-drunk-middle-aged-men-around-for-a-week-to-pay-for-it affordable. It truly must be a Christmas miracle.

Clara and I have our garment bags in hand and are about to leave when she asks the sales associate by the door, "Excuse me, but do you know if there's a hardware store nearby? I need to buy a few pairs of earplugs."

Very Merry
Holly

LET'S PLAY A BRIEF word association game. If I say *snowy-day lunch*, what do you think of?

If grilled cheese and tomato soup came to mind, congratulations! We should be best friends. If it didn't, that's cool, too. If you're sitting there thinking, who the heck pairs grilled cheese and tomato soup? Well then, I don't need your energy in my life.

Mark, actually, was the third kind of person, and that should have been all the red flag I needed to abandon ship.

But the Goodman family? They saw flurries this morning and had the electric griddle heating up when Clara and I walked in the house. They're so into it that I will even forgive them for using mayonnaise instead of butter for the bread. (Nick and I, however, sneak the tub of butter from the fridge and prep our own sandwiches the right way.)

Anyway, all that to say, Nick Goodman and I are compatible when it comes to snowy-day lunches.

After our pre-noon lunch, we bundle up in coats and mittens and more and make our way to the resort's ice rink. It gives major Rockefeller vibes, but with more trees and fewer skyscrapers. There's a set of bleachers for viewing, a food truck selling hot cocoa and chicken noodle soup, and a hut for skate rentals. That's where I drag Nick, though he doesn't protest.

"Do you skate a lot?" I ask as we haul our skates over our shoulders to the prep area where his parents are waiting to take our shoes. (As Nick's dad reminded me earlier, he's "one good fall away from a new hip," so they will not be joining us on the ice.)

"Not much these days," he answers. "You?"

"Hardly ever."

He chuckles, and I watch tiny clouds from his mouth evaporate in the air. "So this should be fun, is what you're saying?"

We plop ourselves onto the bench to change into our skates, and I jab his arm with my elbow, even though he's not wrong. "If I go down, I'm taking you down with me."

He pulls my beanie down over my eyes and pats the top of my head. "Don't worry. I won't let you fall."

My mouth goes dry. I readjust my beanie and think about all the ways I could fall, and the one way I might already have fallen.

No. There's no way. Nick and I are friends, and anything beyond that is a part we're playing quite convincingly, and that's it.

Once Nick has his skates on he kneels in front of me, untying and tightening my laces before double knotting bows at the tops.

"You good?" he asks, rising and pulling me up with him.

I wobble like a newborn deer. "Great," I lie, and he laughs.

"Just hold on to me, okay?" Nick supports my elbow with a steadying hand and guides me onto the ice. Slowly, we make our way around the perimeter; I use a combination of Nick's arm and the outer boards to stay upright.

Clara's in the distance skating backward, twirling, occasionally begging Mark to get off the sidelines and get on the ice with her, but that's a losing battle.

Mark doesn't skate, because he could fall, and falling is a sign of weakness. Mark doesn't show weaknesses, which is sort of a Catch-22, because not showing weakness is definitely the opposite of being a strength.

After fifteen minutes or so on the ice, I start to feel less like a newborn deer and more like a drunk grandma. There's a lot of giddy laughter, a healthy dose of slow stumbling (but miraculously remaining upright!) around the rink, and a weightlessness in my chest I haven't felt in—well, I don't actually know the last time I felt like this.

And Nick is right there by my side through it all, laughing along with me, throwing his head back as flurries swirl around us.

"Are you having fun?" he asks after a few more laps. I've forced myself away from the wall and am now relying wholly on my nonexistent sense of balance and his arm to stay on my feet.

My fingertips are frozen and I can't even feel the tip of my nose anymore. I answer emphatically. "Yes."

"Good. Me too."

"So, what could you do out here if you weren't stuck making sure I don't fall?"

We round a turn at the far end of the rink, curving onto the last straightaway, approaching the exit.

"Could you do what Clara does?" I jerk my head toward her, which threatens to topple me like a sabotaged Jenga tower.

He nods slowly. "Yeah, maybe fewer turns, but I could at least do some backwards skating."

"I want to see." I turn my feet toward the boards and reach for the ledge. "Let me off here and go actually enjoy it."

"I *am* enjoying it." There's a snowflake stuck to his eyelashes, but it melts and turns into a wet dot on the lens of his glasses.

"Still. You deserve a lap without me holding you back." I slip my hand from his and crash pelvis first into the wall. Once I make my way onto the rubber mat just off the ice, I turn and shoo him away. "Go! Be free!"

Nick snorts and shakes his head, and then he skates backward just long enough to shout that he'll be back in a few laps. And then he seamlessly switches to facing forward again, crossing his feet one in front of the other as he casually and effortlessly glides across the ice. He picks up the pace along the far side of the rink, and even from here I can see his beaming smile—and the matching one Clara sports—when the two of them decide to race. First forward along this wall, then backward along the opposite.

Luckily the rink is mostly empty; the line for hot cocoa seems to have attracted most of the families that had been on the ice minutes ago.

"I don't remember the last time I saw those two like this," Mr. Goodman says when Clara and Nick end up doing some sort of skills challenge, complete with jumps and lunges and turns.

Mrs. Goodman kisses her husband on the cheek and drapes his arm over her shoulders. "It's nice, isn't it? Just like when they were little."

"Did they skate a lot as kids?" I ask.

Mr. Goodman answers, "We signed them up for learn-to-skate classes when they were three and five."

"And then again when they were eight and ten," adds Christina.

"Didn't stick the first time, apparently," Jonathan says with a chuckle.

I turn my attention back to the ice, where Nick and Clara are simultaneously spinning in side-by-side spirals. "Well, it sure looks like they're paying off now. They seem to be having a lot of fun out there."

"Funny thing is," Christina says, her voice gentle but matter-of-fact, "I think Nicky was having more fun when you were out there with him."

My cheeks heat, tingling as the internal and external temperatures meet, like two fronts colliding.

I take a deep breath, huff it out on a cloud, and make my way back onto the ice. Alone. Brave enough to build momentum as I pull myself along the boards around the rink's edge.

No, not brave enough, really. Just motivated enough to forget or ignore that I'm afraid of how much it hurts to fall.

I round one turn, two, and then it's a long, straight line until I reach the spot where Nick and Clara are, apparently, challenging each other to various tricks. I push myself off the boards to skate toward them and shout Nick's name.

"Watch out!" comes the cry from the person barreling toward me.

But there's no 'watching out' when someone's skating directly toward you at a high rate of speed, and you're wholly incapable of changing course even if you wanted to.

Fortunately, they veer right at the last second to avoid colliding with me (though there are some choice words after the fact). *Un-fortunately,* panic has latched onto me, and because I was terrible on skates to begin with, I'm now stumbling, arms flailing, trying to stay upright. Reaching Nick is a goal I've completely abandoned; the whole goal right now is *don't fall and die.*

And then there's warmth. A steadying arm around my back, an affirming "I got you" in my ear.

It feels safe, and I decide to trust it. I lean into the arm, the body pressed against mine. My skates steady.

"Told you I wouldn't let you fall," Nick says, his breath warm on my neck. It's a whispered promise. A vow.

My knees buckle like a Tonya Harding husband has come after them.

I've got one arm wrapped around him, but my free hand is pressed against his chest. I pull back and he raises his head, and I search his eyes for any indication that he knows how I'm starting to feel—*really* feel—about him.

"Nick, I—"

"Oh my *gosh*, you two are so freaking cute!" Clara skates over and collides into us with a giant hug. "Are you okay, Holly?"

I don't take my eyes off Nick's. "Yeah. I'm fine."

"Good. I thought you were going down."

"Same," I say.

"Good thing Nicky was here!"

"Yeah. Good thing," Nick echos. His breathing is heavy, like every inhale is a gasp and every exhale carries the weight of a confession.

Clara sighs, oblivious to the silent soul-searching happening before her. "We should probably get back to the cabin. Anyone want some hot cocoa for the road?"

"Sure," I answer.

Nick adds an "Okay."

Clara looks from me to her brother and back. "Cool. You guys are acting weird." Then she skates off with the carefree ease of someone who isn't maybe kind of falling for their fake-boyfriend-slash-client.

"Thank you for saving me." My eyes are still focused on his, with only an occasional and fleeting glance at his lips. I'm transfixed by his focus on me, the unwavering eye contact, the strength of his arm still around my back.

"Of course. I won't let you get hurt, Holly."

My heart flutters like it wants to take flight up through my throat and explode in a million fireworks once it hits the air. "Not with witnesses, anyway."

I gesture toward his right, and for the first time since he caught me, Nick shifts his gaze. I follow suit and confirm: His parents are definitely looking our way, with Clara conspiratorially leaning over her mom's shoulder.

"*Are* we acting weird?" I ask, her words a lingering indictment.

"I don't think so."

We are. One-hundred percent, yes, we're acting weird. Because if we were a real couple and he had saved my life in the most romantic, Tobey Maguire-Spider-Man-cafeteria-scene-on-ice way, I would have kissed him.

So I push myself up to kiss his cheek, just as he turns his attention back to me.

Our lips meet, and every part of me longs to push myself into him, to wrap my arms around his neck and deepen the kiss. If we were a real couple, that's what I would do. I would melt into him like ice in a hot coffee. But Nick's words ricochet in my head:

I won't let you fall.

I won't let you get hurt, Holly.

I can't count on that. It's not his job to keep me from falling, not his responsibility to make sure I don't get hurt. It's *mine*. He's my client, and this is a job, and I need to protect myself.

And that's exactly why I push myself away and force myself toward the exit of the rink.

THAT'S CHRISTMAS TO ME
Nick

AFTER THE MOST ROOM-TEMPERATURE shower I've ever taken (necessitated by the combination of my exterior coldness and my interior—um—feelings), I pull on the green and navy checkered fleece pants and the matching navy long-sleeve T-shirt that Mom gifted me at the beginning of our trip.

Matching pajamas have always been a family tradition—first, in photographs for Christmas cards; then, when Santa's elves made a special delivery early on Christmas Eve and we'd all unwrap matching flannel or fleece, which we'd wear to watch Rudolph and a whole host of animated classics before dozing off on the couch and waking up to twice as many presents under the tree as had been there only hours earlier.

When we were teens and spent most of Christmas day traveling to an aunt's house, followed by my grandparents', leaving our own home by 10 A.M. to be everywhere with everyone else, we would be granted permission to wear our matching PJ's out of the house so we could at least be comfortable. (This was an unpopular choice with one aunt in particular, who insisted on her own children wearing dresses or ties to Christmas dinner, and the animosity with our cousins hasn't really faded since then.)

And now, Mom divvies them out upon arrival at the cabin, and we wear them on Friday night, when we cook a traditional Christmas dinner (with a little help from room service and the pastry team) and open presents before the resort hosts its late-night pajama party in the lobby.

"Look at you, Nicky!" Mom's voice rings through the kitchen. She lowers a foil-covered tray onto the counter and hip checks the refrigerator door shut. She's also wearing navy, but in a silky material with a button-down shirt. If I had to guess, I'd say dad has a matching style but in a deep shade of green.

"Potato duty again this year?" Every year, I peel potatoes to be boiled and mashed and served in volcano form with gravy lava. (Lest you think I am the child at heart who creates said volcano, I shall share that my father is, in fact, the one who insists on such a display.)

But Mom shakes her head. "Nope. Everything is taken care of. I just need to throw this in the oven for forty minutes, and then we're good to go."

A quick glance around the room reveals that the table is set, the fire is already crackling, and everything appears to be ready. "So, what can I do?"

She shrugs. "You want to talk about Holly?"

Holly. Yes, I want to talk about her. No, I don't want to talk about her with my mom. Mostly because the thing I want to talk about most is how I find myself faking the faking, and wondering if that means I'm just really bad at faking in the first place or if I'm so good at faking it that I've fooled myself.

Obviously, that's not an answer I can go with, so I answer with, "Sure! What do you want to know?"

Sometimes, lava-spewing potato volcanos aside, I think Dad is the most sentimental of the four of us, and Mom is the most mischievous. Supporting evidence for this particular assertion can be found in the way her eyes sparkle now and the goofy grin that grows on her face. "Tell me what was happening on the ice today."

Clara and Holly come back from the Santa's Workshop room in the lobby with a tote bag filled with freshly wrapped gifts. It's genius, really, for the resort to dedicate space to a wrapping station next to their lobby gift shop and charge a premium on wrapping basics like tissue, boxes, paper, and bows, but it really comes in clutch and is well worth the money when you have a pile of presents to wrap and not many other options to choose from.

She drops the tote by the tree and helps pour drinks for everyone for dinner, and then we eat. I make a volcano out of mashed potatoes and let gravy lava attack my ham, mostly because Holly does it first and Dad lights up like a kid on—well, Christmas morning.

After dinner, we bound toward the living room, where presents are piled under the tree and the fireplace snaps and sparks and mugs of cocoa sit atop cork coasters on end tables.

And yes, Dad is in hunter green silk pajamas, and Clara is in the kind of nightgown you might expect to find in the early nineteen hundreds: plaid and high-necked with ribbons creating ruffles around the sleeves, and Mark might be rebelling against the tradition because he's wearing black pants and a navy quarter-zip sweater.

And then there's Holly in plaid pants that match mine and a deep green sweatshirt that she cut the neckband off of. The wider neckline keeps nudging itself toward the cliff of her shoulder under the cascade of wild, wavy hair that escapes from beneath a green elf hat that's complete with comically large, pointed ears attached to the sides.

It's not December 25, but this is Christmas.

"Who's up first?" Clara asks.

Before you go thinking my parents have this weird obsession with keeping her chaste via grandma-esque pajamas, please know that A: she likes her nightgown because it "feels like it's from *The Nutcracker*," whence her name comes, and B: she needs something with coverage because her typical position for gift-giving is to sprawl herself out on the floor with her feet kicked up behind her, watching everyone open their gifts with her elbows on the floor and her chin propped on her fists.

That's where she finds herself now, with Mark behind her on one end of the couch, stealing glances at his cell phone.

Mom always volunteers to distribute their presents first, so she and Dad play Santa and pass out presents to each of us. I get the personalized padfolio I've wanted for work, along with a ticket to a concert Dad and I have been talking about going to.

Clara gets new shoes and a special edition of *Pride and Prejudice* with an embroidered cover and painted edges.

Mark gets an assortment of gift cards. (My parents try to be personal and intentional with their gift giving, but, this is Mark we're talking about, and there's only so much to work with.)

And Holly, though she's only been around a few weeks, and though she's not even my real girlfriend, gets a gift as well: a buffalo plaid poncho with *Holly* monogrammed down one of the sleeves and a green-and-red trio of leaves and berries next to it.

"For next year's tree hunt," Dad says, smiling.

"I love it," Holly replies. She examines the custom stitching, holds it out so Clara can feel the fabric (which she deems *'crazy soft'*), and says "Thank you" to my parents so earnestly that it's like she actually plans to wear it to Evermore Evergreens next December.

Mark and Clara pass around their joint gifts, which are so Clara-specific it's clear Mark did nothing to contribute, though he does promise Clara that he has a gift waiting for her upstairs, and I'm sure he'll be making promises about his 'package' later tonight. Ew.

I pass mine around, as well, which are not super thrilling since I tend to add items to my cart when I hear things like 'Why do we never seem to have enough double-A batteries around this house?' and 'It would be so nice to just have a collection of greeting cards and stamps so I don't have to worry about missing someone's birthday again.'

Holly is last, and I forget—until Clara bursts out laughing—that Holly has bought her a copy of *Kama Sutra for Manga Lovers*, which incorporates illustrations of the source material. Shockingly, Mom and Dad find it intriguing, and—less shockingly—Mark's interest is piqued as well.

She gives Mom a mug that she painted at a pottery store yesterday and picked up on her excursion with Clara today. It says *Undisputed Cocoa Champion* in careful black lettering on a burgundy background that's speckled with white. Below the words, Holly inexplicably drew a championship belt (Mom has never been a fan of wrestling) that features a steaming mug of cocoa, flanked by two chocolate chip cookies.

Mom, like Clara a few moments earlier, laughs at her gift. It's not done cruelly; she legitimately loves it. "Thank you," she says, wiping the tears from her eyes.

For Dad, there's a Decorate-Your-Own-Ornament kit, complete with paints and brushes and half a dozen wooden Christmas-themed shapes. "I thought it would be fun if maybe we all painted one while we were here, or something. But it's lame, I—"

"No." Dad interrupts her, examining the red box in his hands. "It's perfect. Thank you."

Holly's cheeks flush, and she nods a silent *'you're welcome'* in reply.

Mark opens his gift and chuckles before launching into a whole story about how he and his former roommates (read: frat bros) grilled a garden gnome on a (very drunk) dare, and I try not to feel the pang of jealousy that stabs my kidney when I think about Holly remembering what could elicit such a response from her typically taciturn ex.

"Cocoa time?" I ask, standing. I'm sure Mom wants to put her new mug to use.

No one else rises.

"Don't you want yours?" Holly's voice is timid; her cheeriness seems like someone's taken a chisel to it and chipped off a piece. And there, when I turn around, is one final gift in Holly's hand.

"Oh. I thought—"

Holly just shakes her head. I hadn't brought anything for her, using the excuse that we were going to exchange gifts later. It's not that I didn't want to get her something. I promise, this was not some *I'm-too-cheap-to-buy-my-fake-girlfriend-a-gift* thing. It was more like a *What-do-I-get-someone-like-Holly?* thing. A *What-do-I-get-this-person-who-makes-me-smile-more-in-a-week-than-I-smiled-all-of-last-year* thing; a *Holy-shit-I'm-falling-for-her* thing.

"This one's a little time sensitive." She pushes the gift toward me again, and the gold curly ribbon flops against the navy blue paper with rows of green Christmas trees stretching from end to end.

I sit down next to her again and hold the feather-light box before unwrapping it.

"Holly—"

She hugs a throw pillow to her chest and bites her bottom lip. "I thought it would be a fun adventure. And hopefully no snake bites this time of year."

Inside the box is a handwritten certificate saying that she's reserved two spots on the Hope's Knoll hawk walk tomorrow with a falconer, where we'll walk through the woods and call trained birds of prey to us along the journey.

How ridiculous I was to be jealous of Mark's gift when this—this is personal and thoughtful and perfect.

"I love—" Emotion forms in my throat, and I cough. "I love it."

Holly nods and smiles, and I would happily kiss every square millimeter of her lips, even with that hat on her head. Especially with that hat on her head.

And I might, too, if Clara didn't jump up and say, "How about that cocoa?"

GLOW
Nick

PAJAMARAMA IS A HIGHLIGHT of our trip every year. The activity is meant to be a welcome event for guests arriving Friday night for the weekend, but for us it's a traditional mid-stay celebration where we get to wear the matching PJ's Mom works so hard to find for all of us and get compliments from families who wish their teen or adult children would partake in such festive gaiety. We also rock our special socks from Clara; mine and Holly's are both black with little holly leaves and berries printed all over.

One of the best parts of Pajamarama is what is affectionately known as the Bedtime Buffet: a selection of cookies and treats available to all attendees. The bar is a favorite stop as well, where guests can enhance their hot cocoa with something more effective at helping them prepare for sugar-psycho kids.

We can never have too much cocoa. This isn't quite as good as Mom's, but it gets an assist from the peppermint schnapps.

The whole family has a great time dancing and dining, but then the yawns begin and increase with exponential frequency, and my parents, Clara, and Mark take the trolley back to the cabin. Which leaves Holly and me in the lobby with the dwindling crowd.

We find an empty corner with a fireplace, a towering Christmas tree next to it, and a tufted-leather sofa in a rich tobacco color. With snow falling outside the windows, piling up on the sills and fogging the glass, the whole scene seems like it belongs in a YouTube yule log video.

Holly lowers herself into one corner of the couch and tucks her feet up under herself. "What a day, huh?" she asks, wrapping her hands around her mug. "Shopping, skating, dinner, gifts, and now—"

"We're wearing pajamas in public like it's two thousand five?"

She laughs a gentle "*Hmm*" and examines her mug, the tree, the fire, the smooth buttons of the sofa. There's a peace to it, but a melancholia, too.

"I'm sorry," I blurt out from my position on the ottoman in front of her.

Her head snaps up and her brows furrow. "For what?"

"I feel like an idiot for not giving you a present earlier."

I once dated a girl who dumped me because I didn't take her to dinner on her birthday. My reason? I was in the hospital for an emergency appendectomy. So when I tell you I'm not used to a certain level of grace, there's the backstory.

Which is why I'm shocked when Holly's lips spread into a grin. "You don't have to apologize. I wasn't expecting anything."

"But you did so much for everyone, I thought—"

"I did hardly anything for anyone, Nick."

I feel like my jaw must be perilously close to needing scooped off the floor. "Well, that's just not true, is it?"

She's silent, which is—and I mean this in the nicest way possible—saying something.

The fact that I have to explain this to her is a bit mind boggling, because it's so clear, so apparent to me. "Did you not see every single person's face as they opened their gift from you?"

Holly rolls her eyes. "They were just being nice."

"No." I stretch my hand out with the word, letting my fingertips settle on her wrist. She glances down at the points where we meet and I draw my hand back like I've touched a live wire. "You somehow managed to find the exact right gift for everyone in my family. Including your ex, which..."

I've said more than I meant to, and Holly's eyes meet mine. "Does it bother you?"

And this is why I didn't mean to bring him up. If I say *yes,* she might think I'm breaking some unspoken client rule by prying too much into her actual life, or worse, that I'm so pathetic I let the fact that my fake girlfriend remembers a ridiculous story about her ex-boyfriend bother me. If I say *no,* well, then I'm lying to us both.

"I'm just surprised, I think. That you still put effort into choosing something good for someone who really doesn't deserve it."

She shrugs and brings her mug to her lips, swirling the warm liquid inside. "If I didn't put the same thought into his gift as everyone else's, that would say more about me than it would about him."

"Would it say that you've set healthy boundaries? That you don't feel the need to pour yourself into people who have hurt you? Who have taken and taken and never given back?"

With a sigh, Holly shifts in her seat and props an elbow on the arm of the couch. "I am who I am, Nick. Gift giving has always been my thing, I guess. It's hard to break that, even if I'm not the biggest fan of the recipient."

I nod, because it's clear gift giving *is* her thing. I doubted it for a moment, when we were scouring the old wooden shelves at the bookstore yesterday and she pulled out a comic Kama Sutra and had the absolute (and completely correct) audacity to suggest it would be a good gift for my sister. But then tonight happened, and all faith has been restored.

I clear my throat. "Can I ask you something?"

"Sure."

It's a question I've wanted to ask for weeks, but I've always been too nervous to bring it up, afraid it was too much, too personal, too real. "What's your story, Holly? How'd you get into this job?"

Her cheeks are pink, wind-burned from the day outside, and she runs a thumb along the rim of her mug of cocoa. "I told you before—I was fired, and I needed a way to make some money to pay for all my expenses for this wedding—"

"But there has to be a reason you chose *this*, specifically. It's not like some headhunter tracked you down and asked if you wanted to date losers for a quick buck."

"You're not a loser, Nick."

"Oh yeah? What would you call a guy who can't even get his cubicle neighbor to notice him?"

"I'd say he's a guy living the human experience."

The thing that's immediately obvious about Holly is her boldness. The way she lives at full throttle when she's comfortable, and even sometimes when she's not. But what I've come to appreciate is the way she soaks up the quiet moments, the way she listens, the way she lets you know she feels everything. It's that version of her that I see now, with her sweatshirt sleeves creeping down to her knuckles and her legs tucked up next to her on the couch, and a hint of a smile that's meant for a memory.

"Did you know that ten percent of American adults report feeling lonely every day? And one in three say they feel lonely every week?" She glances at me, then down to her mug. "I didn't choose *this*. I was driving for Pickup CARtist, and it just kind of happened."

"You accidentally went on a date with someone?"

"No. Not the first time." She takes a deep breath and holds it for a beat, then releases it slowly. Her eyes are glued to her hot chocolate, like all the answers she needs are at the bottom of the mug. "It started with a CARtist client. I was driving him to his dad's funeral."

I wait for more, wondering how she went from death to date night.

"His dad struggled with substance use toward the end. Apparently he'd had a bad accident at work, grew to depend on his pain meds. Once they were gone, he sought out that relief anywhere he could.

He was never well enough to go back to work, benefits ran out, and his wife left. When we pulled up to the cemetery, it was nearly empty. This poor kid—he was maybe early twenties—was going to bury his dad without any support. So I asked if he'd like me to walk with him." She shrugs, like it was so easy, so normal to do. "That was the first time I realized that some people just need to not be alone. A little kindness, a little squeeze of the hand—they go a long way."

"And then you decided to monetize? After that day?"

Holly shakes her head. "No. It's not something I set out to do. But a few weeks later, I was dropping off a guy at his parents' house for this party. His brother got some big job in New York, so they were doing this whole sendoff thing for him. Anyway, we got to talking about how much it sucked that our younger siblings were more successful than us, and how annoying it is in family gatherings when people ask how things are going in your life and you have nothing good to report."

Being Clara Anne Goodman's older brother feels just like this. Clara has always been put-together like a firstborn, with the free-spirited nature of the youngest child, and the ability to connect with others like a middle child. And she has an actual boyfriend, while I have a really complicated web of lies that threatens to trap me like I'm an insect with an unfortunate flight path.

"When we pulled up in front of the house, he randomly offered me a hundred bucks to make his family think I was his girlfriend, just so they wouldn't ask him about work and stuff, and I went along with it."

"And you realized you could help yourself by helping others?"

She cocks her head, turns up one corner of her lips. It's a half smile she doesn't believe in. "I realized that we're all lonely, and sometimes we feel lonelier when we're in situations where that stands out more. And I realized how easy it is to show up for people and give them the companionship they need at the times they need it most."

I do it without thinking: tuck a loose strand of hair behind her ear. Let my thumb stroke her cheek the way hers stroked her mug while she told me her story. Let my eyes fall to her lips.

She inhales, sharp and soft. And then, still not thinking or thinking entirely too much, I kiss her. For real, this time. Not for show in front of Mom or Dad or Clara or Mark or anyone else—just because I want to. And if the way her mouth relaxes against mine is any indication, she wants to, too.

Two weeks ago, for the sake of research, Holly told me to kiss her like I'd kiss a real girlfriend. It was clumsy, but passable. *This*, though? The way her fingers wind into my hair and tug at the strands? The way her face presses my glasses into my skin? The way my teeth graze her lips and the way her tongue tests the boundary between us and my hand cradles her neck and she whispers my name into my mouth? *This* is the way I'd kiss a real girlfriend, and the way a real girlfriend would kiss me back.

She tastes like chocolate and sugar and a dream come true and danger, like hot cocoa spiked with peppermint spirits and attraction.

Like maybe—just maybe—this isn't some job to her, but is instead something special and beautiful and real.

And that would be the greatest gift she could give me.

Kissin' in the Cold
Holly

Kissing Nick—and I mean *really* kissing Nick, not for some hypothetical *maybe-there-will-be-mistletoe* practice—is like stepping out of a shower and into a warm, straight-from-the-dryer towel. It's like seeing a double rainbow after living your entire life in shades of gray. It's like standing in the front row at a concert on your bucket list and feeling every thud of the bass and every decibel of your favorite song course through you like it's part of you, the rhythm of your expanding lungs and the beat of your heart.

It feels good, and right, and like *living* instead of just *existing*.

Nick pulls away without pulling away. His forehead rests against mine and one hand lingers behind my neck while the other seems to realize it's on my thigh and slides more appropriately toward my knee.

He's on the edge of the ottoman, covering barely any real estate there, having leaned in so far for the kiss. And, maddeningly, his lips are a breath past a pucker away.

I spend a lot of my life doing what other people want. Thus is the life of a working woman, but also, I'm going out of my way to make sure I can give Jasmine all the revelry she deserves for her crazy-expensive wedding. My literal job is to take people where they want to go. My don't-tell-our-government job is to be the kind of date people need, to cozy up when they want me to and say the things they want me to say and make them look the way they want to look in front of their family or friends.

And now, what I want is right in front of me, and it's time to go after it.

"Nick—" I close my eyes and swallow. I don't know what comes next, how to say everything I'm feeling; how to tell him he's color and warmth and music.

Not that it matters, because my neck tingles the way it does when you sense you're being watched.

"Excuse me?" The voice comes from behind me, and I drop my head in defeat. "Hi. Sorry. It's just that— Well, this is a family party, and my kids don't really need to see... Well, you know. So if you wouldn't mind."

Nick pulls back; I bury my face in my hands, hiding my burning cheeks. "I do mind, actually," Nick says. His voice is unusually gruff, gravelly. And oh my word, it's sexy as hell.

There's a sputtering, stammering response, like she can't believe he would have the gall not to do exactly what she wanted him to do, despite the fact that she does not own this particular resort, and despite the fact that there are many places to be around the lobby that don't have a direct line of sight to us.

Also, there's the whole *it's-just-a-kiss* thing, but the way my heart is hammering in my chest makes me wonder if it's fair to say it's *just* a kiss.

"Your child is literally wearing pajama pants with the Playboy Bunny logo on them, so maybe he's not really all that affected by seeing some random strangers kiss in a hotel lobby." He pauses and exhales, and his thumb grazes my knee, and I bite my lip and watch it. The way it moves is absent, distracted, like he's touched me like this in car rides and on couches and curled up in bed for years and years and it's just habit now to swipe his thumb back and forth and back again.

"If you wouldn't mind," Nick says, "my girlfriend and I were enjoying a romantic evening, and your family may prefer to spend time with you instead of standing around watching you accost tourists."

There's an amused snort, and when I look up a teenage boy is biting back a laugh. An older girl in a quarter-zip over her pajamas stands behind him, her cheeks matching the rose-colored mark that peeks out from the neckline of her sweatshirt. I think to myself *I doubt it*, a theory that is all but confirmed when the mom storms off and the kids roll their heads as they turn, like rolling their eyes isn't quite dramatic enough for the havoc their mother wreaks.

"That was... something," I say to Nick, and when I turn to face him again he cups my jaw in his hand.

My smile fades as he scans my eyes, searching. "Are you okay?" he asks.

I answer with a nod, which has the added bonus of nuzzling my cheek deeper into his hand. "I'm okay."

He smooths a thumb over my skin, and then his eyes dip to my lips, still searching. He leans in again, and the skin on my hands tingles. And there, with his mouth so close to mine and everything I want just an inch away, I suck in a breath and sigh it out in a word: "Nick."

"Holly."

I've heard my name so many times before, from parents and teachers and friends and strangers and bosses and colleagues and clients; I've heard it yelled and laughed and screamed and barked and admonished; I've heard it groaned by brothers and moaned by lovers; I've heard it in songs and commercials and in rhymes and jingles.

But I've never heard it the way Nick says it now: adored, revered; a whispered plea to stop stopping, to pick up where we left off, to let us happen. To try.

It's absurd, really, that we started this whole farce for a few hundred bucks, so I could buy a designer dress I'll wear for one day, so he could impress a girl that is decidedly not me, and now here we are, losing track of all of that.

Laughter bubbles in my lungs, nervous and unexpected, and I clench my jaw shut to hold it in. Not that it helps to keep my mouth shut when my body starts shaking with it, but I did what I could.

Nick looks at me like I'm losing my mind (which is generous, considering I feel like I lost it ages ago), and I can't hold it back when confusion wrinkles his forehead. I giggle, and he chuckles, and I chortle, and thoughts of kissing are nudged aside by this shared amusement.

"You saw the hickey on the daughter's neck, too, right?" I ask.

"I didn't want to sell her out to her mom, but yes."

I can barely get my words out between fits of giggles. "I can't—re-member—the last time—I had—a hickey."

"Can you imagine," Nick starts, and I cut him off like I've had eight spiked cocoas instead of—checks notes—one.

"What if we saw them at breakfast tomorrow and I had a giant hickey right—" I form my hands in a circle on the side of my neck.

Nick's hand gestures in a large circle toward my upper body. "Just... hickeys. All over."

If you've ever wondered how to get two people who are laughing hysterically to stop laughing entirely, might I suggest gesturing in a large circle and saying "Hickeys all over." It might not be an effective method on everyone, but I can attest that it is quite adequate for people who are not-really-but-maybe-(?)-wish-they-were dating. At least, it is for us.

Immediately sobered from that one drink that wore off forty minutes ago and the high of having been kissed to make-out Utopia, I clear my throat. "Should we go back?" I ask, certain that we should go back but unequivocally loathing the thought.

Nick nods. "Do you want another hot chocolate?"

"If I drink any more, I'll turn into the chocolate river in Willy Wonka's factory." I leave out the part about the schnapps and the free feeling it gives me and the intoxicating compound it creates when it reacts with the free feeling *he* gives me, like I could fly (obviously not), or run for days without stopping (I can barely run for *minutes* without stopping), or float (I'm not made of helium, though I've been told I've got a lot of hot air), or simply live without worry (in this economy?).

So I deposit my mug on a large tray with other dirty dishes, and we pass by the mom who approached us just a few minutes ago (as expected, her children look as though they want to be anywhere but here), and we stumble giddily into the cold. I immediately curl into Nick's side, and he wraps his arm around me.

"Do you want to take the trolley?" he asks, even though we're walking away from the pick-up gazebo.

I shake my head, a gesture he surely feels more than he sees. "I want to walk with you." Those last two words feel especially important to vocalize.

His arm tightens like a physical echo of the words, and we stroll along the lighted path with flurries falling all around us.

"It's really romantic here, especially with the snow tonight." And then, either because I'm afraid of growing too attached to someone I can't have, or because I'm the biggest moron in the world, or because of both of those reasons but definitely not neither, I add, "You should bring Catherine sometime."

Under My Tree

Holly

I HATE MYSELF FOR saying it as soon as the words leave my mouth.

You should bring Catherine *sometime?* No. He should bring *me* again. Next year, and the year after that, and maybe for Valentine's Day and in August, just because.

He doesn't acknowledge the remark verbally, but he pulls his arm free and tucks his hand into his pocket, which speaks volumes. "What are your plans tomorrow?"

I shrug against the sudden rush of cold. "Well, we have the bird thing before lunch. Unless you wanted to take your dad or someone else."

"I think it would play into our cover story best if we went together."

"Sure." I nod, even though he's not looking at me. "And then after lunch, I'm spending the day at the salon with your mom and sister. And then there's the ball."

"Busy day," he says, his eyes glued to the pathway ahead, his voice even.

I nod for my own benefit. "What about you? After the hawk thing."

"Not really sure," he answers. "Probably some combination of hanging out with my dad while trying to avoid Mark. Maybe log in and get some work done."

The thing about reflexes is, they're things our body just does without conscious thought, so even if we *know* it's a bad idea, we don't have an opportunity to reason the reflex away.

On an unrelated note, I reach out and grasp Nick's forearm.

"You're on vacation, Nick. You shouldn't be working."

He shrugs, and his arm goes rigid under my touch. "You're working. What's the difference?"

The difference, I want to say, *is that this hasn't felt like work.* Instead, "Touché" comes out of my mouth, and I retract my hand and shove it in my coat pocket.

We spend the second half of our walk in silence, wasting the snowfall that glistens in the golden glow of streetlamps and the slow, jazzy music playing through speakers hidden in rock beds that line the sidewalk.

Just outside the cabin Nick pauses, sighs, and holds out his hand. "We should probably—"

"Of course." I slide my hand into his and try to ignore the rush of warmth that snakes its way from my fingertips to my palm and up to my shoulder. Then I plaster a smile that I hope looks real across my face, and he nudges open the door.

The living room is deserted, save for Mr. Goodman snoring softly in the recliner. Mrs. Goodman is rinsing a mug when we walk in, and she sets it in the dishwasher before drying her hands. "Good, you're back!" She hides a yawn in her elbow. "I wanted to wait up until you made it back, but it's getting late."

"Sorry," Nick says.

"Don't be," his mom replies. "Did you have fun?"

Yes, I think. *Until I opened my stupid mouth and talked about stupid Catherine.*

"We did." Nick smiles but drops my hand. "You didn't have to wait up, though."

"Sure I did. You'll understand when you have kids." She glances between us with the wide eyes of a mother who has said too much and adds, "If. *If* you have kids."

Now that things are infinitely more awkward due to her eyeballs' implication that if her son *does* have kids they'll be with me, she pushes herself to her tiptoes to kiss his forehead, hugs me, wishes us both goodnight, and shakes Mr. Goodman awake on his recliner before dragging him upstairs with only a cursory glance back.

"That was something."

"Uh-huh." Nick scrubs a hand through his hair and straightens his glasses on his nose. "I'm going to get ready for bed." He deadbolts the front door and saunters toward the stairs.

It seems like he's trying to get away from me, but I'm tired and frustrated and I also need to get ready for bed, so I follow close behind.

We brush our teeth in silence, stealing glances at each other in the mirror and looking away quickly when we fear we've been caught. Then he props his toothbrush on its charger and leaves the bathroom to gather his pillows and blanket for the couch.

The thing about reflexes is, they're things our body just does without conscious thought, so even if we *know* it's a bad idea, we don't have an opportunity to reason the reflex away.

Which is, I'm certain, why I find myself leaning against the door-frame with my arms crossed, watching it all unfold in front of me, and say, "I don't actually think you should bring Catherine here. I'm not sure why I said that."

He pauses. I'm staring at his slightly hunched back while he grabs a blanket from the edge of the bed, and he doesn't finish the action. Instead his hand flexes like he's Mr. Darcy himself and he's just helped me into a carriage.

I want to stop him, to say *Nick, talk to me*; or *Nick, can we please discuss how you kissed me?*; and *I kissed you back, Nick*; and *Nick, I know you have to know how I feel*; and maybe even *I think you feel the same way, Nick*; but in the torrent of words that floods my brain, only one makes its way through the dam.

"Nick."

"Why did you say it?" he asks.

"I told you, I'm not sure."

He sighs.

"Why did it upset you so much?"

A-*ha*. He freezes at the question, turns, and drops onto the bed. "I don't know."

"The whole reason you hired me was so that you would look good in front of her."

"I know why I hired you, Holly." There's a roughness to his voice, but not a cruelness. More like an exhausted, hard-edged tone. I let him wallow in it, turn the answer over and over in his mind like it's an unsolved Rubik's Cube he's examining on all sides, trying to piece the puzzle together.

"You kissed me," I finally say. There's the minor detail that I kissed him back, but that's not something we need to discuss right now.

"I know," he answers on an exhale.

"Like—you *really* kissed me. To the extent that some random—"

"I *know.*" He flops backward, the edge of the bed behind his knees, his feet planted on the floor, his body sprawled across the quilt. He whips his glasses off his face and rests them on his chest before pressing the heels of his hands into his eye sockets, and it softens me. Makes me melt like a marshmallow over red-hot coals.

I copy his position from the other side of the bed so our heads are aligned with the other's torso, and I watch him. "I kissed you back." I gently lift one of his hands in mine, lacing our fingers together.

He drops his other hand to his side and turns his head toward me, first regarding our joined hands, then meeting my eyes. "You did."

"Mhmm. Promise you won't tell HR? They tend to frown on that." This earns a promising (or maybe just playfully exasperated?) chuckle from him. "No guarantees."

"Fair enough."

We lay there like that, hands clasped, our elbows pressed to each other's sides, for minutes. There's so much that needs to be said. Or maybe there isn't. Maybe 'you kissed me' and 'I kissed you back' is all we really need to acknowledge right now, and tomorrow is a new day and a fresh start and we'll go back to being who we were this morning, which I would classify as two-people-who-really-want-to-kiss-but-haven't-yet-done-so-or-made-that-desire-known-to-the-other.

It's comfortable right here, just like this, and I find myself dangerously close to saying so. That is, until Nick rises and lets his fingers fall from mine and says "We should get some sleep," and then he grabs his pillows and blanket and crosses the room in one awful, fluid motion.

The thing about reflexes is... well, you know. And when my brain computes that he's grasped the doorknob, the eleven million bits of information floating around up there somehow force a very specific set of words out of my mouth.

"What if you stayed?"

Time To Fall In Love
Nick

THERE'S SOMETHING ROMANTIC ABOUT trudging along snow-covered pathways with your fake girlfriend, a falconer, and a hawk that eats tiny, sometimes-discernible pieces of animal flesh from your gloved hand.

Maybe it has something to do with the memory of waking up with my arm draped over her as a streak of sunlight highlighted the reddishness in her hair; the lazy way she rolled over to greet me with a closed-mouth kiss; the sparkle in her eyes as our bare legs lay twisted together; the heat of her pressed against my chest; the pile of clothes on the floor; the easy way we fit together.

Yes, actually—now that I think about it, shivering in the woods with a meaty mouse head pinched between my thumb and forefinger is definitely not doing it for me, but the way Holly's eyes widen in wonder and her smile beams at me with every visit from our assigned hawks... these are aphrodisiacs.

"Did you like it?" she asks, bounding away from the Hope's Knoll Zoological Education Center where we started and ended our hawk walk.

I'm a few paces behind her, which is entirely too far away for my personal preference. "I loved it. Thank you again."

She twirls to face me and stops in the middle of the sidewalk. "I wanted you to have something real to talk about. Something we *actually* did together."

Without thinking I draw her to me, pull her close, kiss her deeply. I feel her smile against my own. We had something very real last night, but I guess I shouldn't talk about that with my coworkers.

"What was that for?" she asks, tugging her beanie down over her ears.

If the moment was right I would tell her. I would tell her it's for the way she put in the effort with my family's gifts, the way she makes the weight on my chest float off on a breeze, the way she makes me laugh. I would tell her what I was moments away from telling her last night, what I almost let slip out and then agonized over and resolved to tell her right before we were interrupted by the angry mom.

But maybe the moment *is* right, because it's *a* moment, and our arms are around each other and the feeling bubbles in my lungs like I've been breathing champagne.

"It's because I think—" I begin at the exact time a car pulls up next to us and my sister shouts out of the rear window.

"Come on, Holly! We're going to be late for the spa!"

I finish "I love you" into the too-full air, with music blasting from the car's speakers and Clara audibly urging Holly toward her.

"Good timing," Holly whispers with a wink, like it was all for show. Then she kisses my cheek and strides toward the car, glancing back before climbing in.

"You guys are ridiculously perfect." Clara's gushing fades as the window slowly rises.

And here, alone on the sidewalk, I consider that the next time I'm prepared to make such a heartfelt declaration, I will absolutely wait until a *better* right moment.

What Christmas Means To Me
Holly

I demand a refund on all my spa services. Not because they weren't relaxing (holy shit, were they ever!), but because they were *too* relaxing.

Spa time with Clara and Christina should have been a great time to socialize over manicures and talk about the ball and the week so far, but instead Christina has surprised us with 'bonus gifts' and has booked us each a massage. So I end up in a quiet room for seventy-five minutes with nothing to do but physically relax and let my ruminating mind do anything but.

Obviously I wonder what Nick had wanted to say before I was kidnapped for the spa adventure; a tiny part of me—like, nail-of-my-pinky-toe tiny—considers that what I heard is what he meant, and then reality smacks me in the metaphorical face and I go back to wondering what he'd wanted to say.

After the massage, I sit sandwiched between Clara and Christina while we get our nails done. Christina opts for holly berry red, Clara chooses a holographic pine green, and I select glittering gold at Clara's urging.

"It'll look so great with your dress," she says.

And then, when the polish has cured, I sit at the end of a row of hair stations while we get blow-outs and light styling for the ball. When I make a comment about everything looking great except my makeup—because I learned makeup application techniques from a woman who never wore it and I couldn't get into the up-talky tutorial videos online in recent years—my hair stylist offers to also do my makeup for me at no extra charge.

At the risk of jinxing it, I think as she wiggles a mascara wand against my lashes, *things are going really well.*

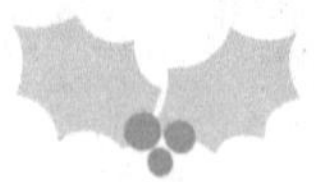

By the way Clara tries to keep Nick from seeing me before the ball, you'd think it was my wedding day and he was a waiting groom. "You look super hot," she says. "But you can't let him see half the package. Once you're dressed he can see you."

Normally I would balk at the idea that someone could dictate to me where I can go and who I can see, but two things are true. First, this is Clara, and it's nearly impossible to say no to her. Second, I kind of like the idea of Nick seeing me with the whole look put together. And I like the idea of seeing him seeing me; I'm getting so much better at reading his expression and knowing what he's thinking, and I have suspicions about what I might intuit at the big reveal.

Not much hiding is necessary when we return to the cabin.

"Where's Nick?" Clara asks when we walk inside. Mark's lounging on the couch, scrolling on his phone with an action movie on the TV.

He barely looks up, and shrugs. "He left a little while ago."
"Left?"
Mark raises his shoulders again, but offers no clarification.
"Where did he go?"
He answers with a sigh.

"And how did he get there?" I wonder aloud.

"Oh. Right. He took your car."

Christina closes the door behind us and expertly maintains her even tone, even though her face betrays her nerves. "Will he be back in time for the ball?"

"I'm sure Cinderella will be here before the ball starts."

Clara wrinkles her face and looks at me. I'm simultaneously holding back both laughter and the desire to smother Mark with a throw pillow.

"That's not how that story works, babe," Clara tells him, but Mark just turns up the volume on the TV.

"Want to get ready together?" she asks.

It takes me back to junior prom at my best friend's house, listening to boy bands and spending more time lip syncing than doing our makeup. A bit of girl time is good for the soul. "I'd love to."

Turns out, when your hair and makeup are already done, getting ready together turns into socializing and helping each other with your zippers and accessories.

Clara turns on a playlist of poppy, festive tracks and rummages through her travel case for earrings that would complement my outfit. "What about these?" She dangles a pair of golden bows in front of me.

"Those are cute."

"Here—" She shoves them into my hand. "Wear these if you want to. They'd look great with your dress."

I push the posts through my ears and check the clock on my phone. The ball starts in twenty minutes, and we still haven't heard from Nick.

"Anything?"

I shake my head.

"This is so unlike him."

Not that I know him—*actually* know him—well, but tardiness is not a trait I'd associate with Nick Goodman. "Is he a big fan of the ball?"

Clara chuckles and shakes her head. "No, not really. But he's a big fan of *you*."

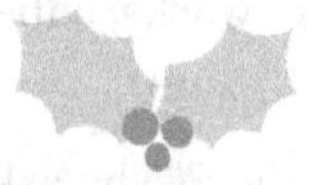

Clara and Mark and Mr. and Mrs. Goodman and I arrive in the ballroom three minutes after dinner is scheduled to begin. Nick texted Clara fifteen minutes ago and told her he'd meet us here, but no matter how I crane my neck I can't see over the throngs of people milling about between the bar and the ballroom to see if he's here yet.

If I was impressed by the lobby a few days ago, I am absolutely floored by the ballroom setup. There are twinkling lights every-where, from the dessert tables to the centerpieces; glistening white branches that look like they were dipped in vats of glitter line the walls; Christmas trees fill every corner, and there seems to be mistletoe affixed to each of the chandeliers overhead. All the glitter gives the appearance of fresh-fallen snow, and I stop my search long enough to close my eyes and replay this morning's kiss in my head.

And then there's a shriek and a commotion; I jump and look to my right just in time to see one woman pull another up off her knee. A white leather box is still in her hand and she is wielding a rock on her finger that could make Dwayne Johnson look small.

The crowd applauds as much as they can around martini glasses and champagne flutes, and then they go about their business while

I'm still transfixed by the moment. I'm not sure how long I stare at the two women, but it's long enough that they move on with their night and I find that I've been staring at the spot where they'd been, where people mill about now, laughing and partying.

Clara, who's been next to me the whole time and whose one-sided conversation with Mark provided the soundtrack for my trance, sucks in a breath, which snaps me out of it.

There, just beyond the spot where the proposal happened moments earlier, holding a bouquet of red ranunculus and white mini calla lilies, stands Nick.

THE ONLY GIFT
Nick

I SPENT THE DAY carefully planning for tonight, from a new suit jacket to a specific bouquet of entirely unnecessary flowers, from a quick perusal through a vintage store to a gift I hope she'll love, from what I want to tell her to exactly how I want to say it.

But when I see Holly standing twenty feet away from me, an almost worried look on her face, the whole plan goes out the window.

I take the first few steps toward her but she closes the gap, rushing toward me and throwing her arms around my neck. "Where were you?"

I bury my face in her hair, breathe her in, feel the silkiness of satin and skin against my palm.

"I missed you." And then, because I need her to know it and not just hear it, I kiss her. It's a drop-the-flowers-on-the-floor-and-hold-her-face-in-my-hands-like-the-precious-thing-it-is kiss, a truly-madly-deeply kiss, a kiss that says *I love you* and *none of this is fake to me* and *please tell me you feel the same.*

To my surprise and eternal delight, she kisses me back with the same voracity.

She bites her lip at the kiss's end. "I missed you, too."

I swear Mark grumbles *"It's been six hours,"* but I don't care.

"Sorry I'm late. I was out doing a little shopping and I hit a few snags. I hope it's okay that I borrowed your car."

"Mi carro es su carro." She slips her hand into mine.

I bend and pick up the flowers, which look a little rougher than they did three minutes ago, and hand them to her. "These are for you."

She beams at them and squeezes my hand. "How did you know that ranunculus are my favorite? Or was it a lucky guess?"

With a shrug, I say, "It looked like you really liked the flowers at your grandma's place, so I wanted to get the same kind."

Holly leans in and kisses my cheek. "Thank you. They're gorgeous."

"Nowhere near as gorgeous as you."

Her answering smile could heat this entire resort for a week. "What about you, dressed like you're ready to star in a sexy Santa calendar?" Her fingers slide up the dark green velvet of my new jacket and toy with the black satin lapel, tugging me closer to her mouth again.

There's a less-than-subtle reminder from Mom that we're not alone. "We're going to get started with dinner, but take your time and join us whenever you're ready."

"Sure, Mom. We'll be right there." Once she's gone, I hang my head with a groan and meet Holly's forehead with my own. "Do you think we could talk, then? Maybe after dinner?"

She nods. "I'd love that."

And there's that word again: the one I thought I felt days ago and now I'm sure I do; the one that fills me, improbably, with excitement and calm, all at once; the one I want to say and hear and repeat over and over and over again until my voice is hoarse.

"Shall we?" I pull away (with great effort) and extend my elbow to her.

She gives her best *Bridgerton* impression with a half-curtsy and prim "We shall" before she links her arm through mine, and we follow my family to our table.

Dinner is, like everything else the resort does, incredible. The food is delicious, but even better is the time we have as a family to laugh and remember and tell stories, like when I tell Holly, "We used to save one gift each for the night of the ball so that we could all sit by the tree and open something in formalwear because Clara wanted to feel like a Kardashian," or when Mom talks about me sitting in a diaper at two years old, playing my new drum set the day after Christmas, and the drum set mysteriously vanishing shortly after New Year's, or when my parents are visiting the dessert stations and we're debating our worst Christmas ever when Holly joins in on the fun with her own tale.

"One Christmas, my parents had made this incredible dinner, as usual. But my boyfriend was late getting there, so we kept pushing dinner back fifteen minutes, then another twenty, until finally the ham was dry and the stuffing was burnt and everyone was hangry. We waited and waited all this time and when I finally heard from him, do you know what his excuse was for not showing up?" She looks around the table for an answer, and everyone sits rapt as she prepares for the punchline. "His fantasy football team was in the playoffs and one of the games went into overtime, so he just *had* to stay until it was over."

"That's terrible," Clara says.

Holly's wine-stained lips are an indication that maybe the drinks should have waited until after story time was over. "Well, that's Mark for ya." She raises a glass toward Clara. "Cheers to you, my friend, for being more worthwhile than I was."

The mood at the table shifts as Clara quiets and scoots her chair inches away from her boyfriend. Holly sets her glass down and turns toward me, apparently unconcerned by the drama unfolding across the table. "I should really take these flowers back and put them in water."

"I'll come with you."

"No." She braces a hand against my chest. "Stay with your family. The trolley will have me there and back in twenty minutes." Then she kisses my forehead and takes off.

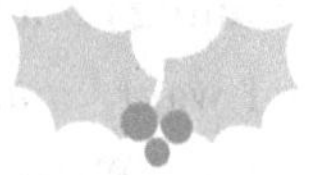

"Have you seen Holly?" I ask Clara over the bass of the song that is blaring through the speakers. There was a jazz quartet that played during dinner but now the night has turned its focus to dancing, with colorful lights projected onto the walls and a DJ set up next to the stage. It's been an hour since Holly left with the flowers, and I have spent the last half hour searching for her near the bars, the dance floor, and—awkwardly and unobtrusively—a few yards away from the women's bathroom (just in case). Now, back at the table with my sister, I am still without my girlfriend.

Clara shakes her head.

"Where's Mark?"

This time she shrugs as she twists her cocktail straw around her fingers. "Probably tracking his fantasy stats."

"Clara." I'm officially in Protective Brother Mode, but it's hard to know the best way to do that these days. "People can change a lot in a year." It's a simple phrase, completely true, and even if I happen to doubt it applies to Mark, I don't need to push my negativity onto her. She has been giddy in love with this guy for months.

The way she looks at me, though, with her eyebrow arched and a wry smirk on her lips, tells me she doesn't really believe it either.

"Well, at least *some* things that never change are *good* things. C'mon." She grabs my hand and pulls me out into the lobby where a tiny hut has been set up all week but is now inhabited by none other than Santa Claus(*) himself. We've always met with Santa together, even when I was well over the age of believing but had to sit with Santa and Clara at the mall anyway for a photo op. In our late teens it became a fun tradition for us to find him at amusement parks and hotels and shopping centers; we'd each take a knee (careful not to rest our full body weight on him) and we'd tell him our lists (often phrasing it like we were auditioning for a Spice Girls cover band, with me saying 'I'll tell you what I want,' and Clara tacking on 'What I really, really want' before rattling off the most out-of-the-box things our adolescent brains could conjure), and we'd get a photo to keep as a souvenir for Mom and Dad's fridge.

So now, here, of course we need to visit Santa, just like we've done every December since we started coming to Hope's Knoll. What's nice is, with the number of tipsy fifty-somethings in line, we don't even feel out of place for doing it.

When it's our turn, we take our seats on the plush white couch where Santa sits.

"Ho, ho, ho, who do we have here?" Santa bellows in his jolly voice. Just like everything else here, the resort splurges and gets a Santa with a real gray-white beard and no padding needed under his red suit. If he didn't have to ask for the names of everyone who came to call, I'd insist he was the real deal.

"I'm Clara, and this is Nick," Clara says, her voice regaining some of her typical cheer in the last few minutes.

"Welcome!" Santa says. "And what do the two of you want for Christmas?"

Clara looks at me, and the twinkle in her eye turns to a laugh that threatens to burst out of her pinched lips. I wink back at her and say to Santa, "I'll tell you what I want."

"What I really, *really* want," Clara adds, barely getting the words out. And then she rattles off a few items, like a lower electricity bill, and for the comments sections on most news articles to be disabled, and for Tom Hanks to be immortal, and for someone to look at her the way Jonah looked at Amy on *Superstore.*

"And what about you, young man?" Santa asks me, and kudos to him, because he doesn't seem all that fazed by my sister's list. Granted, when you're probably used to getting kicked and cried on all day, a prankish twenty-something doesn't seem all that bad, I guess.

Just over Clara's shoulder, I see her: a waterfall of red satin, a cascade of brunette curls. The woman I undeniably love.

I answer Santa simply and honestly. "Her. I want her."

YOU'RE A MEAN ONE, MR. GRINCH

Holly

TONIGHT HAS THE POTENTIAL to be the best night of my life.

Yes, I once sang a rousing, standing ovation-inspiring rendition of *Call Me Maybe* at O'Donnell's live band karaoke night, but I feel like *maaaaybe* hearing the words 'I love you' travel from Nick Goodman's delicious mouth to my waiting ears will be a tiny bit better.

I know it's improbable, but something about us feels special. Different. Right. Which is why, after putting the flowers in a vase, I go up to our room and tuck my flannel shorts into a drawer, laying out the ice-blue babydoll I picked up at the department store instead. It's satin with lace accents and little silver snowflake embroidery, and I thought it was the perfect choice for a romantic winter trip. It's sparkling and new, just like this next phase for Nick and me.

The trolley drops a handful of us off at the rear entrance; from there it's a short walk to the ballroom and the man I—

"Holly?"

I spin on my heel at the sound of my name. There's a vaguely familiar face in front of me, one I can't quite place but know I should be able to, which is never a good feeling.

"I thought that was you." He snuffs out a cigarette on the sidewalk. *Chef Ben* is scrawled in royal blue cursive across his heart, and bile rises to my throat as he stands and holds out his arms for a hug. "How ya doing?" he asks, but he doesn't give me time to answer. "I wasn't expecting to see you here. Joey said you couldn't make it."

"Oh, yeah... I *couldn't*, but then my schedule changed, and I thought I'd surprise him." It feels like a convincing lie. "Anyway, it was great to see you, but I really should get inside—"

"I'll come with ya!" Ben matches my stride toward the door.

My hands go clammy, and despite the freezing air around me I'm sweating. If you've ever wondered if it's a good idea—even for a hundred bucks—to pretend to date a guy so he can impress his family, let this be a lesson.

"You really don't have to—"

"Are you kidding? My brother hasn't stopped talking about you for months. You think I want to miss the look on his face when he sees you?"

I'm sure it will be quite the look, considering I couldn't pick my first paying customer out of a crowd. How Ben remembers me from that one, brief meeting, I'll never know.

I feel like a Bond villainess, wearing a gorgeous gown in a room full of well-off, well-dressed people, constantly checking over my shoulder to make sure I'm not discovered.

"Hey, bro." Ben claps a hand on Joey's back. "You'll never guess who Santa just dropped off for you."

Joey turns, and a look of sheer terror flashes where his jovial smile had just been.

"Holly! Oh—oh my god! I wasn't expecting—"

"Surprise!" I give tiny jazz hands to try to look excited.

Joey rises and gives me a one-armed hug, careful not to spill the drink in his opposite hand, and whispers in my ear so no one else can hear him. "I'm so sorry, and I will get you two hundred bucks when this is over if you can give me thirty minutes."

My immediate reaction is *definitely not*, because Nick is waiting for me and I've already been gone longer than I told him I would be. But Joey's voice is so doleful, so hopeless, and I don't know how to walk away without humiliating him in front of his family.

"Sure, sweetie," I whisper back.

He steps beside me and slides a hand to the small of my back. "Two fifty," I say quietly through the gritted teeth behind my outward smile.

His mom shifts to the corner of a luxe couch so there is room for both Joey and me, and once we're seated Joey dedicates both hands to holding his drink.

For the next twenty-nine minutes, I field questions about work (apparently I'm an attorney), and life in North Carolina (I make up something about barbecue and try not to be surprised that Joey has lived there for two years), and I try to highlight how incredible Joey is (this proves to be the most challenging, because I know absolutely nothing about Joey other than that, apparently, he has lived in North Carolina for two years). I also find out that Joey and his family are all booked in separate rooms instead of in a cabin, which is helpful for my exit strategy.

At minute thirty, per the intricate wooden clock that's a centerpiece of sorts in the lobby, I excuse myself to the bar, dragging Joey behind me. "Tell everyone I'm heading back to the room, and whenever you feel like ditching your family, say you're going to join me."

"That won't take long." He rolls his eyes and laughs, and it's the most at ease I've ever seen him.

"Joey?"

"Hmm?"

"Stop the charade. Soon. Just live your life and be proud of who you are. They won't respect you if you don't even respect yourself."

I kiss his cheek, leaving a smear of red there for good measure, and he counts out bills from his wallet.

"Thanks, Holly. I'd say see you 'round, but—"

"Joey, I mean this with so much kindness." I rest a hand on his shoulder and eye him like he's my own brother. "I hope I never, ever see you again."

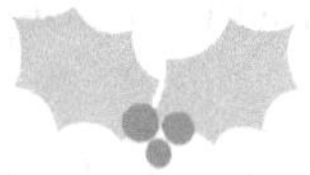

The signature cocktail of the evening is dubbed Jolly Juice, which feels like it would be more at home at a frat house. It is, however, incredibly delicious, so I arm myself with two glasses and scour the crowd for Nick or any of the Goodmans. I do, after all, have a very important conversation to have.

Instead, I find Mark slouched and manspreading in an armchair, his cellphone in hand.

"Hey! Do you know where everybody else is?"

"Nope," he says with a smirk, popping the 'p' at the end of the word. "Last I saw them, they were out by the trolley stop, maybe a half hour ago."

Ice races through my veins and I try to keep my composure. "They were?"

Mark purses his lips and scratches a finger against his temple, that maddening sneer just beneath the surface of his false confusion. "No, wait... That was *you* out there."

"Mark, I—"

"It's really fascinating to see you out there with some other guy, but I guess I shouldn't be surprised, considering you're basically doing that for a living now." With one arrogant wiggle of his cell phone, I know that he knows about Holly Dates.

"I can explain," I start, even though I can't. Not in a way Mark could ever understand.

"What I want to know is, does *Nick* know? Is he in on your little side hustle, or will it break his little loser heart when he finds out?" Mark stands and takes one of the cocktails from my hand, downing half of it in one gulp.

Nick called himself the same thing last night, and now I have no question who was feeding him that idea. "He's not a loser."

"Sure. He's just fallen for a girl whose job is to make people believe she's in love."

If there is one silver lining—and I am working *very* hard to find any tiny hope worth grasping onto—it's that Mark appears to have no idea that Nick is or was ever a client. I'm happy to fall on the sword if it means saving him and his reputation with his family and coworkers. It's one thing to be duped by a woman who normally gets paid for dates; it's another to need a date so badly you have to resort to paying. That's how most people will see it, anyway. "What do you want?"

Mark sighs with an inhale that expands his chest menacingly. "Well, I didn't love it when you called me out in front of Clara earlier."

I nod. "Sure, of course. I'll go talk to her, smooth it over."

"I don't know if that's good enough, actually."

My skin prickles with suspense. "Okay, so what *would* be good enough?"

His eyebrows rise and he chuckles and crosses his arms, and I realize that he's won. Our whole relationship has been an ongoing chess game with no time limit. When we broke up, I thought we'd reached a stalemate, but now he's lining up his rook and queen for a battery I can't escape. There's no *check* anymore; *checkmate* is imminent, and I've lost the game.

"I'm not entirely comfortable with my ex being around my new girlfriend so much. Especially when she's proven she's willing to lie and deceive people for her own benefit."

"Mark—"

He *tsk*s the interruption and puts a condescending hand on my shoulder. Just like always, he's pushing me down. "I don't think there's room for both of us around the Goodman family. You can leave on your own and try to save face, or I can let everyone know that precious little Holly is a fraud who duped their son."

"I don't care what they think of me."

"Yes, you do. But you also have to consider what they'll think of *him.* And not just his family, but everyone at work, too. I mean, *Garrett* might get it, but what about Catherine? George?" Mark pauses like he's deep in thought. "I wonder if George will let him keep his raise, or even his *job*, or if even unknowingly dating an escort violates the morality clause."

"You wouldn't..." I say, but we both know Mark absolutely would.

He swipes the other Jolly Juice from my hand and relaxes his posture, knowing he's got me trapped. "Tomorrow, Holly. I want you gone by tomorrow."

Red Dress

Holly

Tonight is, quite possibly, the worst night of my life. Not just because of a terrible interaction with Mark (what other kind is to be expected, really?) or because I wasted thirty minutes of the ball with Joey and Ben instead of spending it with Nick and his family, but because I'm somehow supposed to tell this man who means so much to me that he means nothing to me at all.

Of all the lies I've told over the past few days, weeks, months... this is the one I know I'll always regret.

Fortified by a whiskey sour that now threatens to reverse course back up my esophagus, I work my way back toward the ballroom. And there, just outside and sitting with Clara and Santa Claus and looking directly at me, is the man I love.

The thought of breaking his heart breaks my own.

Nick smiles and hops off the platform where he's been mingling with The Big Guy himself, then weaves his way through the crowd to me, and all I can think about is how I should have just gone back to the cabin, left him a note, and taken off under cover of darkness.

But selfishly, I wanted one more night with him. One more chance to hold and be held and to dream that I could be happy.

"You're back!" Nick's hair flops over his forehead as he comes to a stop in front of me. He slips his hand into mine like he's done it a million times, like he knows I need the same connection he seems to crave. "Do you want to get a drink? And maybe find a quiet place to talk?"

I know from my journey the last thirty minutes that the quietest part of the lobby is inhabited by Ben and Joey's family, and I can't show up there with Nick right now. Also, I don't want to talk anymore. I can't bear to hear the words I've been looking forward to hearing all night.

"Can we dance? Just for a little?" I've missed out on an hour of the party—one of my last hours with Nick, it turns out—and I want to experience it all with him. Dinner, dancing, feeling alive as I twirl and twist on the floor with him, feeling whole and free as I sway in his arms.

"Whatever you want." He kisses the top of my head and tugs me toward the ballroom where the DJ is playing a pop song from when I was in middle school, and we make our way toward the middle of the crowd.

"I never know what to do with my hands," he shouts over the music as he bobs to the rhythm, his arms bouncing along to the beat.

"They didn't teach you that at Miss Lisa's?"

He stops, and a smile blooms on his face. "You remembered."

"Of course I remember." How could I forget anything about the night that culminated in our first kiss? Even if it wasn't real then, even if it was just for show, I remember.

The music changes to a slow song, which really solves the whole hand situation, and Nick takes one of mine in his while he rests the other on my hip. "Is this okay?" he asks.

Knowing what's coming for us, it should feel wrong. But I find comfort in Nick's arms, and there's an expiration date on it, so I'm going to take advantage of every second I can until I can't anymore. "Don't let go," I tell him and move my body closer to his.

We sway to the music, and I feel every breath that fills his chest, every hum in his throat. And when he lowers his face to kiss the crook of my neck—when he whispers *"You're so perfect, Holly"* into that same, tender spot, tears well in my eyes until I can't force them back anymore. I bury my face against his velvet jacket and cry silently, grateful for waterproof mascara and the memories we made and *him*.

It's like he knows something is wrong. He pulls away before the song ends and cups my face in his palms, swiping his thumbs over my cheeks and kissing the ghost of a tear. "Talk to me, Holls. Tell me what's going on."

Holls. That's the first time he's used a nickname for me, and it flows so easily out of him, feels so natural, like he's been calling me that for months or years. It weakens me just enough that I want to give in.

But I can't tell him what's going on, obviously, because if I try I'll break down, and I don't want to do that here in front of all these strangers. "I just want to enjoy tonight," I answer, which is not a lie. I thought a little dancing would be the distraction I needed, that it would put off the inevitable ending a little longer, but it's just a reminder of everything I love so much and am hours away from losing.

"We can stay if you want, or we can go back, or we can play Jenga or chess or mahjong or drink Jolly Juice until we puke. Whatever you want. We can do whatever you want."

I sniffle, trying to calm myself. "Do you mind if we go back to the cabin?"

"Anything, Holly. Come on, let's head to the trolley." We walk hand-in-hand out of the ballroom where the crowd is dwindling as the hours pass.

"Actually—" Part of me doesn't want to risk a run-in with Joey's family by the trolley station, and part of me doesn't give a damn about Joey's situation right now, but all of me wants to draw out every moment with Nick, just the two of us, like the slower we move the more time we'll have. "Could we walk instead?"

Nick snickers and glances down at my feet. "You want to walk in those?"

When I packed the red-and-green plaid stilettos that I wore to his Ugly Christmas Sweater party, I didn't anticipate dancing in them, and I *definitely* didn't think I'd walk half a mile in them. Had I known, I would have brought flats. Still, it beats being crammed into a trolley with throngs of other people. And besides, what's a little foot pain when I'm about to rip out my own heart and crush it?

I look up at Nick, and I know he takes pity on my confused little brain, even though he has no idea why it's confused about this particular choice. He shakes his head with a grin and unbuttons his jacket before sliding it over my arms. Then he hoists me onto a nearby chair and turns so his back is to me. "Hop on," he says over his shoulder.

In any other relationship or situationship I would ask approximately twelve-point-four clarifying questions. *Are you sure? Is this a good idea? Are you* sure *you're sure?*

But that's the beauty of this thing with Nick, even if it's almost over. I trust him to think things through before he says anything, and then to mean exactly what he says.

So I hike my dress up with a laugh and climb on (under the curious gaze of many of the ball's attendees) and I let him give me a piggyback ride on the winding path back to the cabin.

Out on the dance floor just a few minutes ago, Nick told me I'm perfect. Even though I'm far from it, I wish more than anything that I could be good enough to deserve Nick Goodman.

IS IT NEW YEARS YET?
Holly

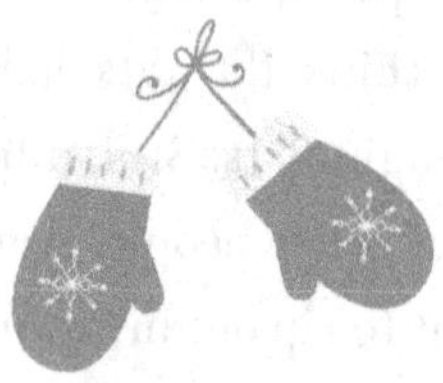

IN A MOMENT OF weakness, I slip into the blue lingerie while Nick retrieves two bottles of water from the refrigerator downstairs. Considering I was crying half an hour ago, then giddily catching snowflakes on my tongue while he carried me on his back from the lobby to the cabin, he is, needless to say, taken aback by this sudden venture to shy and sultry vesture.

His eyes widen as he pushes the door closed behind him with his foot. "Wow," he says, frozen. "I—uh— *Wow.*"

"Is it too much? It's too much. Damn it. I'm sorry." I pull the icy-blue satin robe that completes the set closed around my waist, fumbling with the slippery belt.

Nick sets the waters on the nightstand, then catches my hands. "There is no such thing as too much of you, Holly."

My heart melts, and I'm pretty sure it threatens to come out of my eyes again. But Nick presses his forehead against mine and slides his hands to my hips. I fidget with his tie; the knot is already loosened.

"Are you sure you're okay?"

In time, I'm sure I will be. If I don't find someone else who lets me be exactly who I am, I'm sure I'll forget what it feels like to have found someone who does. I'm sure I can numb myself to this feeling of being special and alive and make an average, respectable life for myself with someone who loves parts of me and puts up with the rest.

I offer what reassurance I can muster, carried on a smile that threatens to crack when I think about tomorrow. "I'm better than okay. I'm with you."

And then Nick kisses me. He kisses me like he's full of promises and hope and joy that all involve me, like he's already missing me. Like he loves me.

I press a hand to his sternum and feel the steady thumping of his heart, and then I undo one of his buttons. Then another. Then the rest.

We move together toward the bed, knees bumping into knees, mouths and noses colliding. He sits and pulls me against him; his fingers are woven into my hair and his breath is ragged. I reach for his glasses. "No," he says, biting his lip. "I don't want to miss anything."

With a hard swallow and a tightness in my chest, I trace my fingers along the stubbled line of his jaw, his Adam's apple, his shoulder, because if I'm going to be left with nothing more than a memory of him, I don't want to miss anything either.

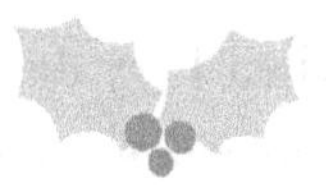

"You really should go to breakfast with your family."

Nick's knuckles brush over my arm, and his voice is muffled by his cheek being pressed into the top of my head. "I don't want to leave this bed. Or you *in* this bed. Or you, at all."

The words sting, because I know what happens next. "*Go.* You need some carbs. Or protein." I shrug against his chest. "Who knows. I'm not a nutritionist."

He chuckles and brushes a kiss across my lips. "And you're sure you don't want anything?" He rolls over and out of bed, then pulls on a pair of jeans and a basic henley from the closet.

"All I want is more sleep," I lie with a groan that I hope will make it seem like the truth.

He stands barefoot in the bathroom doorway while he brushes his teeth. "I'll bring you back a muffin. Lemon blueberry? Or did you want to try the orange and cranberry?"

If he wasn't so thoughtful, this wouldn't be nearly as hard. Who remembers such a specific favorite muffin flavor? And in such a short amount of time? "Surprise me." I force a smile, but the best I can produce is a tiny twitch in my lips.

Nick forgoes socks and slips into his shoes, then twists a scarf around his neck. His hair is perfectly disheveled and he kisses me once more before he leaves. "Promise me you'll be right here when I get back."

I straighten his glasses on his nose. "Enjoy your breakfast, Just Nick."

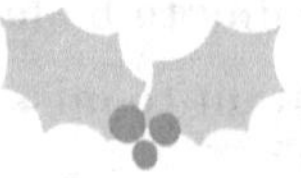

I try driving in silence. Then I try driving with screamy 'music' playing. Then I drive in silence again. I am neither deserving of nor in the mood for festive, feel-good holiday songs. But the silence stings, because it allows my brain to focus on the words I left behind for Nick; nothing more than excuses about how it's not him, it's me. Drivel about *finding myself* when I know that I have never been more found or seen than I was these past few weeks.

But the lies needed to be told, because if Nick Goodman knew the real reason why I had to leave, he would live up to his name and take the fall for the whole mess.

I pull over twice because I can't see the road through my tears.

I turn my cell phone off after the third missed call from Nick, then think better of it in case there's an emergency. When I stop to refuel, I block his number. And then I block Clara's, just in case.

My stomach growls ten minutes after leaving the gas station, which is what puts me over the edge. I'm sure there are two muffins in a bag somewhere, just waiting for me to claim them, because Nick Goodman is the kind of guy that gets you the seasonal flavor that sounds really good *and* your trusty favorite, just in case.

And then I curse Mark Thompson's name for an hour until I get home, see half a dozen familiar cars parked near the house, and curse my timing and our giant family lunch. Then I text Jasmine.

Are you busy?

Never too busy for you. Pepper & Pour?

See you in twenty.

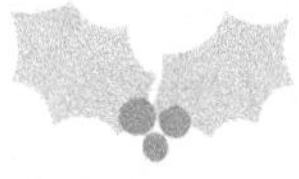

Jasmine is shockingly level-headed about the entire ordeal when I explain it to her.

"You could have told me it was too much, Hol. My mom can cover the shower, and I don't need a huge bachelorette getaway."

"Yeah, but you've been talking about it for months."

"I talk about a lot of things, but that doesn't mean I need or get them all. If that was the case I'd be sitting here with a Fendi Baguette and not a Coach clutch."

Someday we'll have a conversation about how normal people live—that is to say, without three-hundred-dollar handbags—but today we are focused on my broken heart and the mess I've made of things.

I swipe my hands through the air in front of me. "I didn't ask to meet up to talk about the money."

"Right. We're here because you walked out on the man you love and you're trying to figure out how to get him back."

"Or—counterpoint—we're here because I'm sad and people spend time with their friends to be less sad."

Jasmine nods slowly, considering this. "Okay, I'm on board. But for the record, I just want to say that I really hate Mark Thompson."

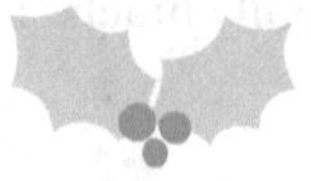

My spirits are slightly lifted by my afternoon appetizers with Jasmine, and then I get home.

Mom is cleaning up from lunch in the kitchen, and I abandon my bags in the doorway to offer my help with dishes. I feel a little guilty that I could have been here for the family gathering but wasn't.

"Hey, kiddo. How was your trip?"

There is no use lying to my mom; she always finds out the truth, and it's always been better for me if I tell her the truth on my own—and fast. But I try to hide the truth now, at least for a little, anyway. "We had a lot of fun." That part is true. We *did* have a lot of fun, until we didn't.

She smiles. "I'm glad."

With my sleeves rolled up I ferry platters from the table to the sink, box up whatever leftovers I can scrape out of casserole dishes, and dry everything Mom washes by hand. I fill her in on the ice skating, on the revelation that there was a ball, the tradition of opening gifts on vacation in matching pajamas, on the panic of not having any gifts with me to share and the fortuitousness of finding the perfect things for each member of the family—Mark, unfortunately, included.

"You always had a knack for that," she says as she drains the soapy water from the sink. "You'll have to invite Nick over for Christmas morning, if his family isn't doing something together. I picked up a few things for him, and I'd love for him to join us if it's not a hassle."

This is when I lose it. When the dam breaks and the emotions I've been walling up inside come flooding out. "I don't think that's going to happen."

Mom takes one look at me and grasps my shoulders with her still-wet forearms. "Honey, what happened?"

There is no use lying to my mom. So I tell her the two things that I know are true, that tell her all the basics in seven little words. "I love him. And I ruined everything."

I Need You Christmas

Nick

GOING TO WORK ON an average Monday is a challenge; harder still the day after a vacation. But it's damn near impossible when you've spent the last twenty-four hours subsisting on a diet of questions and a break-up letter that does nothing to answer any of them. And yet, sleep-deprived and red-eyed, I find myself at my desk on time. I can't say the same for Garrett, who waltzes in twenty minutes late and immediately claps me on the back and motions for me to follow him to the break room.

"So? How was it, man?" he asks as he shoves his mug under the dispenser of the coffee machine and pushes a button to brew his selected pod.

"Which part?"

He cocks his head and studies me, his brow pinched.

With a sigh, I offer an explanation. "The beginning was great. The middle was great. We went ice skating, we walked through the woods with birds. She and my family got along great—"

"Except for Mark?"

I roll my eyes. "*Even* Mark."

"Bro." He smacks my shoulder before gripping it and pointing a finger at me with more seriousness than I would expect. "Marry her. Marry her *right now.*"

"Well, that might be a little challenging, considering I think we broke up."

"No way, dude!"

I switch places with Garrett and start the brew cycle for my own coffee. "Yes way, dude."

"Oh, that *sucks*." He nearly sloshes hot liquid right over the side of his cup when he slaps my back apologetically.

"What sucks?"

Catherine somehow seems immune to both Mondays and mornings. Her hair is perfect, her makeup is pretty, and her outfit is polished. Unlike Garrett, who's wearing wrinkled khakis and a solid black sweater with (what I'm assuming is) powdered sugar on the arm.

"Oh, uh—" I shift my eyes to Garrett with the misguided belief he might offer assistance.

Instead he blurts out, "Dude got dumped on his romantic getaway."

I glare at him, mouth agape at this "bro"-betrayal, and he simply panic-shrugs and bolts out the door.

"Wow." Catherine clears her throat and drops her gaze to her feet. "That sounds terrible."

"Yeah. It is."

"Not to overstep, but can I ask what happened?"

I sigh and take my mug, stepping aside so she can access the coffee maker. "I wish I could tell you, but I don't really know. I thought things were great, and then all of a sudden she was gone."

How she managed to pack and write a note and sneak out in the time it took me to eat an omelet, I'll never understand. I've read and reread the note at least two dozen times, and I still don't understand *why* she did it, either.

"I'm really sorry, Nick." She tucks her hair behind her ear and takes a step closer to me. "If you need someone to talk to, maybe we could meet up for coffee sometime. Or drinks after work, maybe."

I am not an expert on flirting, but this feels like it. My pulse quickens at the realization that Catherine, on whom I have had a crush for the better part of a year, is *flirting* with me. Inviting me for a coffee date or happy hour. And I know that I should feel thrilled; I should feel relieved. I should take the win and feel grateful the plan worked. Catherine never showed an interest in me before and now, thanks to Holly, *she* is asking *me* out for coffee or drinks.

And yet when I look at her, all put together and perfect in front of me in pointy-toed shoes and a crisp emerald-green shirt and black skirt, I don't feel any of those things.

All I feel is empty.

CHRISTMAS LIGHTS
Holly

LANDON IS, WITHOUT A doubt, the best brother of all time. Not that I'm the biggest hockey fan in the world (and I still don't understand any of their fouls or penalties or whatever they're called), but I really like going to the occasional Ferryton Falcons game. Landon buys two tickets to Tuesday's game—Christmas Eve eve—and then forces me to stop moping so I can go with him.

"It'll be good for you to have some fun."

I think what he means is, *'It'll be good for you to have a reason to get off the couch and shower.'*

The game will also be a good opportunity to pick his brain a bit so I can find him the perfect Christmas gift. I'm out of time, and I need an idea tonight to even have a shot at finding him something he wants in the Christmas Eve crowd tomorrow.

Rather, the game *would* be a good opportunity to pick his brain, but he calls me from work twenty minutes before we're supposed to leave the house to drive to the arena.

"I'm sorry. We ran into a huge coding issue earlier that we need to fix, and we're not even close."

If ever there was a reason to curl up on the couch to watch horror movies with a half gallon of chocolate chip cookie dough ice cream,

I think that your own brother ditching you after your ex-boyfriend blackmails you into real-dumping your fake boyfriend is a great one.

"Before you even think about bailing on the game, just know that I have summoned reinforcements, so you still need to leave in twenty."

"Reinforcements?" My chest tightens, hoping it is and praying it isn't Nick.

"Don't worry," Landon says, which means it isn't. "And you'd better snag me one of the free Mac Bernard bobble heads. They're handing them out to the first three thousand fans. I wouldn't normally support fighting with children, but if it's between you and a toddler, just remember you're bigger than they are."

I know he's joking, and I roll my eyes. I don't know much about the sport or the team, but I've heard so much about Mac Bernard since he joined the team two seasons ago that I could co-author one of those "Who Is..." children's books about him. "Twenty minutes, meet a mystery guest, fight a child for a free thing. Got it."

"Cool. I'll send you your ticket now. Have fun!" And then the line goes dead.

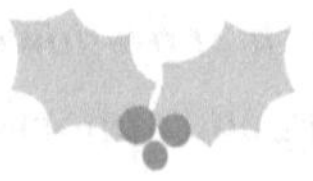

Jasmine, who knows less about hockey than I do, is waiting on the plaza outside the arena when I show up. Her bedazzled Falcons sweatshirt shimmers in the bright white of the shoebox lights around the plaza, and I'm not surprised to see she's wearing a full face of makeup and heeled booties on her feet.

"Surprise!" She throws her arms around me. "Twice in one week! It's like college all over again."

"But with fewer Jell-O shots."

She chuckles and scans my outfit, which includes black leggings with sneakers and Landon's Bernard jersey, which I'd seen draped over the chair in his bedroom as I passed by just before leaving the house. "So you're, like, actually a fan?"

I shrug. "I like the games. I stole this from Landon, though. He just doesn't know it." I link my arm through hers and start tugging her toward the security line. "Let's go in. If I don't bring home a bobblehead, I might not live to see Christmas."

A few minutes later, the four of us (Jasmine, me, and two plastic Mac Bernards) are seated right behind the glass—and right next to the Falcons' bench.

"Wow. Landon really splurged on these tickets."

"I think he wanted me to be so focused on the pucks flying at my face that I couldn't focus on being miserable."

"Or—" Jasmine gestures toward the bench, where some players are chatting with the coach while others warm up on the ice, "he wanted you to be so focused on the hot professional athletes that you couldn't be miserable."

As if the universe bends to her will, one player takes off his helmet, shakes out his blond curls and runs his fingers through his not-yet-sweaty hair.

"Mac!" Jasmine yells, jumping out of her seat and waving, and Mac Bernard and his glorious head of hair turn toward us.

He smiles and waves before Jasmine yells again to ask for his autograph on her bobblehead.

There are a few children behind us who are far more prepared than we are, and after they get their own bobbleheads signed, they let us borrow their Sharpie. Mac signs both dolls, then looks at my jersey. "Want me to sign that, too?"

"That would be awesome! Thanks!" My cheeks burn red and I turn around so he can sign the number stitched onto the back. "My little brother is your biggest fan, but he couldn't come tonight. He's going to be so jealous that he missed this."

Mac caps the marker and passes it back to the kids behind us. "Tell you what. I'll make sure he gets a little something special before the game's over."

"Oh, I mean—" I want to tell him that a signature on his lucky jersey is probably good enough, but Jasmine can never say no to a gift.

"Thanks, Mac. Have a great game!"

And he does. Mac scores twice in the first period and has an assist in the second. He out-skates the defense and puts pressure on the goalie and gets the crowd excited and loud.

Jasmine and I visit the concourse during the second intermission in search of soft pretzels and moonshine cocktails, dividing and conquering to get back to our seats in time for the third period.

And it's there, waiting for pretzels, that I see a familiar face.

"Hey, Holly." And when he picks up on my curious expression he adds, "Garrett. I work with—"

"Yeah, sorry. Hi."

The tiny woman next to him, who seems a little tipsy, leans toward me with growing eyes. "You're Holly? *Nick's* Holly?"

Garrett and I exchange a glance, and I wonder if he's heard the news yet. "This is Catherine," Garrett says. Catherine.

"Ah. I didn't realize you two were—"

"We're not. A couple of us from work thought we'd check out the game."

My breath hitches and I scan the crowd, like all of a sudden Nick will be there in the middle of the concourse crowd with a spotlight shining on him like he's Gabriella in the stands of a high-stakes Wildcats basketball game.

"He's not here," Garrett tells me. "He's been a little bummed yesterday and today."

"A *little?!*" Catherine screeches, indignant. We shift forward in the stuffed pretzel line. "He's all sulky and gloomy. He didn't even eat the cake they brought in for Tammy's birthday yesterday."

"I mean, that's not that unusual, is it?" Garrett asks.

Catherine and I exchange a look like *'Who turns down cake?'* and I smile, aware for a moment that in an alternate universe we might have been friends. But we're in *this* universe—the one where I fell for a man who hired me to get to her, because he liked *her,* wanted to be with *her.*

"It was triple chocolate, from Sweet Tooth, and you know that's his favorite."

Garrett chuckles. "I'm proud to say I had *no idea* that's his favorite."

Catherine blushes, and everything is suddenly clear. "You should ask him out," I say. And then, because I know how awkward that is to say about a man I just supposedly dumped, "He talked a lot about you."

She answers with a snort, then covers her mouth with her hand. "Okay, I know this sounds ridiculous or desperate or whatever, but I *did.* Yesterday."

"Oh." The idea that Nick would move on so quickly somehow stings and soothes at the same time.

"Yeah. And he shot me down, so..." Catherine bites her lip.

I order my pretzels and pay in a haze, wondering why Nick would turn down the very thing he's wanted for so long.

"Holly!" Jasmine's voice rings out over the crowd. She's across the concourse and hoists our cocktails in the air in victory. "It's starting soon!"

"I have to go." I grab the pretzel bag when it's handed to me. "Nice to meet you and see you again," I tell Nick's coworkers, and then I bound off toward my friend, ready to escape the whole situation.

I couldn't tell you how many goals are scored or how many times the fans boo the refs or whether we sing *Don't Stop Believin'* or *Sweet Caroline* during the third period, because Nick turned down a date with Catherine.

And I can barely process how excited I should feel when the game is over and Mac Bernard hands me a signed game-used stick, because Nick turned down a date with Catherine.

And I forget for a moment that I'm sad, and I hug my friend goodbye without the energy she deserves, and I drive to a house that isn't mine, because *Nick* turned down a date with *Catherine.*

Like a creeper (but without the creepy intentions), I park across the street from Nick's house and turn off my headlights so I don't draw too much attention to my idling car. And then I just look. I look at the house where Nick and I reviewed our faux relationship history before the party, the place where we practiced kissing. The driveway where I picked him up nearly a week ago, on our way to our romantic escape after he thoroughly charmed my grandma. The front door that I carried a giant potted Christmas tree through.

Then the window, where a tiny tree wrapped in colorful lights illuminates the dark room beyond it.

And the railing along the front steps, wound in matching multi-color strings.

And the lawn where an inflatable mug of hot cocoa rustles ever so slightly in the winter wind.

I didn't notice it last week in the daylight when we were in a hurry to pack the car and start our trip, but I notice it now—every last thing. Even down to the sprig of mistletoe hanging above the door.

Nick loved me. I'm sure of it. And when the sight of a home where we should spend the holidays laughing and snuggled on his couch, exchanging gifts by his potted tree, becomes too much, I turn my headlights on, wipe my tears, and drive home.

SANTA DOESN'T KNOW YOU LIKE I DO

Holly

HOCKEY STICKS ARE NOTORIOUSLY (or maybe, not notoriously enough) hard to wrap, so I enlist Dad's help with finding a giant box to put the signed Bernard stick in to disguise it. He finds a refrigerator box, and frankly, I think that's my best option.

Luckily it's lightweight, so Mom and I can easily maneuver it around the living room while I use two full rolls of gift wrap to cover it in paper that had me laughing out loud in the store. (I'm sorry, but it's covered in Santa hat-wearing T-Rexes with gingerbread men in their hands, looking flustered that they can't get the cookies to their mouths, and a little word bubble with *'phew'* coming from each confection, and it's incredible.)

Once we have it shoved into the corner and surrounded by a plethora of other, smaller gifts, we clean up our wrapping supplies and take in the merry little scene of our living room. Misshapen tree? Check. LEGO gingerbread house assembled on the mantle? Check. Stockings hung? Presents wrapped? Throw pillows thrown? Check, check, and check. We're ready.

"Once again, Holly Grace, I think you're going to win Christmas." Mom crosses her arms over her chest as she surveys the room.

"One would argue that you guys are the real winners," I reply with a wink.

She bumps her shoulder into mine. "You should start a personal shopper service or something."

"Ha," I laugh on an exhale. "Right."

"I'm serious! There are so many people who have no idea where to start when it comes to gift giving, and even though it should be easy to find things online with the whole retail world at your fingertips, who has the time to sift through hundreds of sites and reviews and determine what's legitimate, what's garbage, what meets the criteria in the right budget? Having someone to do all that for you? That's a convenience I bet a lot of people would pay for."

She kisses my cheek and picks up her book from the end table. "I'm going to take a relaxing bubble bath, and then do you want to bake cookies so we can eat them during a cheesy movie and spoil our appetite before dinner?"

I give Mom a smile, and I don't even have to force it. "I'd love to."

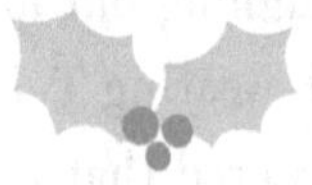

Landon gets home from work while dinner is in the oven, and I obnoxiously bother him pretty much from the moment he walks in the door. However, we've silently agreed that this is acceptable, since I have given him a signed bobblehead and returned his lucky jersey with a matching autograph. Once he opens his gift tomorrow, I'm pretty sure he would forgive me if I microwaved his laptop just for fun.

But today's task is reasonable, and I don't think it'll take all that much work, because the foundation has been in place and tested for months.

"What's up?" he asks, dropping his messenger bag on the floor by his desk.

"I need your help."

"For my favorite sister? Anything. Almost anything."

For a long time, I've been unhappy with myself. And not just because I've felt like a failure in relationships, or because I couldn't find a job in my field, or because when I had a job that got me closer to my professional goals I got fired because rich people didn't want to cut golf from the budget, and I allowed myself to feel like that was my fault.

No, I've been unhappy because I've felt like I haven't done any-thing positive in any aspect of my life in a while. But seeing the decorations at Nick's house last night, getting Landon the perfect Christmas gift, spending time with Mom today, seeing the look on Grandma's face when we visited on her birthday... It all makes me feel like I've had a larger, more positive impact than I'd realized; like I've put my psychology degree to work after all, in meaningful, special ways.

That's why I plop myself onto the corner of his bed while he takes out his laptop and sits in his office chair, swiveling around to face me. And with great conviction I tell him the plan I've had in my head all afternoon.

"I need to change the Holly Dates site."

Christmas Isn't Canceled (Just You)

Nick

I APPRECIATE THAT MY family has allowed me to wallow without criticism for the bulk of the week, but Christmas morning is the expiration date on my self-pity.

Even though we spend most of the day at our family's houses, my parents always start us off with breakfast at their place, followed by the ceremonial opening of stocking stuffers, and then we carpool the rest of the day—first to my aunt and uncle's house, then to my grandparents' old rancher.

Personally, I think the carpooling is less about the lack of parking that my parents claim ails each neighborhood and is more about holding us hostage so we can't bail early when our uncle starts talking about the 'good old days' or when my cousin tries to get us all signed up for her MLM scheme.

This year there will be no exceptions made for heartbroken brothers, for sullen sons. This year there will be cinnamon rolls and sausage and stockings and Mom and Dad and Clara and Mark and me, and there will be joy and smiling until we leave the last house, and then I can go back to being grumpy.

These, of course, are my rules, because my family shouldn't have to put up with a Scrooge with no redemption arc on their favorite holiday just because I made a mistake and hired a stranger to pretend to be my girlfriend to impress someone else.

I get to Mom and Dad's first, and there's already a pot of coffee brewed and waiting.

"You're allowed to talk about it, you know," Mom says, leaning over the kitchen island and sipping from her own mug. "Even today."

I add cream to my mug and swirl it until there's a white hurricane pattern across the black-brown surface of coffee. "Merry Christmas to you, too."

"Merry Christmas. And you're allowed to be sad. You don't have to act like you're magically better after four days just for our sake. If you remember, we all liked her, and we all love you."

She pats my shoulder and navigates toward the front door when it opens. Clara and Mark shuffle in out of the cold, and after a brief greeting, my sister makes a beeline for the kitchen. She looks left and right and then at me.

"Damn. I was hoping she'd be here."

"You and me both."

"I don't get it, Nicky." Clara takes out a mug and a glass, fills the latter with ice from the refrigerator door, and pours coffee into both. She passes the hot coffee to Mark and pours flavoring from a tiny bottle in her purse into her iced coffee, then adds cream and takes a sip. "You guys were so great together."

Mark snorts into his coffee, and Clara whips her head toward him.

"What was that for?"

Mark swallows and has the good sense to look slightly ashamed, though like the moron he is, he quickly hides it in favor of a more defiant approach to the conversation.

"Oh, come on. You guys really think that Nick and this mystery girl, who you all didn't even meet until a few weeks ago, were madly in love? *Really?*"

Well, when he puts it that way...

"Yes." I can say it confidently, because I know how I felt. I know how I still feel. And I know that this kind of hurt doesn't come when something fake ends. You don't feel this kind of pain at the end of a movie or a book or a TV show you've watched for fourteen seasons. You only feel this pain when you're mourning something or someone you truly loved.

"I still don't understand why she left," Mom says. "And with nothing more than a note?"

I shrug, unable to share all the specifics with my family. "She just said she needed to move on and find herself before she can be in a relationship." She also told me to be myself with Catherine, that I am perfectly lovable just as I am. That part hurt the most: I'm *perfectly lovable,* but the woman I love doesn't love me.

"Gimme a break." Mark rolls his eyes, taking his whole head along on the ride. "She left you because she's a *fraud.*"

Mom, Clara, and I exchange a glance. In their eyes I see hesitation and disbelief, and I hope they don't see in mine the paralyzing fear I feel.

"She dates losers for money, and she somehow tricked you into—" He cuts himself off and slaps the granite island. "Holy shit. *You hired her.*"

Clara groans. "What are you talking about?"

I'd tricked myself into thinking that if Holly and I worked out, our origin story would be a funny tale to eventually tell our families. And if we didn't work out, then there would be no need to tell it, because the job would be over and there would be little talk of that girl I dated once upon a time.

But now Mark is preparing to shine a light on all of it, because somehow he knows. "I had no idea *you* actually *paid* her. I thought you were just some sucker that she tricked for fun, or that Garrett hired so you wouldn't seem so lame."

"Don't talk about my brother that way." Clara glowers at him.

Because Mark is an asshole, he makes a *shoo*-ing motion with his hand toward Clara, who takes a step back, her jaw dropped.

"Don't be a jerk to my sister."

"Whatever. Look. I can prove it." Mark picks up his cell phone, and I feel the color drain from my face. "I thought it was self-preservation, you know? Like she was trying to avoid getting caught. But it looks like she conned herself, had a soft spot for you. Left to save you the embarrassment."

"How do you know all this?" Puzzle pieces swirl in my head like leaves and ghosts in *This is Halloween*, which is fitting, because this feels a lot like a nightmare before Christmas. Piece by piece they fall into place and lock together. "Holly and I—"

"I gave her a choice, and she chose to leave." He snickers and taps his phone's screen before passing it to Clara. "Not that it matters, because you're all learning the truth now anyway."

The last puzzle piece clicks into place, and the picture is complete. My heart yo-yo's between my stomach and my throat and I ball my hands into fists that I know I'll never swing. "*You* did this?" I knew Mark was awful, but I had no idea he would sink to the level where he blackmailed Holly and drove her out of my life.

His smug smirk is all the response I need.

"I don't understand..." Clara narrows her eyes at the phone, looks up at me, and passes the device my way.

"I can explain," I reply, taking the phone. Mom and Clara look at me expectantly while Mark drinks his coffee, still smirking. I look down at the display and realize I, in fact, can *not* explain. What's in front of me is something completely different than what I thought I'd see.

In the search bar, I type in the address of the Holly Dates website, and I'm redirected to the same page Clara had shown me: Shop-A-*Holly*c.

And there's a picture of Holly, her arms full of gift wrap, a Christmas bow in her hair, and bold words at the top of the webpage:

Finding the perfect gift? That's a wrap.

I exhale, relieved, and feel my lips form their first smile since Sunday morning.

"What?" Mark demands, stealing his phone from my hands and actually looking at the screen. "No—this isn't— It used to be—" He taps at the screen and types with his thumbs, and then swallows and frowns. "She changed it."

Eventually I will tell my family the full truth, but for now I am ready to bolt out the door and drive to her parents' place, where I know she was planning to spend the holiday.

"You should go," Clara says, and Mom nods. And then, as I swipe my keys from the corner of the counter, I hear her voice darken, and she adds, "*Both* of you."

Underneath the Tree
Holly

It's not altogether difficult to put on a happy face Christmas morning. There's so much energy and excitement in Mom and Dad's modest house when Ian and Micah come home, and a platter of cookies and mugs of frothy hot cocoa being passed around to the soundtrack of upbeat instrumental music creates a festive—dare I say *merry*—little Christmas.

With the stress of the Holly Dates site gone and two inquiries already for Shop-A-*Holly*c, I feel good. At the very least, I feel okay. Which is a huge change from yesterday's 'almost not miserable.'

We're crowded into our living room, ripping open paper from the gifts in stockings Mom and Dad still fill for us. We all get things like our favorite candies, some scratch-off lottery tickets, and other trinkets. Micah gets funky dress socks and I get flavored lip gloss; Ian gets some goop that is supposed to clean his dashboard and Landon gets a wireless charger for his cell phone with the Ferryton Falcons logo on it.

Once we clean up the first round of shredded paper and organize our gifts so nothing gets misplaced in the forthcoming mayhem, it's time to open individual presents. This is the part of Christmas I live for—even this year, when I feel like most of my presents are lacking.

Ironic, considering the website I launched late last night, but with such a restricted budget I did the best I could.

Anyway, Micah loves his cologne, just like always. And Ian gives a hearty *'Let's go'* when he opens a signed art print from an artist he's been following since last year's Comic-Con. And Mom and Dad seem at least intrigued by a gift card I give them.

"You asked if there was room for two more on my trip to Hope's Knoll. Trust me—you'll love it. And you deserve a weekend away."

"It's too much—" Mom protests, but the doorbell cuts her off. "Who on earth could that be?"

"Probably a telemarketer," Ian says, his mouth full of chocolate chip cookie.

"On Christmas?" Micah asks.

"In person?" Landon arches an eyebrow at our brothers.

No one makes an immediate move toward the door, probably because it entails crossing a sea of tissue paper and boxes, but when the knocking starts Mom rises and shouts "Coming!"

Though curious about who would possibly be visiting on Christmas day, I'm more intrigued by the peanut butter cookies we made last night, and I sneak one from the tray.

Landon keeps trying to guess what I got for him (his ideas include a life-size robot, an inflatable hot tub, and a gift card to The Pancakery, and he keeps asking 'What's in the box?' in the same dramatic fashion as Brad Pitt in *Seven*), but Mom interrupts our exchange.

"Uh, Holly? It's for you."

She takes a step back, and Nick Goodman warily enters my parents' home.

"Hey." He gives a little wave and scratches the back of his neck. "I'm sorry to interrupt."

I jump up from my seat. "No! No, it's fine. We were just opening presents."

"Right. I was hoping we could talk, but I should come back later."

"Now's good." I sound a little over-eager, considering I left him a note that practically said I wasn't in love with him and I wasn't looking for a relationship. But right now, I don't care. I *am* eager. I've been missing Nick all week. Seeing him now is like spending three days on a sugar-free diet and then being handed a platter of donuts. I know I shouldn't want him, and I know it's bad for me, but I'm taking every last morsel I can get.

Nick's eyes shift around the room at our audience, so I pick my coat out of the half dozen that hang on the coat tree inside the door, slip my feet into a pair of loosely laced sneakers, and follow him out onto the front porch.

"Despite the excitement in my voice that I'm doing a really terrible job of hiding, I really don't think you should be here."

"Is that so?" He lowers himself onto an old wooden swing while I pace the length of the porch.

Flurries have started falling, and the neighborhood is full of glowing lights against a backdrop tinted white. And Nick Goodman is here, on my porch, with me. Maybe it's *actually* a wonderful life and I'm having a Mary Bailey moment, because part of me wants to shout *'It's a miracle!'* thirty-seven times.

"I told you in my letter that I needed to move on."

"I know you did." His voice is even, which is typically calming for me. But now it just makes me feel like he's biding his time until some big reveal, and after the last few days I'm not a huge fan of surprises.

I pause at the opposite end of the porch and cross my arms. "I don't understand why you're here, Nick. I thought you wanted to be with Catherine. That's why you hired me. Now our little charade is over, and you can ask her out and be happy."

"Well, here's the thing." Nick's breath comes out in tiny puffs, and my mind flashes back to the night when he stood outside O'Donnell's waiting for me. Then to the night of the ball, when Nick carried me on his back the whole way from the lobby to the cabin. Tiny puffs of air, of laughter and promises, floating up and away into the sky. "Just like you promised, you broke my heart so epically that Catherine took pity on me and asked me out less than twenty-four hours after you left."

"Great! Then I did my job." I want to wipe my hands clean of everything related to the Holly Dates site.

"I told her no."

I've known for days that he told her no, but it still catches me off guard to hear him say it. "Why would you do that?"

With a shrug, and with a step away from the swing and toward me, Nick meets my eyes. Holds my gaze. Reads me like I'm one of Ian's comics. "We both know that what I want now is different from what I wanted then."

My breath hitches, and he takes another cautious step closer. I shouldn't be bold right now. I shouldn't ask questions if the answers are going to break me. But I was robbed of the opportunity to hear Nick say—and mean—the words I've been longing to hear, so even though they're going to hurt—even though I might as well be agreeing to wear LEGO flip-flops for the remainder of my days on this planet—I ask the question.

"What changed?"

"I did." A smile grows on Nick's lips and even through his foggy lenses I can see his bright, clear eyes. "I changed because of you. Because you brought a tsunami of joy into my life, and yet I feel like I've been drowning without you. Because you showed me what it's like to live free and be indiscriminately generous in so many ways, and because I had never even let myself believe that I could be as happy as I was when I was with you, and then I lived it, and I'm a believer."

And then he holds out his hands in an invitation, and I accept. I slide my palms into his, which are as icy cold as mine. The touch sends waves of heat straight to my heart, which pumps it to every limb, and soon I don't feel cold at all. I only feel happiness.

"At first I felt like I had to tell you I loved you so people would buy our story, but at some point 'I love you' wasn't just something I said. It was something I felt. Something I *knew*."

"Nick..."

He slides closer to me and I'm rendered speechless (alert the media!) by the look in his eyes. "If I've misread everything, tell me. I know it's improbable, and it's fast, and maybe you don't want to label it as 'love,' which is fine. But we had something real, didn't we? Can you just tell me you at least felt *something* real?"

All I want is to tell him exactly that. In every language possible, in poetry, in music, with actions and kisses and tears. But then doubt creeps in, and it's wearing a Mark Thompson mask, and I know that if he knows the truth, I can't be with Nick without destroying his reputation with his family, his coworkers, and his friends.

The wintery cold stings my teary eyes as I take one long, final look at him, take a calming breath, and shake my head. "I'm sorry, Nick. I just can't."

LITTLE SAINT NICK
Holly

"You can't?" Nick sucks in a breath, and all the color (save for the rosiness of his cheeks and the tip of his nose) drains from this face.

"Just trust me on this, okay?" I give his hands a squeeze, and he promptly pulls them away and runs them through his hair before readjusting his glasses. "I have very much enjoyed the last few weeks, but we just can't be together. It wouldn't be fair to you."

He balks at this, because of course he does. Because why wouldn't he, when he just told me he loves me and I'm telling him it 'wouldn't be fair' to give him what he wants—a matching 'I love you'—in return.

And then, inexplicably, his face softens. "Holly—"

"I really don't think—"

"Are you pushing me away because you really don't care for me, or are you pushing me away because Mark blackmailed you?"

I freeze. "What?"

"I found out this morning. It made for an awkward start to Christmas." When I don't move, he takes a hint and continues. "I was... well, full disclosure, I was wallowing. Very mopey, since the woman I love walked out unexpectedly without even taking the muffins I bought her."

He smiles, but I don't, so he goes on.

"Anyway, Mom and Clara basically tried to therapize me to figure out why you left without warning, and Mark goes into this whole thing about you dating losers for money—"

"That bastard." I should have known Mark wouldn't keep his word. It's bad enough he confronted Nick, but to do it in front of his mom and sister? Does his villainy know no end?

"Long story short, I love the new website." He beams at me sheepishly.

"He wasn't supposed to say anything. That was the deal—"

"If you make a deal with the devil, do you really expect the devil to keep his word? He's not exactly known for being a good guy, Holls."

Holls. There's that nickname again, the one I've heard from him a few times before, in worry, in whispers, and, apparently, in love.

"He told me there wasn't room for both of us, that he and I couldn't both be part of the Goodman family. That he didn't want me spending time with Clara. And that if I left he wouldn't tell anyone about Holly Dates."

I've started pacing again, but Nick rests his gently steadying hands on my shoulders. "I might have some good news for you."

"Yeah?"

He smiles and nods. "Yeah." And then he tells me the rest of the story, which really comes down to Clara kicking Mark out. "So Mark Thompson is a non-issue, as far as I'm concerned."

It gives me a glimmer of hope, and I dare to imagine that Nick and I could be together and be happy. But then there's the doubt—driven by Mark for more than a year, but plenty of others before him—that I couldn't put in the letter; that I couldn't really wrap my head around or put into words. It's a doubt that lives in my brain like a well-watered seed, taking root in my medial prefrontal cortex, growing like ivy, strangling my sense of self.

"What if you get tired of me?"

He exhales one beat of laughter. "I could never."

"But what if I sing too much in the car? Or I dance too much on sidewalks or I'm too loud? I don't even have a real job, and I live with my parents." Some part of me knows that *this* is the real reason why I let Mark win: because what's the point in letting everyone find out about our little arrangement and ruining Nick's reputation with everyone he cares about when we're not going to last, anyway?

"Holls." He smooths a thumb over my cheek and meets my eyes. "If you want to dance on sidewalks, I'll provide the music. I love that you sing in the car like you're a one-woman production of *Rent,* and that you remember details about children's books. I love that you care deeply about other people and that you say what you want and that you show up on doorsteps with potted trees and paint championship belts on ceramic mugs. How could I get tired of joy? And I don't care where you live, or what you do for work—I just want you to be happy doing it. Ideally, I want you to be happy doing all of it *with me.*"

Tears threaten to freeze in my eyelashes. Nick hasn't given me reason to doubt him yet. *I won't let you fall. I won't let you get hurt.* It might be too late for the first, but I'm going to trust him with the latter. I take a deep breath, letting winter fill my lungs, and I meet his gaze. "He's really gone? It's safe for us to be together?"

He kisses my forehead and wraps me in his arms. "Other than the impending frostbite, yes, we're safe."

"Come inside," I tell him. "If you can stay."

He takes my face in his hands and smiles down at me, then kisses my lips with a gentle ferocity that is the stuff of period romcoms and first-kiss dreams. "There's nowhere else I'd rather spend Christmas than right here next to you."

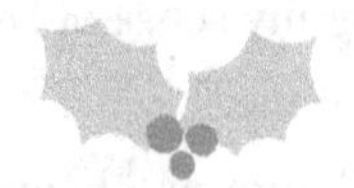

Nick might be regretting the whole 'nowhere else I'd rather spend Christmas' thing, because my brothers have been obnoxious since we walked in the door with frozen limbs but gooey, melty hearts. Landon has continued to harass me about his gift like I never even left the room, Ian starts grilling Nick on his 'intentions' with me, and Micah makes a show of deleting Mark from his contacts like this is the first he's hearing about Mark being the absolute worst.

I finally let Landon open his gift, and to no one's surprise he's obsessed with the signed stick. I get a few small things, and then one box with a tag that says it's from my whole family, and inside is an airline gift card that will cover the cost of a flight for Jasmine's wedding.

Having such a huge expense practically paid for is a relief. I don't normally find gift cards to be personal or special, but this one is absolutely perfect. It feels like a weight has been lifted from my shoulders, and with Nick next to me, his fingertips brushing my back, it feels like another has been lifted from my chest. Like I can breathe, and like I might float away on a wisp of winter wind.

Nick passes me a box he brought with him—a carefully but imperfectly wrapped rectangular box with a large gold bow—and under a layer of sparkly tissue paper I find a familiar Wilde Lake crest on a worn, heathered gray sweatshirt. *GOODMAN* is arced across the back in blocky white letters, and reflexively I bring it to my face. Sure enough, it smells just like Nick.

"I love it. Thank you."

"You're welcome." He brushes my hair back off my face and then wraps an arm around my waist while I snuggle my cheek to his shoulder, and we sit this way to watch the rest of my family open the remaining gifts.

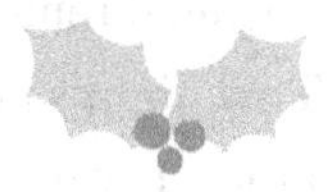

"I have one more present for you."

We're curled up on the couch together; he's stroking my hair while I cradle a mug of hot cocoa, which is basically just melted marshmallow sludge at this point. Mom has just retreated upstairs after a group viewing of one more cheesy holiday movie with an invitation for Nick to stay the night and a final *Merry Christmas* to us both.

So now it's just us, the TV turned to a crackling fire and jazzy Christmas instrumentals, and windows frosted with a fine dusting of snow.

"Oh you do, do you?" I ask, craning my neck to kiss him.

"Mmhmm." He stands and pulls a small box out of the pocket of his coat by the door. "Don't get too excited," he says when he sees me eyeing up the box, which is just the right size and shape for a piece of jewelry.

"Of course I'm excited. It's Christmas, and you're here."

"Good save, Holls." He winks, then kneels (on both knees, so calm yourself) next to the couch, and fidgets with the object in his hands. "The day of the ball, I went into town to try to find the perfect gift for you. Turns out, it didn't really exist. But I thought about the mug you made for Mom, and I was inspired to have something made just for you. I hope you like it."

And then I'm opening a box with a pair of earrings inside: two dangling earrings shaped like little sweater dresses, black, draped across the neckline with red, green, and gold dots that resemble garland.

Dumbfounded, I stare at the earrings. "They're exactly the same—"

"As the one you wore on our first 'date.'" He uses air quotes around the last word. "I wasn't sure if you'd remember."

"Of course I remember! That night's pretty impossible to forget."

His eyes crinkle with a smile. "I agree."

"You know what I remember most about that night?"

"Those little pies?"

"No, but now I really want one."

"Was it my incredibly sexy sweater?" He straightens his glasses and waggles his eyebrows, and I giggle like a tween with a crush.

"Not quite."

Nick drapes his arms across my knees and lets his chin rest at their intersection. "What, then?"

I think for a moment, remembering how—at the time—I thought I'd screwed everything up. But now I know that the part of that night that I thought was a mistake was exactly what led me to *this* night, to this incredible man in my house, his sweatshirt on my body, his chin in my lap, his eyes locked on mine.

"That's the night I said I had fallen in love with you."

"Ah, yes, I think I remember that," he says with the air of a man who remembers it, in fact, very well. A hopeful but wary smile crosses his lips.

"I feel like I'm supposed to say that I couldn't have guessed then how I would feel now, but I think I somehow knew. I think from that first meeting, from when you told me I'd been bitten by a snake in your fantasies—"

He interrupts defensively. "That's not quite what I—"

"Nicholas Goodman, are you going to let me tell you I'm in love with you or not?"

He stops, and he chuckles silently, and he nods. "Please. As many times as you'd like."

"Perfect." I tell him again, and I bend to kiss him, and he winds his fingers into my hair. "I love you, Nicholas Goodman," I say when we pause to catch our breath.

He rolls his eyes lovingly. "Holls, you know it's just Nick."

But I shake my head. "No. You're not *just* anything. You are absolutely everything."

He grins and kisses me again: gentle, slow, sweet as gingerbread and soft as marshmallows and comfortable as home.

The TV fire crackles and the snow glitters under streetlights outside and Christmas lights illuminate the corner of the room, and Nick Goodman is here, his arms around me, his cocoa-flavored lips pressed to mine, and *this*—this perfect night—is the best gift I could ever ask for.

KISS ME AT MIDNIGHT
Holly

It didn't take much convincing for me to agree to come up to Hope's Knoll with Nick for two nights; we deserve a do-over of the end of our last trip here. And while we don't have a cozy cabin on this visit, we also don't have someone trying to actively sabotage us, so I like to think this is an upgrade.

Instead, our room is perched on the top floor of the main hotel, and we've got a balcony that overlooks the lobby, which is now full of guests in tuxes and gowns attending the Midnight Masquerade.

I brought the same red dress I wore nearly two weeks ago, and I've gotten a bajillion compliments on it, though I think most of them were either because it was one of the only dresses in the room that wasn't black or silver or gold, or they were from Nick Goodman. And he *has* to compliment my dress, because he's—officially—my boyfriend. Which feels weird, considering we're adults and he's a *man*, but it sure sounds better than 'this guy I'm dating,' so we'll keep it.

Nick's wearing that same green velvet jacket he wore on our last visit, too, paired with a Phantom-style black and gold mask that makes me think I might have a weird Stockholm fetish, but that's something to explore later. Suffice it to say, the look works.

When I picked out my mask, I went with delicate black lace, which matched both my black lace heels and some other, unseen black lace apparel.

The heels are, of course, painful, and after an hour of dancing I decide a break is called for and flop onto a tufted leather chaise in the lobby while Nick gets us drinks. I take in the scene around me: the couples of all ages, the shimmering silvers and glistening golds of the banners and balloons spread around the lobby, the families in pajamas just passing through the lobby on their way between the kid-friendly pajama party and their rooms, and it's all so perfect, and right, and fun, and free.

And then I notice him. He's across the room, one drink in his left hand, taking a sip from the drink in his right. Our eyes meet, and he makes his way toward me.

I know I'm smiling like an idiot, but I don't care.

"Excuse me," he says. "Is this seat taken?" I shake my head and he passes me a drink as he lowers himself into the spot next to me.

"I'm sorry if this is too forward, but I spotted you from across the room, and I just couldn't take my eyes off you."

I tuck a rogue strand of hair behind my ear and blush unnecessarily. "I'm flattered, but I have a boyfriend."

"Is that so?" His grin is obvious, even with one corner hidden behind his mask. "I heard you were just dating him for show."

"Nope. I'm dating him because I'm madly in love with him."

"Madly, huh?"

I nod, and our smiles collide. Nick's hand on the small of my back is firm and warm and needy and protective, all at once. And his lips? They're perfect. Soft but greedy. Wanting. Mine.

"How much longer until midnight?" My heart is racing, and even though we spent a good chunk of the day twisted up in each other, I wouldn't mind spending a good chunk of the night that way, too.

Nick looks past me and checks the giant clock in the center of the lobby. "Still an hour until midnight."

"Damn it."

"You're not enjoying the party?"

"I am. But I think there are other things I'd enjoy more."

With a wink, Nick weaves his fingers into mine and jerks his head toward the elevator bank. "Let's go."

"I'm thinking of keeping this on all night. What do you think?"

Nick turns from the balcony door to face me, and I swear he nearly chokes on his drink. "It's definitely a choice."

"But is it a *good* choice?" I rotate for him like a rotisserie chicken, showing off the previously mentioned black lace, including the mask. Though I may have added a gray sweatshirt that we both know well.

"Holls. You can make any choice you want, just please keep choosing me."

Warmth courses through me. Warmth, like a crackling fire. Like a mug of Mrs. Goodman's hot cocoa. Like a cozy college sweatshirt or a pair of fuzzy socks or sandy beaches in the summer or a trip to the sun.

And I slip my mask off, because Nick doesn't want or need my disguises. He's chosen me exactly as I am. Unmasked, I affirm, "Always."

He bridges the distance between us in two steps and holds me, wrapping his arms around me, burying his face in the crook of my neck and in my hair.

Then he kisses me, his tongue dancing with mine, his hips pressed to mine, his heart hammering against mine. And he keeps kissing me, while the clock chimes twelve times and champagne corks pop below, while merry shouts swirl in the air around us and for minutes after.

We begin the new year the same way we end an old one: mid-kiss, together, and so very, improbably, and freely in love.

LIKE IT'S CHRISTMAS
Nick

I VERY MUCH ENJOY snowy winter mornings with Holly, waking up in flannel sheets and fuzzy blankets and drinking coffee and cocoa, and curling up in the evenings to watch action movies together or to read while we share a bottle of wine.

But being on a tropical island together? Waking up to a breeze rolling in off the waves and through billowing sheers, carrying the aroma of sea salt? Sun-kissed skin scented with coconut lotion, and staying out late to dance under the stars? This might be unbeatable.

"I should probably get going." She should—she has to meet Jasmine and the rest of the bridal party for hair and makeup in half an hour, but instead she's still sprawled facedown on the bed. "Who in their right mind schedules hair and makeup for 8 A.M. after a rehearsal dinner that only ended at eleven?"

"I'm not sure the 'eleven' is the problem, Holls." We got back to the room just after the dinner ended, but who are we to try to deny the gravitational pull of a moonlit night and the urging of a hibiscus flower in flowing, salt-waved hair, or the hint of a mojito on the lips of someone you love?

She groans, and I pass her a cappuccino that room service delivered five minutes ago. Once she's seated crosslegged on the pillowy mattress, I hand her the plate of fruit I ordered for her as well. "You're too good to me," she says as she picks up a grape.

"Nonsense."

She finishes some pineapple and the coffee, and now, caffeinated, she announces she's going to take a shower. "Join me?" she asks with a kiss on my cheek.

"Maybe later. You don't have that much time right now." (Yes, it takes great restraint to say no when she's got a sheet wrapped around her and bed-mussed hair.)

"Fine." She pouts, but she showers alone. I have her bridesmaid's dress and her emergency kit—all the things she swears are essential for her maid of honor duties—ready when she emerges from the bathroom in a flowy floral dress.

"Have fun."

She smiles wide, and I know she's looking forward to celebrating her best friend today. Even if it's early, even if it's been a long and costly journey to get here. And then she kisses me again, less chaste this time, and tells me she loves me before she bounds out the door.

Jasmine and Bradford, together with the resorts' wedding planners and their parents' bank accounts, know how to throw a party.

The ceremony takes place on a private portion of beach, with guests mostly in linen suits and pastel colors; the bridal party wears all white, save for sky-blue pocket squares in suit jackets that match the shade of the bridesmaids' bouquets perfectly. (Lest you worry about anyone losing the bride in a sea of white, I assure you, she was impossible to miss in a blinding, crystal-encrusted gown that reflected every ray of sunlight. Mostly into our eyes. A surefire way to guarantee everyone cries during the nuptials.)

Cocktail hour is on the sand as well: piña coladas and mojitos are passed around with honey-colored lagers in sweating glasses. I mingle with a few people throughout and try to catch glimpses of Holly through palm trees and privacy screens.

Finally at dinner, after a grand entrance featuring an intricately choreographed dance routine, she takes a seat next to mine in the brick-floored courtyard of the historic hotel and squeezes my hand as a greeting.

"Having fun?" she asks, and I nod.

"Absolutely. More importantly, are you?"

"The most. Though I need to write a letter complimenting the chemists behind my mascara, because it has *definitely* proven its waterproof-ness."

She holds my hand and rests her head on my shoulder during the speeches and toasts that follow her own, and we socialize during dinner, and then, finally, I get to wrap my arms around her waist on the dance floor and hold her close to me.

"Is it cheesy if I say I've missed you today?" I ask her with a kiss to her forehead.

"Yes. It absolutely is."

"Ah."

"I love cheese."

"Well then—" I twirl her once and pull her back in close. "I've missed you today. And I am very grateful to have you back here with me."

Old stone archways, draped with gauzy whites and gentle blues and twinkling lights, encircle us. The sun has started to set, and the sky is alight in pastel pinks and purples and streaks of gold. It is, in a word, stunning. And yet it pales in comparison to the woman in my arms, whose white dress floats around her as she spins, whose hair is perfectly imperfect after hours in the salty air, whose smile I'm still not sure how I've earned.

"What other responsibilities do you have, Madam Maid of Honor?"

She surveys the courtyard around us; Jasmine has changed out of her bejeweled ceremony dress into a white minidress covered in sequins, and she seems perfectly content dancing to, of all things, Chumbawamba's *Tubthumping*.

"I would say I am probably done, actually." She exhales like it's the first chance she's had to breathe all day.

And then she peers up at me, her smile going a little crooked, a little wicked, and she presses up on her toes until her forehead is against mine, and she whispers, "Wanna get out of here?"

Without waiting for an answer, she drags me through an archway into the encroaching night, the sky now blazing reds and violets, the sun low on the horizon. The water glistens.

We stand side by side, each with an arm around the other's waist. "I've always wanted to spend Christmas in a place like this," I say. "Away from the hustle and bustle, just relaxing on the beach."

"We could, if you really want to."

When I turn my attention from the water, I see her gazing up at me.

"Too presumptuous?" she asks. "Just planning a trip together that's eight months away?"

We've only been dating for four months, only known each other for five. And yet looking into a future that's longer than our past doesn't seem presumptuous. It seems joyful, hopeful, exciting. Possible. Incredible.

"No," I finally answer. "Not too presumptuous at all."

She smiles, then twitches with a shiver. I slide my sleeves out of my jacket and wrap it around her shoulders, and it instantly takes me back to that night at Hope's Knoll: the night everything changed and I just hadn't known it yet; the night before she left and I thought I'd never find that same spark, that same joy, again.

I turn my back toward her and say over my shoulder, "Hop on."

She pauses, and then a smile spreads across her lips before she hikes up her dress and climbs onto my back. Her thighs are warm in my palms, and I take off walking across the sand.

"Where are we going?" she asks as she tightens her arms around my neck and shoulders. She plants a kiss on the side of my neck.

"Not sure," I answer. But I carry her until we're far enough away from the party that the ocean is our soundtrack and the thumping of the bass is replaced by the beating of her heart against my back, until the water licks at my feet and I feel the burn in my legs from walking across the powdery sand.

And then I set her down, lay my jacket in the sand, and we sit, her in front of me, and just *be*. I nuzzle my nose into her neck, kiss her bare shoulder, and hold her in my arms, and we stay like this until the sky turns black with specks of stars.

And then, guided by the lights from the party still raging further up the shore, we trek back through sand so white and light it might as well be fresh-fallen snow, pausing briefly to take in the scene through an archway.

"You did it. You got here."

She sighs and leans against my side. "And all it took was dating a few duds, deceiving my friends and family, and breaking a few hearts—my own included."

"Bright side—you know I won't break it. I love you, Holls."

She reaches up and kisses me, her fingers tracing the stubble along my jaw. It's the kind of kiss that ends with ruffled hair and displaced glasses and clothes on the floor. "I love you too."

In bed, an hour later, with the sea breeze blowing and a gentle rain pattering against the sand, she says, "An airline gift card and four thousand dollars."

When she catches the confusion on my face, she repeats it. "That's what it cost me to get here. In addition to the duds, the deception, a little tax evasion, and the heartbreak. And I wouldn't change any of it, because I got to see my best friend get married in the most beautiful place, and—more importantly—I got to meet *you*."

She tucks herself in closer to me, resting her head on my bare chest, and I stroke her arm with my thumb as I press my lips to the top of her head. "Who says you can't put a price on love?"

Put a bow on it.

ACKNOWLEDGMENTS

Every book is a unique journey, but one constant is that many people have a hand in bringing it to life. I want to thank all the people who helped to make Holly Dates happen.

I am incredibly grateful to my writing buddies who sat with me—sometimes for an hour and sometimes for five, sometimes bringing me food or coffee and sometimes letting me ask eighteen million questions. Ashlinn, Crystal, and Lisa, you are incredible writers and creatives and women and moms and humans, and I'm so blessed to also call you friends.

Ashlinn, thank you for making this book better with your thoughtful conversation and insight!

A huge thanks goes out to my team of researchers, Crystal and Jeff, for finding one obscure movie reference I needed help identifying while I was in the middle of a marathon session.

My proofreader, Deb, is an absolute gem of a human. Generous, kind, loving, hilarious, and smart. Thank you for lending your detailed eye to Holly's story. Please know that even though I kept some of my beloved em dashes, I very much trust and appreciate you!

RJ: Always my first reader, always a trusted voice. Thank you for all that you do!

In chapter 11, I reference Love + Kindness Candles. This is a real company, close to home and closer to my heart. I love the people, the background, the mission, and the candles. (Christmas Tree and

Hearth + Home are recommended scents while reading *Holly Dates* or for any winter activities.)

The goal was to release *Holly Dates* before my birthday, which meant that in a busy back-to-school season with multiple extracurricular activities, we were extra busy putting the finishing touches on this story. So thank you Jeff, L, and Z, for your patience, your support, and your excitement about this particular project. I love writing, but I love you all so much more. (Wuv iz tiz.)

As always, I owe a great deal of gratitude to you, dear reader. Thanks for taking a chance on me and this story and for picking up a copy of this book.

When I was an older teen, I was told, "You're too happy—it's annoying." I'm still trying to reclaim the joy I thought I had to hide to fit in, and writing characters like Holly helps me do that. I love writing quirky, messy women who are "a little much" but a lot awesome, and I hope you love reading about them. And, if you need them to, I hope their stories help your heart heal.

These words are from my brain and my heart, carefully and oh-so-painstakingly arranged in this particular configuration, and that's really hard to do. It took decades to chase my dreams, but I finally did it. I know we're taught not to cheer ourselves on—that it's not polite to celebrate ourselves—but y'all, I've published four books, and it's my birthday, and it's the holiday season, and you can bet I'm celebrating all of it.

Happy Birthday, me.

Happy Holidays, you.

XOXO,

Megan

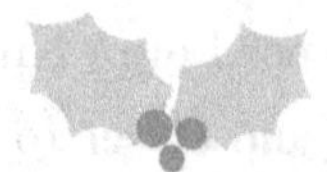

Megan Becker's Additional Works

The Mates & Dates Collection

Coffee Dates

Ship Mates

Band Mates

About the Author

Romance author with imposter syndrome seeks spot on bestsellers list.
I'm Megan, a contemporary romance author. I enjoy snuggling my furryocious rescue pup and cheering on my kids in their athletic, scholastic, and creative endeavors. Additional hobbies include playing card games, making friendship bracelets, and drinking coffee. I'm currently seeking fame and fortune as an author because my husband would love for us to have a tiny vacation home in the mountains, and because I would love reassurance that I'm not wasting my time writing. Are you the bestseller list that wants to take a chance on me? (Probably not, because lists don't typically read author bios. But just in case...) I have a heart for love, a quirky sense of humor, and a passion for writing relatable characters.